OF LIGHT & LIES

A novel by

Darrell Denny

DD

DOUBLE D PUBLISHING

Santa Ana, California

*For all who feel their lives have no value
because of things they've done wrong.
May you find light in the darkest corners
and remember that redemption
is always within reach.*

*And for my mother,
whose unwavering love
has been a beacon of light in my life,
thank you for teaching me the meaning of
true grace and compassion.*

Introduction

———— ••• ————

BE HONEST—YOU'RE TEMPTED TO SKIP THIS INTRODUCTION and maybe even the Prologue. Don't do it. Read both. I've kept them short.

The Prologue is essential. Look for clues to help you piece things together.

This novel takes place on Mustang Island, one of the barrier islands in the Gulf of Mexico. Along with its six brethren, it shields the beaches, communities, and ecosystems of coastal Texas. Spanning 113 miles, it forms the longest undeveloped barrier island chain in the world. Yet, most people know it more for being the Spring Break epicenter of Texas than for its significance.

While the narrative unfolds in the present day, it weaves in references and recollections stretching back 162 years. Don't worry—it won't be hard to keep up.

With a title *Of Light and Lies,* you might wonder what is true and what is deception.

As for truths:

❖ The 20th Regiment Iowa Volunteer Infantry of the Union Army was, indeed, stationed on the island; they helped capture two Confederate forts in 1863.

❖ Surrounded by sand and seagulls, the Chapel on the Dunes overlooks the old town of Port Aransas. This humble, beautiful white church is just 225 square feet, with colorful frescoes adorning its interior walls.

❖ The Voss Iron Works is a real, multi-generational family-owned company based in San Antonio, Texas. It's still renowned for skill and artistry.

❖ There are old .22-caliber rifles that require the manual safety to be disengaged before every shot.

As for lies:

❖ I've taken liberties with the island's dimensions and, at times, the topography. Distances in the book versus reality are—shall we say—iffy.

❖ If a man named Samuel Holcomb was the 2nd Lieutenant and Acting Quartermaster of the 20th Iowa in 1864, I'd be shocked. I dreamed him up.

❖ If there's a concrete tidepool on the island, it's a coincidence. I made it up.

❖ Oh, by the way, don't waste your time looking for Mustang Manor. I imagined the mansion as well; it doesn't exist.

How about things that could be true or a lie or something in between?

There's long been rumors that Jean Laffite—pirate, slave trader, privateer and spy—died before he could recover treasure he'd buried on one of the Gulf Coast islands that became his operating base. Lafitte had a problem; he was wanted by the United States government for years of piracy, smuggling, and spying. He was running out of places where he could spend or invest his ill-gotten booty.

Lafitte helped a still coltish America win the Battle of New Orleans in 1815. Ever the dealmaker, Lafitte warned the Americans that England was willing to pay him to turn coat and fight against the United States. He wrangled a total pardon from President James Madison for a lifetime of crimes in return for aiding the Americans. Lafitte and his men fought in a naval battle that most thought they'd lose. They triumphed, keeping England from peeling off Louisiana and much of the Southeast of the United States.

Fact or fiction, I hope you enjoy the read.

~Darrell Denny

Prologue

————— ••• —————

February 22, 1864

This dispatch to be conveyed
via flag-of-truce schooner LAURA
on station, Gulf of Mexico

From:

Regimental Headquarters, 20th Iowa Volunteer Infantry
Sand Point, Aránzazu Pass, Texas

To:

N. B. Baker
Adjutant General,
20th Iowa Volunteer Brigade Headquarters
Des Moines, Iowa

Herewith, I send a list of supplies both expended and
requested. Also, a list of alterations and casualties incident
to the 20th Regiment Iowa Volunteer Infantry.

We thank God for victories a few months ago. General
Ransom led us on an attack of Fort Semmes. Once we
started shooting at them the Reb skirmishers ran away into
the fort. We was joined in by the USS Monongahela and
our men poured fire down on them. They gave up quick, an

unconditional surrender. I was not there but we captured Fort Esperanza two weeks later. I think maybe these Rebs are on their last legs, at least in these parts. A lot of them prisoners are ill fed and sick. I thought I might feel sorry for them but they've kilt too many friends so I will not.

The regiment has seen a great deal of hard service. We may not have been in as many battles as some others but have done as much hard marching as any. The regiment has lost eighty-six men by death. Of the three hundred and forty-three men present, there is only eight sick. In forwarding new recruits, please remember the Twentieth.

We are now stationed on Mustang Island in Sand Point near the Aránzazu Pass since November 17th, 1863.

I am yours respectfully,

Samuel B. Holcomb
2nd Lieutenant and Acting Quartermaster
20th Iowa Volunteer Infantry

P.S. Another soldier and me, we found something when we was digging the corner posts for the barracks we are building. It is a fancy silver dagger in a metal box. Inside the box we found a piece of wood with numbers and French words burned into it. Billy went to the University of Iowa for two years and he learned a little French. Billy says this knife is hundreds of years old. He told me a story about a Frenchie pirate who might have left the dagger to mark where there is a mess of buried treasure. Can you imagine? We got more digging to do tomorrow, so wish us luck and God's providence.

CHAPTER ONE

The Many Twists and Turns

"I don't like expeditions where it is a total lottery
whether you live or die."

~Bear Grylls (1974–present), British adventurer, writer, wilderness survivalist

—————— ••• ——————

IT'S DARK. EVEN THE MOON IS HIDING. THE ONLY LIGHT there is, she carries with her.

Fat raindrops, liquid meteors, hammer the roof making it vibrate as though electrified. Shrieks and moans accompany her, the byproduct of angry wind flurries and protesting tires fighting for traction on the saturated roadway.

Windshield wipers set on high whine, indignant at how quickly rainwater reappears after having just been swept aside. The ambulance shudders—and sometimes hops—when wind gusts slam into the top-heavy vehicle.

The van's beams illuminate needles of rain that slash diagonally across the glare to explode onto the road's surface. Despite their valiant fight, the vintage headlights only give her, maybe, thirty feet of visibility into the blackness.

Juanita's face is bathed in the glow of the instrument panel, the light so mild and frail that it is hardly there at all and most of what can be seen is merely suggestion. A hint of sturdy chin. A whisper of generous lips. An insinuation of carved cheekbone.

Her chestnut-brown eyes are framed by thick, chocolate-brown eyebrows. Her skin, a rich shade of medium-roast coffee, complements her hair—mostly brown but streaked with deep reds, creating a mahogany hue. A few curling tendrils escape from beneath the snug ball cap on her head.

Unmistakable and contemptuous of the poor illumination is her nose on which her driving glasses are perched. It is a blade, and it's beaked, too. It's a nose that Juanita's kindest and cleverest of friends have characterized as regal or stately or imperial, even. Her personal favorite: opulent.

It's a nose about which she is, alternatingly, proud and self-conscious. It's an inheritance, after all, from her father, passed on to him by her grandfather. Juanita's nose is the first thing a person will see and often the only thing a person will remember after meeting her, and she knows it. Her favorite retaliatory witticism she keeps to herself:

I can see past my nose. Why can't you?

This storm has the surrounding sky, land, and ocean fully in its quaking embrace. It isn't a hurricane; those typically threaten the South Texas coast in late summer and early fall, not in December. Still, this tropical storm is a gully washer in its own right.

Juanita wonders, not for the first time, why she's out on a night like this. She could have waited a few more hours—the worst of the storm wasn't supposed to hit until morning. But after driving through its fury, she finds that hard to believe.

She hopes the rain will ease by mid-day. She's been hired to pick up a passenger and drive her to Houston, and the deadline has just been moved up. Originally, Juanita was scheduled to pick up Helen Chesterfield tomorrow. But at the last minute, the legal firm that hired her decided they needed Helen in their office a day early to review her testimony—something about new evidence. The call came just before the storm knocked out phone service, leaving Juanita unable to warn Helen she's arriving ahead of schedule.

Errant weather forecasters or no, Juanita cannot afford to see this assignment as optional. She needs the money. More, she needs to keep the dispatch firm, and its clients, as customers. So, as promised, she is on her way to do her duty despite nature's attempts to make her regret her choice.

Juanita reflects on the passenger she's on her way to collect. Helen is a 66-year-old paraplegic woman whom Juanita has transported several times in the past. Every previous trip has been unpleasant, so she's not looking forward to this one. Juanita's strategy is to ignore Helen's sling and arrows commentary.

She'd learned, truly, the less said the better. After a while, even Helen seemed to get the hint. It stands to reason this mutually honored vow of silence was never voiced as an agreement. It's an implied pact, one that rides with them like a third, pouting passenger.

A licensed emergency medical technician, Juanita owns a private ambulance service. It's a fleet of one. She provides transport for mobility challenged and health compromised persons. The business, which she reluctantly took over from her deceased father, provides mostly interfacility, discharge, and scheduled transport. Given she's included in the state-wide first responder database, she can be called upon for emergency services in the event of extreme need. Juanita's training gives her an advantage when transporting special need persons.

Yeah. Special needs persons. Like Helen. Who thinks all her needs are special. And all her opinions are special, too.

Given it's just past midnight and, technically, already Wednesday morning, the best Juanita can hope for is to get there, grab a quick nap on a couch, load Helen up, and begin the four-hour drive into Houston. Juanita calculates the likelihood her unexpected arrival will be met with understanding rather than indignation.

Zero chance. None.

Even though she needs a break from battling the wind, rain, cold and dark, she knows she is driving through one kind of storm and into another kind.

Not much I can do about it. She clearly doesn't like me. Far as I can tell, there's nothing unique about that. She doesn't like anyone. Well, guess what, Helen? It's vice versa across the whole universa. You reap what you sow.

To Juanita's knowledge, Helen has not one friend. She talks about the evil of liberal socialists—*all liberals are socialists, my dumplin'*—and the great decay of America including how it's no longer safe to go into the women's bathroom because you are likely to run into a man who claims he's a woman in a man's body but he's only a sicko man who's just pretending because he's really a pervert. Juanita can't imagine any person willing to put up with the constant criticism, sarcasm, cursing, complaining, and irritating personal habits.

To wit: the chain smoking.

Helen insists—this allowance agreed upon only after heated negotiation—on a smoke break every hour during her trips in the ambulance. Since Juanita will not allow smoking in her vehicle (duh) that requires frequently repeating the cumbersome job of transferring Helen from her fixed seat into the wheelchair, onto the lift, down to the roadside, and rolling her far enough to be a sufficient distance away so the second hand smoke does not invade the open van and, then, the same procedure in reverse, only not until after Helen has smoked two or sometimes three cigarettes back-to-back, lighting the next one with the dying embers of its predecessor.

Juanita is both enthralled and appalled by Helen's smoking. She doesn't so much puff as suckle. Her intakes are tenacious and cause her cheeks to cave into her face creating temporary dimples. Her inhalations cause the cigarette's end to bloom and run red along the cigarette's length like a wildfire racing up a dry, brushy ravine. Ash grows too long and falls away onto the ground and sometimes, unnoticed, onto her lap where she sits perched in her wheelchair, eyes fixed on some unknown point in the distance. It reminds Juanita of the black snake fireworks she'd light and toss for her squealing brother on Cinco de Mayo and Fourth of July.

Helen will suck so deeply on her cigarettes that when her peach-fuzzed upper lip finally releases its vacuum hold, it makes a popping sound. Juanita cannot imagine an appetite for anything—food and sex included—that can match Helen's hunger for her smokes.

When not smoking, Helen uses her mouth in other ways. Put simply, she says mean things—not just nasty, but wittily cruel. Especially about gender and sexual preference.

On her very first ride, Helen asked Juanita if she was a dyke. She remarked that Juanita must surely be trying to attract a lesbian, given her gender-neutral clothing, short haircut, and stingy use of makeup. Then she followed up by asking if Juanita liked "grinding muffins" and why a man wouldn't do for her, as nature intended.

Why the anger at everybody and everything? Why the weird obsession with sex? Is it jealousy? She sure as hell isn't having any sex. Given the paralysis and her lovely personality, I can't imagine anyone who'd want to have sex with her even if she can. Maybe sex of every kind is repugnant when you can't have any?

The worst was when Helen called Juanita's developmentally challenged brother, Alex, a "retard." Juanita had introduced Helen to her Abuelo and Alex in the waiting room of the physical therapy clinic they all used. The moment the slur left Helen's mouth, Juanita's eyes narrowed into a steely glare. For the first time, she saw a flicker of realization in Helen—a rare moment of understanding that she had truly crossed a line. Helen apologized. Well, sort of.

Despite her having been asked many times not to do it, Helen calls Juanita '*dumplin*'. She says it in a voice that suggests genuine southern affection, though Juanita knows that's not true. Helen claims that *dumplin*' is an endearment, a word she grew up hearing and saying and she simply cannot help but let it slip from her mouth and, oh my, the word just seems to have a mind of its own.

Helen will bat her eyes and pretend a smile as though she is a kindly aunt, fully aware that Juanita is alert to the fact that she's curvy and being compared to a blob of dough.

She should talk. She's a five-foot nothing bag of bones, she is. Skinny as a matchstick. She can't weigh a hundred pounds, withered legs included. Who does she think she is, judging any other body as inferior? She's the winner of the worst body contest, hands down. Worst personality, too.

Of all the insults, though, the ones that grate on her nerves most are Helen's jabs at her ambulance. Helen mocks the vehicle's age, the lack of a sound system beyond AM/FM radio, and the absence of back-seat air conditioning controls. She calls it the 'Scambulance' and suggests she's getting economy service in exchange for a first-class ticket. Juanita reminds her that she's never transported Helen unless someone else was paying the bill—so what makes her think she had a first-class ticket to begin with?

Juanita is strict about maintenance and inspection. She keeps the ambulance meticulously clean, inside and out. She's seen lots of ambulances, some of them only a few years old, all beat to hell inside. She'll take the Chevrolet her father bought 25 years ago over any of them. It might be older, but it's clean, well maintained, and dependable.

That nasty debilitated bitty should be so lucky to be looked after like I take care of my ambulance. And it sure as hell smells better.

Helen lit up a cigarette in Juanita's van. Once. It was the first time she'd been Juanita's passenger. She'd waited until they were off the island and over the bridge just onto the mainland and into a stretch of stop and go traffic. Despite having already been told not to, she'd rolled down her window anyway and stuck a cigarette in her mouth and flicked her lighter. She'd sucked in a throatful and blew it out the side of her mouth, never once taking her eyes off of the rear-view mirror in which she could see Juanita's widening eyes meeting hers.

"No shit," Juanita had said. "You think you can do that in my van?

You are in for a rude awakening." That retribution had included having her cigarettes confiscated. Juanita dropped the mostly full pack and the two other reserve packs she'd found in Helen's purse into the first trashcan she could find. That was a trip where Helen wasn't allowed any breaks since she wasn't going to be doing any more smoking after that.

Well, if it's still raining this hard, there won't be any smoke breaks on the return leg. That's going to make her even more crabby. It's going to be a long drive back, even if the worst of the storm has blown over.

Eyes on the road!

She reminds herself of this as her eyes detect light and movement. Something is coming toward her. The vague shape reveals itself to be another vehicle going the other way on this farm-to-market road. It's supposed to be two lanes but, as is often the case with these island causeways, it's narrowed into a single lane as sand has encroached from both sides.

The approaching headlights—she can see it's an SUV or van—are so highly set and hot white that they temporarily blind her, searing dancing spots onto her retinas. She despises the ultrabright headlights on new cars.

Come around a curve at night and, boom, it's like you're being interrogated by the Gestapo. Please. Just turn off the lights. I'll tell you everything!

The two automobiles edge as far as possible to the right to pass each other, tires feeding vibrations from the rougher surface of the road-way's shoulders. Water is forced up and out by the prow of the passing vehicle and this wake slaps her van as though it's a petulant child. Between the lights and the wall of water enveloping her van, Juanita fears a collision is as unavoidable as invisible. Despite her white-knuckle anxiety, though, the other van manages to pass her by. She cannot help but be angry as to why anyone would be driving so fast on a narrow, squall-ridden road.

With what starburst-compromised sight she has left, Juanita glances in her rear-view mirror to see the passing van growing more distant, taillights hemorrhaging red into the darkness. It takes longer for her adrenalin to bleed away and her breathing to calm.

The ambulance's headlights are older and weaker than their newer descendants. Despite that, she prefers them. In her mind's eye, the slightly yellowed lights are warmer and, well, kinder. She wonders if car makers know or care that their newest generation headlights blind drivers coming the other way. It appears not.

Headlight evolution won't be denied. Survival of the brightest.

The deluge, seemingly perturbed by having been upstaged by the drama of the near bout of vehicular chicken, chooses that moment to double in intensity. Thick and heavy, it feels to Juanita that this storm is a living, malevolent creature. It's hungry and indiscriminate. In the distance, the black sky is pierced by throbbing flashes. The lightning is stalked by thunder that adds its rumbling, aggrieved voice to the night's cacophony. The rainwater's density is shocking, so Juanita tilts her foot back off the gas pedal slowing her progress forward to less than 20 miles per hour.

A small mercy, the headlight-induced night blindness begins to dissipate and Juanita concentrates, again, on navigating the many curves, rises, and dips of the sodden road. Finally, she gets to where the road is mostly straight and level for a stretch. It's an act of will for Juanita to relax her grip. Her fingers feel cemented to the steering wheel, and it hurts to uncurl them even a little. Her wrists and forearms, shoulders and neck protest as well.

Unexpected by Juanita, this stretch of road has been repaved since she last drove on it. Even with her windows rolled up and the storm washing furiously, she can smell the newish asphalt. A black, oily miasma coats her sinuses and throat. She hawks something up and wants to spit it out, but the window is rolled up on account of the rain, so she grimaces and swallows it back down.

This newly blackened road is embedded with reflective buttons and husbanded by reflective signs. Out of the darkness, they emerge—rain-blurred, sparkling infantry marching in neat lines that start abruptly and end with equal brusqueness.

Seen through the waterlogged windshield, the reflected light melts into a hypnotic kaleidoscope. She feels rewarded when the light from her kinder, gentler headlights bounces back. The reflections are some-times proud and sometimes meek and sometimes only there to play on the very periphery of her vision. The light flashes and dashes, projected onto the lenses of her glasses for only a crumb of a moment before winking away, trailing wiggling phosphorescent tails. Shy sprites back to the black.

Ghostly apparitions materialize, literal signs that warn of dangers ahead: *hairpin turn, narrow bridge, watch for wildlife.* The signs reminding her of possible low water keep Juanita on high alert. There is keen competition among the hazards.

Danger comes in many forms, Juanita thinks—not for the first time. To quiet the thought, she forces her mind to steady itself.

Yea, though I walk through the valley of the shadow of death, I will fear no evil.

These words are her mantra, a whispered prayer against fear.

Despite the rededication to keeping her eyes on the road, it has been a very long drive. She knows it's a false security, but she relaxes on this less challenging straightaway. She pulls her elbows back and back again until she feels a satisfying crack between her shoulder blades. Her eyes complete their recovery from the rude high-beam headlights. Her pupils dilate, now drinking in whatever little there is to see. She increases her speed a bit, eager to reach her destination but with growing apprehension as well.

Juanita has been driving almost nonstop against strong wind and hard rain since before the sun went down. That was nearly six hours ago. It's nearly 2 a.m. now, though the frozen dashboard clock has long since decided to display a time that can only be correct in some other dimension.

Her fingers absentmindedly trace the rim of the paper cup in her cup holder. It's empty now, save for the ghost of green tea long dried at the bottom, but the feel of it still soothes her. Sam had given her that tea, just like he always did when she visited. His quiet wisdom has helped her navigate the grief of losing her Papa and Abuela.

I hope you're warm and safe from this storm, Sam. Wish I were on my way to visit with you instead of picking up Helen.

Left to her own habits, Juanita prefers coffee and seldom drinks tea, though her grandfather still drinks disgustingly sugared iced tea, and her father does, too.

Well, did.

Juanita wedges the cup back into the center console amongst the jumble of paperwork, flashlight, energy bars and a mostly empty french-fry container that was part of tonight's dinner on the road. Her stomach is slightly queasy from the meal.

The straightaway ends and the road, once again, is serpentine. Juanita coaxes her way around another curve, and her timid head-lights pass briefly over something prostrate at the bend in the road. Juanita takes her foot off the gas and glances through the cascading rain at her passenger-side mirror. There's not enough light behind her for another look. Still, she's pretty sure she knows what it is.

It's a body, small and hairy.

Juanita pulls her lips firmly against her gritted teeth. Given the deluge, she regretfully accepts the truth.

Not all of God's creatures will survive this storm.

CHAPTER TWO

A Poverty of Self

*"The mind can weave itself warmly in the cocoon
of its own thoughts, and dwell a hermit anywhere."*

~James Russell Lowell (1819-1891), American poet, critic, editor, and diplomat

————————— ••• —————————

A FIERY DOT BOBS IN THE DARKNESS. IT SWELLS BRIGHTER and reddens, a smoldering comet small against the black. It remains bright for almost exactly a second before dwindling away to near invisibility.

Helen, in her ever-present wheelchair, has rolled herself out the still open front door and onto the screened-in porch to smoke. She wears a down-filled vest over a tee shirt. It's chilly outside and her arms are bare, but she likes the numbing effect. She imagines this is how her legs might feel. If they could. The gift her husband had given her a long time ago lays across her lap and onto her unfeeling legs. The blanket is a comforter in name only.

She listens to the rain pounding the metal roof of the Casita and counts the seconds between the distant pulses of lightening and the growls of thunder in pursuit. The interval between light and sound is shrinking.

Storm's comin' closer. Come on, then. Show me whatcha got.

The gusty squall has long since knocked the power out. Shortly after the few lights she'd had on in the Casita went suddenly out, she'd checked her phone—not even a dial tone. Deader than the proverbial doornail.

No lights. No phone. No problem.

Who gives a fuck. Ain't nobody I want to talk to anyway. Sides, I like the dark.

She doesn't mind being cut off from the rest of humanity, having been alone much of her childhood. She wishes mobile phones had never been invented. She'd bought one years ago but, after experiencing unwanted telemarketing calls, unreadable emails, and unnecessary texts, she'd decided she didn't want it. Without ceremony, she'd tossed it into the marsh abutting the Casita. She figures whoever invented smart phones is pretty dumb.

Just because she won't own a cell phone doesn't mean she's illiterate when it comes to computers. She does her banking, medical appointment scheduling, tax filing and paralysis care research on her computer. Two days ago, she'd started downloading onto her new laptop years' worth of pictures and videos from Ben's old desktop computer. It's a task she'd been putting off for a decade. She hadn't yet begun sorting the downloads other than deleting some of the more obvious spam, ancient emails and some unnerving old porn.

Helen prefers a laptop computer for reasons both obvious and personal. Unlike the old desktop, she can use the laptop when she climbs out of her wheelchair and into bed at the end of the day. And she despises talking on her landline phone even more than dealing with bothersome emails. It's easier to say 'no' online.

People with way too much time on their hands. Bunch of pity disguised as concern. Experts at pretendin' to care, pretendin' that the reason they are callin' is what they can do for me when, really, it's all about what I can do for them. And what they want is usually to check off a box on a form so they can collect their fees as doctors or blood testers or therapists or, worst of all, social workers who must get paid by the spoken word given how much they blab. I can do without all of it, thank you very much.

She's most comfortable in quiet, but not irritated by tonight's sounds. She's soothed by the torrent of rain that pings her roof, plops her yard, and plunks the marsh that is close by but cannot be seen in the dark. Though the sound of the downpour gaveling her roof is loud, she does not consider it to be unwelcome noise. It doesn't disturb her peace. On the contrary, she enjoys being shrouded in this auditory curtain of static where she can blend into the dark to watch, listen, smoke, and smell the tobacco fumes mingling with the earthy odors being whisked up and around by the huffing wind.

Inhaling again, Helen holds the vapor in; then, she lazily lets the smoke slide from her mouth and nose to dissipate into the murk. It's a disgusting and expensive habit, smoking. She'd previously quit, but she took it up again ten years ago. She'd restarted when she'd come back to the Casita after weeks of unconsciousness. After months of surgeries. And tests. And more surgeries and more tests.

When she could bear it no longer, and over the recommendations of the doctors, she'd insisted on going home.

Alone.

Alone after learning her husband had died in the crash. Alone after learning he'd been buried while she was unconscious in a hospital bed. Alone with the knowledge it was too late to tell Ben…anything. Alone to a home where there were no welcomes. Alone to a home where there were no goodbyes.

Home sweet home. Piss on that. This ain't home. My real home, anyway. This here? It's temporary. Gonna kick 'em out. Soon as I can. Gonna put an end to it all. The parties. The noise. The stink. It'll stop. I live for the exact moment I kick 'em out and make it all stop.

Helen resists lighting up another cigarette. She understands on a fundamental level that smoking will likely shorten her lifespan. To her, this doesn't seem all bad. Cigarettes may be gradual, a slower acting and cumulative kind of killer, but they are unsurpassed in their ruthlessness. If anything, cigarettes are too slow and unpredictable for Helen's taste, the lowest limb on the suicide tree.

She'd almost gone the whole nine yards, once. She'd downed a bottle of oxycodone that had been prescribed for chronic pain, the ghostly, inexplicable pain in her legs that felt nothing else. The pain doctors said shouldn't be there. But she'd chickened out and pushed her fingers down her throat until she'd gagged and vomited cheap wine and pills into the toilet. Even then, she'd reached back down into the milky toilet water, angry at her cowardice. She'd tried to collect the now slippery pills that eluded her pinched fingers. At the same time, seemingly independent and of contrary purpose, her other hand had reached up and pulled the handle and flushed the sour water and pills swirling down the toilet drain.

Not for the first time, Helen wonders if it matters if she were to off herself. It's not like she's afraid of committing a mortal sin. An atheist, Helen does not believe in God. She gave that up when she was a child. When she learned it was all a big lie.

When life ends, that's it. Anything else is wishful thinkin', fairy tales to make the end of things more bearable.

Unlike the poet Dylan Thomas, she has no intention of 'raging against the dying light.'

Everlastin' and eternal light? Fantasies for the stupid and the gullible. God? God's a con man, a con man we allow to live inside of us, one who tells us to do things his way, follow his rules, follow his self-selected mouthpieces. Bow to his will? Do it or else. Disobey? You'll pay.

The three rules of religion: location, location, location. Heaven. Hell. Purgatory. Those are the most valuable real estate properties to own, aren't they? Tell people you control all the after-death retirement homes and there'll be no shortage of self-deceivers lined up to believe whatever they're told to believe. In public, they'll pretend to be good, say good things, do good things. In private, they'll twist the rules to their advantage. They'll assure you those things that feel wrong are not wrong. They are part of God's will. They'll tell you to obey even though you know in your stomach that what has been said to you, what has been done to you, cannot be right.

If there is a God and he's been watchin', he oughta be ashamed.

Fuck that. Fuck him. Fuck 'em all.

The thought of *endness* has a gravitational hold on her. It's a moon that calls to her blood, coaxing both surge and ebb, an elemental and seductive tide. She is drawn toward absoluteness, toward inarguable finality. It gives her strength, adds substance to her conviction that whatever little there is to be remembered about her after she's gone will disintegrate, quickly, until there's nothing to be remembered at all. As it should be.

Since her husband's death, there's no one worth remembering. Even a fleeting one-time fling only confirmed what she already knew—she's better off alone. And so, too, there are things she's done in her life that will be forgotten as well. That, she believes, might make dying worthwhile. That's what made suicide tempting.

Like Mama. I should've seen she was hurtin' as much as I was. More, even. I wish I'd understood how bad it was. It was too much for her. It was almost too much for me. I had to make a different decision. I took a stand. I made endings.

Endness, the great justifier. Helen doesn't have to pretend she isn't bitter, spiteful, vengeful. She can be who she is.

Fifty years ago, she'd spit on one grave and lain flowers on another. Ten years ago, she'd grieved, alone, looking down at grave soil that had barely begun to settle. A headstone had been ordered but it hadn't been placed yet. Everyone she's loved—and most she's hated—are dead or gone. All that's left in her world are empty people doing inconsequential things. Including herself.

Helen feels triumphant about not having to explain why she prefers to be alone. There is no need to bluff anything. Endness is the one, the only, the final judge of what is, and is not, true.

That she should think of truths is ironic given that she still pretends, without success, not to be a bold-faced liar.

They have accumulated, her deceits.

Helen figured she'd be maudlin tonight. It's the ten-year anniversary of Ben's death and only two days before she's to testify, again. The case for which she's been subpoenaed is akin to the one in which she was interviewed for years ago, except the new one is a civil suit, the older a criminal investigation.

It's taken decades for this lawsuit to rise from the dead and come to life. This new trial is no longer about conviction and jail time. It's about land. Ownership. Money. It's about secrets. And the lies that preserve them. It's about her birthplace, her birthright, and a secret that, if revealed, might prove to be the death of her.

Helen is grateful in one sense. Due to her paralysis, she's incapable of feeling butterflies in her stomach. She used to, before the crash. She'd had them as a girl, at school, in class, whenever she was asked to standup and speak. She'd had them when she was around boys, too. She'd had them whenever Willy was around, though for a very different reason.

She'd had butterflies the night before and day of her interview with the sheriff. The butterflies were with her as she waited in the hall and with her while she sat huddled in the interview room and with her when the sheriff told her she was obligated to tell the truth about what had happened.

As if.

To her surprise, as soon as she sat down in the chair in the interview room, the butterflies simply evaporated.

Helen wants another cigarette, but she puts it off. Of their own accord, her hands find their way to her abdomen. Back in those days, it was talked about in hushed tones. It was called a medical complication or woman's issue, antiseptic terms for something no one wanted to talk about. Not that there was anyone for her to talk to about it anyway.

Ben came to know the truth. Well, some of it. Ben married her knowing she could never bear him children. Ben tried gallantly to pretend that he didn't want or need children in his life. He'd never made her feel bad about it or, at least, not on purpose.

But she'd seen his smile seeing little kids squealing as waves of warm salt water rushed up their legs, grinning at the sight of runaway drips of ice cream that trickled down cones onto tiny fists or booing when he saw kids chase after a seabird who'd just stolen one of their french fries.

Helen cups her abdomen tighter. Nothing. She remembers having been given a pamphlet as she lay recuperating from the accident: *If you listen to your body when it whispers, you won't have to listen when it screams,* she'd read. She'd thrown the pamphlet away and nearly screamed while doing it.

Listening to the whispers? Does that work for a half body like mine? I'll tell you the answer. It's no.

She wonders if those butterflies in her stomach had been there for a purpose beyond confirming anxiety.

Why had I felt those butterflies so strongly? What did they want? To distract me? To help me? To appeal to my conscience? To bear witness? To hear the lies?

She wonders if maybe the butterflies left when they knew she had chosen to lie. They didn't care about her reasons. She had broken their good hearts. She didn't deserve them then and can't conjure them now. Helen feels just like she did at that very moment years ago when she'd decided how she'd dodge the sheriff's questions.

Abandoned.

She thinks of butterflies, now, because she dreamed of them last night. In the dream she's wearing a silver sparkling dress, tiara on her head, glass shoes on her feet. She's stepping down the aisle of a church. The train of her dress is long and flows behind her. Dozens of multi-colored butterflies are flitting around her head and shoulders keeping pace. She glances back over her shoulder and sees some of the butterflies are helping to carry her dress' train down the aisle. She should be happy because she must be getting married but, rather, she's distressed because she knows she's not worthy and those around her know it, too. It's like a Disney movie but one that becomes something else, becomes a horror flick where the butterflies vanish and the train of her dress falls to the floor to become heavy and dirty, and she sinks down and into the floor where there is cold water and it's dark and she cannot breathe. And all the time, the vague heads of the wedding guests nod in solemn assent that this is just. This is deserved.

Fuck it. Fuck 'em all. They don't know shit.

Helen shakes out another cigarette from the pack, lights it and, with gusto, she smokes it down to the filter. She stubs it out amongst the other butts in the ashtray on her lap. She leans back and closes her eyes, giving herself to the vibrations, the white noise, the tastes, the smells, and the feel of the hairs on her arms standing up, swaying, dancing with the charged electrons in the stormy air. She drifts, otherworldly, as though her body has altered its fundamental state. She is liquid and blends with the rain. She is gas and mingles with the wind. She is something else entirely, something that moves freely and encounters little resistance, something that moves swiftly and effortlessly and, above all, unapologetically.

A sharp sound breaks the spell.

"Goddammit!" she hears.

It's a man's voice. The wind carries it to her. Anger in the voice. Some hurt, too?

Lightning takes that very moment to strobe the sky and Helen sees, less than thirty yards away, a man halfway across the metal footbridge that spans the creek to her Casita. The man is hunched but Helen is somehow sure he is rising up after having fallen or stumbled. She figures he slipped and barked himself on something.

Stupid motherfuckers. I told 'em. Put up an aluminum bridge in this salty, humid climate? It's slippery as shit and a fuckin' magnet for lightnin'. It's a miracle a bolt hasn't hit the bridge. That man oughta be fried to a crisp. Shit for brains idiot. It'd serve him right to fry for stupidity.

But her smugness evaporates.

Still light-blinded from the flash, she can't see anything else so her mind dwells on the still-life photo imprinted on her mind. Like a Polaroid picture developing right before her eyes, it's a snapshot of the image the lightning captured. It's a stark, frozen, whitewashed photograph of a man on a bridge. She sees his face clearly but cannot make out his face at all.

That doesn't make sense. How'd he even get through the locked gate on the other end of the bridge? Why's he comin' here? In the middle of a lightnin' storm?

This feels wrong.

CHAPTER THREE

A Mansion by the Marsh

"Every doorway, every intersection has a story."

~Katherine Dunn (1945-2016), American journalist, novelist,
and prolific writer on boxing

———— ••• ————

MEAGER HEADLIGHTS POINT FORWARD AND SO ARE OF little aid as she peers out the rain-streaked driver's side window.

The turnoff is...right...about...here.

She'd driven it once, years ago. It's a crushed stone and gravel drive-way, long and curvy.

Foot off the gas pedal, Juanita lets the van's forward momentum peter out. Engine purring, wipers whipping, defroster chuffing, Juanita knows she is both figuratively and literally idling. This unscheduled sight-seeing detour is adding, in a negative sense, to the duration of her drive but, also, subtracting, in a positive sense, from the length of time she will have to spend at Helen's Casita.

Usually, at night, this is lit up, this archway of stone and iron. Were the power not out all over the island, light sconces would be high-lighting the metal that has been cast and bent, welded and shaped by the famous Theo Voss, founder of Voss Metal Works. The iron parabola is anchored on each end to tall rock pillars. The mansion, itself, cannot be seen from the road even during the day given the setback is nearly a mile.

The wrought iron script, if she could see it, would read: *Mustang Manor.*

Juanita is willing to bet everything she has that the gate she cannot see in the dark is closed and locked. It's accessible only by code and keypad. It's a private driveway. Unanticipated visitors are not welcome.

Juanita knows this from first-hand experience.

The first time Juanita had gone to pick up Helen, she'd struggled to find her house. The secondhand directions she'd received didn't match her phone's GPS, and she'd driven past the porte-cochère twice, once in each direction. Both times, the gate had been closed. There was a keypad, but no call box or intercom.

Exasperated, Juanita had reached for her cell phone to call Helen. She'd not been looking forward to telling her she'd gotten lost. Though they'd yet to meet in person, Juanita had instinctively known she didn't want to give the woman any more ammunition with which to complain. There'd been plenty of that, already.

Juanita started searching for Helen's phone number, remembering it was an unpublished landline. Her best guess? A rotary phone. Just as she found the number and was about to dial, she saw the gate swing open. A pickup truck tore through like a bat out of hell, speeding away from her idling ambulance. It fishtailed down the road, kicking up dust and gravel.

Juanita had hesitated. The gate was still open. With no other ideas, she'd figured the driveway had to lead to Helen's house—or at least to someone who could point her in the right direction. So, she'd turned in, passing through the gate at a slow, cautious pace.

The land was stark but beautiful, baked by the relentless Texas sun. Sand layered over shell and rock, forming dunes dotted with sparkling salt crystals—leftovers from evaporated Gulf seawater. Panicum, Sea Oats, and Dropseed clung to the highest points, battling for dominance, while Bluestem and Beaked Spikerush huddled in the shelter of the dunes.

At first, the property seemed like pure sandy grassland. But as she neared the sprawling house and its circular driveway, she'd spotted marshland in the distance. Tall cattails waved in the breeze, marking an inlet or creek.

She'd cranked down her window, taking in the scent of marine decay, ozone, and something she recognized from freshman biology—the pheromones that gave fish eggs their distinct smell. The memory had stung. She'd once dreamed of becoming a marine biologist, but when her father died, college had slipped away. Now, she was an ambulance driver, ferrying people instead of studying sea life.

She'd passed a patch of forbs where pocket gophers peeked out and Longtail butterflies spiraled in playful chases. Grasshopper mice halfheartedly stalked their prey, waiting for the midday heat to pass before resuming the real hunt.

The Mustang Manor estate stretched toward the wildlife refuge. A tall stone wall and arched gate secured the front, while taut steel cables fenced the sides and extended past the marsh at the rear.

As Juanita drew closer, she couldn't help but notice how striking the three-story house was. Juanita recalled the style of architecture is called Regency. It did, indeed, look fit for a king. The mansion was symmetrical across the front and there were—she'd counted—seven windows on each of the three levels. It had made her wonder:

If there are 21 windows facing just the front, how many rooms must it have when the house seems to be nearly as wide on the sides as it is across the front?

The massive home's exterior was a lavender stucco façade. Ornate wrought-iron detailing surrounded the first level porch and four balconies that jutted out from the top floor. The rooftop sported a squared wooden balustrade around a viewing platform. *The view from up there must be wonderful*, she recalls having thought. Ground level colonnaded breezeways provided shelter and shade from the brutal sun. Those paths connected to a large garage on the right and what appeared to be a newish pavilion on the left.

Altogether, the manor was impressive but also imposing, heavy. The house felt to Juanita as though it had not been assembled from parts but, instead, had been chiseled from a single monolithic cube of granite, the doors and windows sculpted, and the voids that became rooms inside were the result of some lost godly art of cavitation.

Juanita eyeballed the mansion as she pulled into and stopped halfway around the circle at the terminus of the driveway. She turned off the ignition and recalls sitting for a few moments, listening to the ticks and sighs from the ambulance as the engine began to cool down and the interior began to warm up.

Before getting out she inhaled again, her nasal passages picking up a hint of decay that blended with the botanical bouquet. Altogether, it was like breathing through a beach towel that had been left outside to dry but was still damp and heavy.

No sooner had Juanita stepped out of the ambulance and begun straightening her wrinkled clothes when a very big man in suit and tie came charging toward her from the breezeway between the house and detached garage. He approached Juanita with arms flapping wildly like a goose defending hatchlings. There was a half-smoked cigarette in one enormous hand. Juanita could see that sweat had drenched his underarms and the wetness bled right through the jacket. Given how hot it was, she had wondered why the man was wearing a suit jacket outdoors on a sizzling, sticky Texas afternoon.

"No!" the man shouted. He seemed angry.

Juanita had sighed. *Interrupted his smoke break. Fantastic.*

The man in the suit stopped a few feet away from Juanita and looked back to the house. Then, he'd bent down and crushed out the cigarette on the sole of his shoe. His hand made to flip the butt away, but he seemed to change his mind. Instead, he closed his hand around the still not entirely extinguished cigarette, squeezing it in a massive fist. It'd looked like a scene from a gangster movie.

Well, at least he's not a litterbug.

"You no here," the man said to her, wagging a finger from his other hand like a metronome. "This private road. You go now," he added, pointing toward the gate and the road Juanita had come in on. Juanita realized the man had a foreign accent. It was Russian, or something close to it.

"Go now," the man said to her again as he waved his long arms around. His suit jacket was unbuttoned. Juanita glimpsed a holstered pistol strapped to his left breast under his jacket.

A mail order security guard? How'd he get the job? Picked out of a catalogue?

Not eager to overstay her welcome now that she'd seen the man was armed, Juanita launched into an explanation as to why she was there. Halfway through she realized the man was looking at her with confused, blank eyes. He didn't understand.

"Other persons here?" she asked him. "Other persons? Speak English?"

The man turned to look at the house again and, for a time, said nothing. Eventually he turned back to Juanita, frowned, and said, "You talk me," and pointed a kielbasa-sized finger at his own chest.

Juanita had sighed again. *Fine. If you can't beat 'em, join 'em.*

She'd resorted to caveman speech.

"Me here," she'd said, pointing at the ground. "Me drive," she added, miming a steering wheel. "Me look woman." She shielded her eyes, then gestured exaggerated curves. It struck her that her speech and motions had made her feel like an actor in a lame Cowboys and Indians movie.

"Woman," she'd tried again. "Go in this." She pointed to her ambulance. "Helen Chesterfield."

No recognition.

Juanita tried a different approach. "Old." But how to act out old? Then it hit her.

"In wheelchair," she said, crouching and rolling imaginary wheels.

Finally, his face had lit up with a smile, something Juanita had assumed he wasn't voluntarily capable of.

"Yes! Old woman. She live there." He'd pointed beyond the marsh.

No roads. Just open land.

"Directions?" she'd asked, hands up in surrender. She hunched her shoulders and held her palms out and up to show she was lost. Or poor, maybe. Both were true.

The man had gotten the gist of it. She will never forget his directions.

"You go road," he said, pointing back toward the gate. "You go left." His hand executed a karate chop in time with the word.

"You go road, umm, three minutes," he added, holding up three fingers.

"You go left," he said again, repeating the chopping gesture.

"You go road to this," he said. Juanita recalls how she'd, at first, interpreted his fingers as a peace sign. Then it dawned on her, and she knew what it was he'd been trying to tell her.

"A fork," Juanita replied. "Road. Fork," she said, also making a V with her fingers.

"Yes," the man said. "You fork."

Juanita remembers the man's accented pronunciation of "fork" had sounded like "fuck." She decided not to point that out to him, disinclined to look this gift horse in the mouth.

"You go road. You go left," the man said again. This time the man and Juanita made the chopping motion at the same time. She was catching on. She recalls the man grinning at that, a full Cheshire cat ear to ear.

Wow. Two smiles in one day for this guy. Probably a personal record.

"You go leeeeetle bridge," he said, holding up two fingers close together. "You go road. You go leeeeetle house," he added, still holding the two fingers an inch apart.

Juanita repeated the directions back, the man nodding that she'd remembered correctly. She thanked the man and turned to leave when he called to her again and asked, "How you here? How in?"

Juanita told him as best she could that the gate was already open. She explained that a blue pickup truck had come out. She thought he'd understood but was startled when he slapped his thigh and cursed.

"Lazy fucking bastard," the man declared.

"Who? Me? I'm a lazy fucking bastard?" she asked.

"No, uh, sorry" he said. "Other man. Truck," he added, waving his arm toward the distance.

Fair enough.

With a nod, she'd climbed back into the ambulance and driven off, following the Russian's choppy but surprisingly memorable directions.

Juanita's prevailing takeaway from that encounter several years ago is that the tenants of Mustang Manor really value their privacy. Still unknown to her, Juanita hadn't asked the suited guard his name. She wonders if the large man still works there.

Is he still prowling the grounds, even now, in the rain?

Still idling in the downpour at the intersection of road and driveway, Juanita recalls the romance and tragedy of Mustang Manor.

Built in the early 1900s, the estate had been home to Robert and Lilly Chesterfield, progressive thinkers and ecologists. Robert, a geologist and inventor, patented devices to reduce oil spill waste, making him wealthy. Lilly, a suffragette, co-founded the Petticoat Lobby, a powerful women's advocacy group that helped pass the 19th Amendment.

Disillusioned by politics, the reemergence of the Ku Klux Klan and the rise of religious fundamentalism, they had purchased the island land as both a wildlife sanctuary and personal refuge. Given both considered themselves to be scientists, what worried them most was seeing references to evolution ordered removed from high school textbooks to be replaced by creationism around which there was no science at all. Darwinism equaled Satanism among the illiterate and among the congregations of Baptist churches that were sprouting up in Texas like bluebonnets.

Robert died in the Manor's basement, exactly one week after Lily succumbed to injuries from a horseback riding accident. Friends said he died of a broken heart. The estate then passed to their son Hamilton, and later to his son Benjamin.

Ben lost his fortune in the dotcom crash and the 2008 recession, forcing him and his wife, Helen, to lease out the Manor. They moved into the smaller guest house, the Casita, across the marsh. Shortly after, Benjamin died in an unsolved hit-and-run, leaving Helen land-rich but cash-poor—and paralyzed.

Juanita hadn't known on that hot summer day back then who was living in Mustang Manor. She does now. The tenant is Georgi Kask, a Russian immigrant and hedge fund manager. He and his two sons had been looking for a secluded place to live and recover from the loss of the boys' mother who'd passed away abruptly.

The parties thrown by Georgi Kask are legend. Mostly it's barbecues and lawn affairs with businesspeople, financiers and politicians whom Kask supports. Juanita's also heard that, on occasion, the parties will turn into real ragers with heavy drinking and liberal drug use. This is especially true if the parties are thrown by one or both of his sons, Dmitri and Andrei. At these parties, guests are more likely to be musicians, podcasters, and actors, many of them known for their reality show television roles.

Juanita remembers meeting Andrei once—literally bumping into him while she and her friend Betsy Clark waited in line at a taco truck. His dilated eyes and exaggerated swagger screamed stoned. He came on strong, ignored her refusals, and only backed off after she swatted his hands off her bum and warned she'd put him on the floor if he tried again.

"Guess what?" Betsy asked Juanita after Dmitri swaggered away. "Never mind. You'll never guess. There are swingers in the area. And he's one of them."

"Swingers? You mean, like...swapping partners?"

"I mean, like, an orgy," Betsy replied, glancing left and right conspiratorially to ensure they weren't overheard. At the same time, she made a circle with her left-hand fingers and penetrated it with a finger from her right. When Juanita asked what she meant by "the area," Betsy just waved her formerly copulating fingers around her head and said, "I don't know. Just... around."

Even Juanita couldn't help but be curious. She couldn't imagine how someone might bang the bank teller one night and look him in the eyes when cashing a check on the next day.

Eww. Gross.

"Supposedly they're rich people," Betsy had said. Juanita recalls that, for a while after hearing this, she mentally profiled every wealthy person she knew or met on the island.

Being pawed by Andrei and learning he'd orchestrated an orgy at Mustang Manor cemented his perfect 10 rating on Juanita's ick scale.

She gets, to a degree, why Helen loathes her tenants.

What's it like for Helen, owning a mansion and grounds but not being able to afford to live there? She sits there, in her wheelchair, in her little Casita, in a home that had once been servant's quarters. Given how much she brings it up, it galls her.

Helen often lamented her exile in the Casita, convinced Georgi had forged Benjamin's approval for renovations to the grounds and inside the mansion. The most contentious change was the replacement of Ben's handcrafted wooden bridge with a narrow, locked aluminum one, effectively cutting Helen off from the Manor. Georgi dismissed her protests, claiming she was supposed to stay on her side anyway, so it was a case of no harm, no foul.

Despite Helen's complaints, the Casita is in excellent condition—renovated, modernized, even outfitted with a wheelchair-accessible elevator. The grounds, though small, are shaded and pleasant. Juanita recalled her first arrival, the afternoon heat softened by a steady onshore breeze, rustling the leaves and gently swaying a bench swing under the tallest tree.

When's the last time that lover's swing has seen any love? Still, this place is a lot better than anywhere I've ever lived. If it were me, I'd rather live in the Casita than in the big house. Mustang Manor is too damn big and the ocean and marsh view from the Casita is way better. Plus, there's good shade there.

Far as Juanita can tell, the Manor home doesn't have a ramp or elevator or any modifications to make it handicap-friendly. To be fair, though, Juanita has only seen the outside.

Maybe it's so grand inside that you'd be willing to give your right arm to live there. Or your two legs?

A particularly strong gust of wind rattles the ambulance and Juanita surfaces from her daydreaming state. She knows she can delay no longer. Juanita coaxes the ambulance forward and leaves the gate and driveway hidden behind a veil of black and a curtain of rain.

Destination in mind, she sings her ditty and hacks with one hand:

Go road
Go left (chop)
Go three minutes (fingers up!)
Go left (chop)
Go Fork (pronounced fuck!)
Go left (chop)
Go leeeeetle bridge
Go road
Go leeeeetle house

CHAPTER FOUR

A Violation of Personal Space

"Small rooms or dwellings discipline the mind;
large ones weaken it."

~Leonardo da Vinci (1452–1519), painter, draughtsman, engineer,
scientist, sculptor, architect

———————— ••• ————————

THE EXPIRING EMBER FADES FROM ORANGE TO GREY AS
Helen sets the ashtray onto the porch floor. Without taking her eyes
off the bridge, she wheels herself slowly backward through the front
door and into the house. She closes the door as quietly as she can
manage and slots home two deadbolts, newer ones she had installed
at waist level when she'd renovated the place.

She hopes the fading odor of cigarette smoke will make him curious
and hesitant. Any reason to give him pause, to buy her time.

Helen seizes the wheel rims and thrusts herself into the kitchen,
one that has been remodeled taking into consideration her impair-
ment. Her familiarity allows her to navigate despite the darkness.
She goes, first, to the pantry where she takes down a box of cereal.
She rips it open and casts it out onto the kitchen floor by the handful.
Discarding the mostly empty carton on the floor, she wheels herself
over to a low-set countertop and selects two things.

One is a flashlight. The other is a meat cleaver. She's reminded this
sharp butcher's tool helped save her life once before. Maybe it can do
so again.

She pivots and wheels herself back into the central hallway and
pauses, torn by indecision.

Up or down?

Up, she decides.

Elevator or stairs?

She chooses the elevator.

She reckons she will need to preserve her arm strength, but taking the elevator triggers its own set of complications. She did not activate the solar-powered generator when the power went suddenly off, opting to preserve the battery in case the outage lasted a while. Instead, she'd been planning to ride out the storm with just candles like she'd done when she was a kid. Much of her childhood was spent in the dark during storms, electricity being a finicky thing at her Mama's little house.

But, with the power out, the lift won't work. She wheels herself to the generator installed next to the elevator shaft and hits the power button. She's grateful for the near immediacy but also cringes at the high-pitched whine it emits as it comes to life.

Within seconds the kitchen lights up like an operating room. Helen utters her own "Godammit." She's forgotten that lights in the kitchen and also upstairs were on when the power went out. She'd never turned them off.

She wheels back to the other end of the kitchen and turns those lights off as fast as she can, leaving the downstairs mostly dark. The only remaining light is spilling down from upstairs.

Ain't no use pretendin' otherwise. No way he missed that. Now he knows for sure I'm here. Worse, he knows that I know he's here, too.

She wheels herself into the elevator, closes the folding grate and engages the lever. The elevator begins the ascent, but it runs at a deliberate pace and may well be the '*slowest motherfuckin' lift in the world,*' Helen believes. The minutes it takes to deliver her to the second-floor landing adjacent to her bathroom are excruciating.

She thinks on the ride up.

Scream? No. No one will hear me.

Hide? No. There's nowhere he wouldn't eventually find me.

Weapons? Fuckity-fuck. Just what I've got in my hands.

She doesn't know what to do with the flashlight. She certainly isn't going to turn it on. That would only make his job easier. She's not sure why she grabbed it in the first place. She wishes she'd selected something else.

I shoulda grabbed another knife instead. A really long one.

She uses the last seconds of her ascension to practice a few chops with the cleaver.

She's not feeling optimistic. But then she remembers something that might help. She doesn't know for sure how to use it but maybe she can figure it out.

It's old. It's so old it might not even work anymore.

She can't think of anything better.

As soon as the lift delivers her to the second floor, Helen rips open the grate and casts herself to a paneled wall at the back of her bedroom. She pushes on one of the wooden slats and it gives, clicks and springs open to reveal a neatly hidden storage room. Helen reaches up and pulls a string attached to a chain. The bare bulb light is so harsh it's almost debilitating.

She whisks herself into the deep room and rolls to a metal industrial bookcase that fills the full length of the back wall. She thinks what she's looking for is on the fourth shelf but that's higher than she can reach from her chair. Helen latches onto a shelf and she hauls herself up, partly out of her wheelchair, useless legs dangling under her.

Still not high enough, she pulls on that shelf and is able to get one hand onto the next, the fourth shelf. She can't pull herself high enough to see what she's looking for but her fingers brush against cold metal. She wraps her hand around the object and pulls it into her lap. It's longer but not as heavy as she had thought it would be. She pulls herself back up and her fingers find a box but, in dragging it toward the edge, she tips it over and spills the contents deeper into the shelf. Stretched to their absolute limits, her fingers find one, then a second and, finally, a third of the spilled cylinders. She cannot reach any more and is running out of time, anyway. She drops these into her vest pocket, falls back into her wheelchair, spins and wheels out of the closet.

As she passes it, she, again, snatches the string turning off the harsh closet light. Dancing spots compromise her vision. She glides to the bedroom light switch and turns that one off, too.

She doesn't have to guess whether the man is inside her home. She hears the crunch of his shoes on the corn flakes as he passes through the kitchen. She pauses, now no longer sure if she has time to also turn off the bathroom light. The man's voice calls to her from downstairs.

"Howdy Ma'am! I'm Mike. Mike Smith. I'm with the power company," she hears a man say in an unhurried Texas drawl. "We're out making sure our customers are okay. Are you?" he says, and after a moment adds, "Okay, that is?"

Her security system should have restarted when the generator kicked in. She doesn't know how, but she figures he must have jimmied the backdoor without tripping the alarm.

He's got skills. He knows what he's doing. Fuckity-fuck.

The man says more.

Blah, blah, blah, storm. Yap, yap, yap, transformer.

The man's words fly past Helen. She can't waste another moment listening to his bullshit cover story.

She yanks her tires so hard that she does a wheelie and almost falls backward onto the floor. Steadying herself, she shoots across her bedroom and heads back to the elevator. She pauses there, listening. She can't believe her luck. The man downstairs is a real talker, his raised voice projecting all the way to the second floor. He's still talking.

He might be a killer, but he must moonlight as a telemarketer. Is it too much to hope his plan is to talk me to death?

She's grateful for every word he says and the seconds it takes him to say them.

Helen worries that her lack of response will spur the man to come upstairs. That would be a disaster. As if on cue, she hears the creak of the second step from the bottom on the stairs. The man is coming up.

Cupping her hands around her mouth, Helen calls out as cheerily as she can manage. "Hello young man. Thank you so much for coming. I'm taking the elevator downstairs now. Can you meet me at the bottom?"

Not waiting for his reply, Helen wheels back into her bedroom, grabs two pillows and a coverlet, and goes back to the bathroom. She lifts herself out of the wheelchair and onto the toilet, a maneuver that is old hat. She arranges the pillows on the wheelchair. She drapes the blanket over the pillows. She shoves the wheelchair into the lift, closes the grate and reaches through to pull the lever, snatching her arm back just as the lift begins to trundle down.

Never thought I'd be thankful the elevator is the 'slowest mother-fuckin' lift in the world.'

Helen takes the metal and wood object she'd retrieved from the closet and fixes the sling to her shoulder. She tucks the meat cleaver into her waistband and pats her vest pocket. She considers scenarios, dismissing them one after another. She can't think of any plan that doesn't end in her death.

The man doesn't answer at first, but the hum of the elevator in motion must have reached his ears because Helen hears him answer, "Why, sure, ma'am." After another moment, he adds, "Meetcha there."

Still, Helen does not yet hear the creak of the lower stair that would reassure her the man has taken the bait. She senses that he lingers and listens, poised to rush up the stairs where he will catch her out in the open, utterly exposed and vulnerable. Helen holds her breath until she finally hears the familiar creak from the stair, a small but telling sound letting her know he's gone back down. She gasps a lungful of air and kicks it into high gear—or, at least, whatever gear can be managed when one crawls without the benefit of legs.

She knows he will be able to see, at least partially, into the lift before it even gets to the ground floor. She hopes that the bedding stuffed wheelchair will buy her a few additional moments. Any reason to give him pause, to buy her time.

The noise from the lift retracing its way down gives her sound cover as she crawls from the upstairs elevator landing through the bathroom and into her bedroom. She uses the legs of furniture as handholds, arms pulling herself forward like she's on a horizontal wall at a climbing gym. She thinks she may still have time to get to the linen closet in the hall when she hears the elevator's soft ping. It's reached the bottom. She hears the grate being yanked open.

"Mrs. Chesterfield," the man calls. "You are being trickyyyyyyyy," he says, drawing the last vowel sound out.

He's on to me. He'll come up now quick like and kill me.

His steps are no longer careful. Cereal crackles loudly as the man marches back through the kitchen. Helen knows he is no more than a few strides from the stairs. She realizes she can't get to her intended place before she's found. Panicked, she crawls under the bed, pulling her possessions in with her. She's angry at herself.

Hidin' under the bed? That's the best I can do? Fuckin' pitiful. He'll find me, sure as shit. I'll be dead and embarrassed.

Her view from under the bed is limited since she's turned away from the door and toward the interior of her bedroom. She hears but does not see the man who has rushed up the stairs and down the hallway to dash into the bedroom.

With a swish of nylon, the man trots past the bed toward the bathroom. In the dim light she sees his wet, sandy boots pelt the floor. The boots disappear around the doorway into the bathroom which has the only light on in the entire Casita. Helen struggles to rearrange herself under the bed, but she's twisted half onto her stomach and her unresponsive legs are pretzeled the other way.

The sandy boots return to the bedroom and pause before they march, again, out of Helen's field of view, this time toward the walk-in storage room. She'd left the door open. He's in there no longer than a few seconds before the boots reappear very near the bed.

The man says nothing at first but then offers, "Mrs. Chesterfield? I'm here to check your fuse box and, well, check on you too. There's no reason to be afraid. You can come out."

Helen doesn't believe him. The man's chuckling confirms her suspicions.

"Woo ha! No reason to be hiding now. Come out, come out wherever you aaaaaaaare." He croons it like a lullaby.

Helen's mind races through her options. She cannot bring the rifle to bear. It's still strapped to her back. She'd never get it off and pointed in the right direction in time. Even if she could, she's pretty sure it isn't loaded.

Even if it was loaded? What's the best I can do? Shoot him in the ankle?

Bad goes to worse when one boot slides back to be replaced by a knee. Then, a hand goes to the ground as well. Helen torques herself around as best she can to allow her some room to swing the meat cleaver at a more advantageous angle. She takes some satisfaction in knowing she'll take off some of his fingers as the price of her death.

She's an instant from bringing the cleaver down, hand already trembling in anticipation, when she hears a raised voice. It's calling from downstairs.

"Helen. Are you here?" a woman's voice beckons. "The door was ajar. And why is your wheelchair down here? And your kitchen? It's a mess. Are you okay?"

Helen sees the man's hand on the floor spasm, and it very nearly causes her to chop into it in response. But the hand disappears and so, too, does the knee and then the boots. The man has moved away from her vision, but she can feel he's standing just inside the bedroom doorway. He's surely peeking down at what little bit of the downstairs can be seen from that vantage point.

"Helen? Helen? Should I come upstairs?" the woman's voice asks from downstairs.

The voice is familiar, but Helen can't place it.

Helen doesn't hear him step down the hallway but the reliable, squeaky lower stair groans under his weight. He's gone downstairs.

She hears some voices, his and hers. She can't tell what they are saying but she hears a yelp that might be caused by surprise but, more likely, pain.

Redoubling her efforts, Helen starts crawling, again. She doesn't know how much time she has left—surely not much.

CHAPTER FIVE

Fit to be Tied

"Drama don't arise by surprise; it is summoned, undisguised."

~T.F. Hodge (1969–present), American writer, blogger,
wordsmith, graphic designer

———— ••• ————

THE ALABASTER BEAM OF LIGHT FROM HER HAND BOUNCES and wobbles as she skips, hops, long jumps, and tiptoes her away between and around the many puddles that have flourished and grown to become temporary ponds. The sand is saturated and sucks at her running shoes.

Juanita had followed the Mustang Manor guard's well-remembered lyrics to the fork in the road and had taken the final left-hand turn across the one-lane bridge. Once over, however, Juanita's tires had begun to spin as she'd climbed the final incline to the Casita. Not wanting to get stuck, she'd driven to a patch of higher ground that appeared to be less flooded and had decent drainage. She'd parked there, realizing she would have to run through the rain to the Casita—but that had seemed a better choice than getting stuck in a quagmire when it came time to leave in a few hours.

Before exiting the ambulance, she'd pulled on her raincoat and grabbed her small overnight backpack containing a change of clothes plus minimal toiletries and makeup. She'd slung the backpack over one shoulder.

Halfway out of the driver's side door of the ambulance, she'd realized she couldn't use the flashlight function on her still-not-getting-a-signal cell phone without it getting wet in the rain. She'd tucked the phone into her rear pocket and grabbed a flashlight from the center console.

Walking toward the Casita, water droplets fly off in globs when she moves her head. She can feel the bill of her cap is getting soaked and heavy. She hopes it isn't ruined. It's her favorite. Wearing it reminds her of the football games she'd watched on TV with her Papa before the Oilers left for Nashville and before Papa left for heaven.

As Juanita had expected, the early morning is inky dark, the power out at the Casita, obviously. She recalls Helen has a generator and wonders why she hasn't turned it on. Even more surprising is the back door. Highlighted by her flashlight, she can see it's ajar.

Juanita quickens her walk, but she doesn't go directly to the door. She goes, instead, to the side. There, she turns, faces out, and flattens her back against the wall. She turns off her flashlight, waits, and listens.

Is there someone in the Casita? Someone other than Helen? Did she go outside? Did she leave for some reason?

Juanita sees mud and sand on the concrete step under the door's overhang. There are footprint ridges that look like they might have come from boots. Large ones.

Since she's off the landing and out from under the overhang, rain pours off the brim of her Oilers cap and down the back of her neck.

She tilts her chin down and shakes her head, throwing water off like a dog. She opens the door wider and eases herself into the laundry room. She considers for a moment and decides to leave the backdoor open.

You know. Just in case.

It's pitch black, so Juanita switches her flashlight back on. She cocks an ear. Suddenly, a fan—part of the motor of a meat freezer beside her—whirs to life, and she nearly jumps out of her skin.

The generator is on after all? What the hell? Why aren't there any other lights on?

Juanita slips off her backpack and rechecks her phone once more to confirm what she already expects. Still no working cell signal. Sliding the phone back into her pocket, Juanita considers the best course of action. Under normal circumstances, finding a home's door ajar when all the lights are out spells danger. That said, Juanita reasons, it's not likely anyone has been out breaking into homes during a heavy thunderstorm. Juanita is becoming more convinced that Helen must have not secured the door well enough before she went to bed.

Still, the quiet unnerves her.

Juanita takes a couple more steps into the hallway and, again, pauses. She hears nothing beyond the barely audible electric hum coming from the freezer. Her flashlight reveals nothing.

Juanita sniffs the air.

Something smells…off?

"Helen?" Juanita says, as much to herself as anyone else. "Are you home?"

No answer.

Advancing further inside, Juanita slinks a few feet from the laundry room to where it intersects with a hallway. To the left is the living room; to the right, the kitchen.

Juanita shines her flashlight into the living room. It's a spartan space with a flatscreen television, two matching bookcases, a loveseat, and enough uncluttered room for a wheelchair. If Helen isn't on the porch, this is usually where Juanita finds her.

Not here. Maybe the kitchen?

Seeing nothing disheveled in the living room, she turns and goes the other way, down the hallway, and follows the flashlight's beam into the kitchen. There's something spilled across the kitchen floor. It glistens and Juanita isn't sure what it is, but it crunches beneath her tennis shoes as she walks across the tiled floor.

Stepping all the way to the rear of the kitchen, she sees Helen's wheelchair. It's curiously stuffed with bedding, and it's sitting halfway in and halfway out of the lift.

Maybe it got stuck there when the power went out? Is Helen upstairs?

She can see a green light on a panel fixed to the wall next to the elevator landing. The generator is definitely on.

"Helen. Are you here?" Juanita calls out more loudly. "The door was ajar. And why is your wheelchair down here? And your kitchen? It's a mess. Are you okay?"

No answer. Scenarios run through her mind. She's trained to deal with exigencies. Her chief worry, now, is that her passenger is injured or sick. Or dead.

"Helen? Helen? Should I come upstairs?" All decorum is forsaken; now she's shouting.

There's no answer for a few seconds. Just as Juanita starts toward the stairs, she hears a man's voice call down to her from the upstairs.

"Hello," the voice says. "I'm Mike Smith, with the power company. The storm has knocked out the power and I'm checking on our more vulnerable customers. I'll be right down."

Juanita can hear the man is coming down the stairs, talking as he's walking, saying he's here to check the fuse box or, maybe, fix the transformer, but the words seem to run together. Juanita cannot understand what the problem is or, rather, what the man is planning to do about it. As the voice reaches the ground floor, it occurs to Juanita that the man doesn't have or isn't using a flashlight and that seems weird.

Come to think of it, where did he park? I didn't see a service truck.

The man keeps on walking and talking nonstop, and it seems to

Juanita that he's repeating himself. The voice floats from the stairs landing and around a corner until the man steps into range of Juanita's flashlight beam.

Into the glare strides a man dressed entirely in black. He's wearing some kind of beanie-like knit mask and it obscures all of his face except for dark eyes and a wide, toothy mouth. Juanita recollects the ski mask is called a balaclava, and she associates it with movies about terrorists. And assassins.

The hairs on Juanita's neck stand up and she involuntarily shudders. She knows this is trouble.

Seeming to have used up all of his words the man strides forward, reaches out, and snatches the flashlight from Juanita's hands. The man wraps her in a bear hug and tackles her to the ground, his weighty body landing on top of hers as she topples to the floor. Air whooshes from her lungs as she hits the ground.

"No!" Juanita yells. Before she can say more, a gloved hand clamps over her mouth. She cries out again—a muffled bark beneath the smothering grip. She writhes and bucks, desperate to shake off the suffocating mass. The man raises the flashlight and brings it down. A sharp pain erupts across her cheek, followed by a tingling sensation.

"Shush!" the man says, mouth next to her ear. "You need to be quiet. If you make another sound, I'll hurt you. Don't talk. Nod if you understand."

Juanita is petrified but her trembling mutates into a nod, though it's difficult to do with her head on the floor and a hand across her mouth. Juanita feels her body being turned over and now she's on her stomach. The thought of rape enters her primal consciousness, and she struggles again.

She yells "No!" and "No!" again.

She yelps when her arms are pulled behind her back. She hears the sound of plastic teeth zipping. Her wrists have been secured together behind her back. He swiftly does the same thing to her ankles. Juanita pulls in a breath and opens her mouth to yell for help, but she's barely begun when something is thrust into her mouth, filling it. It tastes like a dishrag. She tries again to scream. It comes out a baffled moan.

The zipping sound is loud, right next to her ear, and the pain is instant. A zip tie has been put around the back of her neck and over her mouth. The man applies another zip tie under her skull and across her lips to help hold the gag in place. A third tie joins, this one flattening her nose. The zip ties are excruciatingly tight, and the constriction pulls painfully at her mouth, cheeks, and neck.

The man rolls Juanita over onto her back and holds the flashlight just a couple of inches in front of her eyes. It's the SUV headlights all over again. Except, this time, she's certain, they're not going to slide on by and leave her be.

"Listen," the man says to Juanita. His voice is higher pitched than she expects. "I am not here to hurt you. I'll let you go in a few minutes. But for now, I need you to just stay right here. If you do that, you'll be fine. If you don't, I'll have to shut you up," he says. "Nod if you believe me."

Hooded eyes hover just above the shaft of light pouring into Juanita's face. His eyes feel cold and hard and the image blurs as tears flood her own eyes. She's grateful she cannot see his clearly, but she can't look away either. Juanita nods even though she does not believe him.

"I'll be taking this," the man adds when he yanks the cell phone from her back pocket. Juanita winces as she hears boots stomp, plastic crack, glass break. It's a river dance of destruction.

My phone! He smashed it. Shit. Shit. Shit!

The man stands, looming over Juanita. He turns off Juanita's flashlight causing the house to plunge back to darkness. Juanita can tell there's a trickle of light coming from somewhere upstairs, but very little of it penetrates the hall in which she's been left cruelly bound and gagged.

"See you later alligator," the man sings in falsetto.

Juanita hears the man go down the hallway and turn right into the laundry room. Soon she hears his voice again. A faint and tinny sound reaches Juanita's ears after the man has stopped talking.

He's talking to someone. On a phone? How? There's no cell service unless it just came back on. Is he using a walkie-talkie? A radio?

Juanita can't tell what's being said. She's filled with certainty her survival might depend on knowing.

Can I do it? What will he do if I don't stay put? He said he wouldn't hurt me. I don't believe it. Shit. It's now or never.

Rocking her shoulders, Juanita rolls herself like a log partway down the lightless hall to where she can hear better.

"...here for sure. She's upstairs somewhere. Hiding. Woo hee, like that's going to do her a bit of good."

Tinny squawk.

"Yeah, but there's a complication. There's a Mexican girl here. She came in after me. Showed up out of nowhere. I got her tied up so she's not going anywhere."

Tinny squawk.

"No, I have no idea. What do you want me to do?"

Tinny squawk.

"Both of them? Okay, okay. But I'm going to need help with the, uh, disposal and cleanup."

Tinny squawk.

"Sure. That'll work. How soon can they get here?"

Tinny squawk.

"Three hours? Fuck me. Well, make sure they bring two body bags."

Juanita's eyes widen at that.

Two body bags? One of 'em sure to be mine.

Tinny squawk.

"Don't worry, I'll recover the computer and bring it with," the man says.

Tinny squawk.

"Okay. I'll confirm when I have it. After that, radio silence for the next several hours, then. Gotta go. Woo hee. Work to be done. No rest for the weary."

Shit! He's done. Roll back. Roll back. Roll back!

Juanita barrel rolls herself back to where she was or, at least, where she thinks she was. And just in time.

The man comes back as Juanita is trying to disguise her heaving. Rolling with hands and legs bound and a gag in the mouth has made her pant. The man sinks down next to Juanita and pats her face hard, just short a slap.

"No reason to be this anxious. Be a good girl and you'll be fine," the man says.

"After while crocodile," he sings as he rises, turns, and steps away to dissolve into the gloom.

CHAPTER SIX

A Game of Hide and Seek

"Don't wait to be hunted to hide, that's always been my motto."

~Samuel Beckett (1906-1989), Irish novelist,
short story writer, theater director, poet, literary translator

———— ••• ————

A BLANCHED GLOW WASHES FORTH FROM THE BATHROOM'S open door. Some of the light trickles into the bedroom. Helen crawls away. She needs to put distance between herself and the light.

She'd started out scootching herself. It's not the fastest way to move, sitting on your butt, looking at your legs, lifting and shoving yourself backward. It may be reliable, but it's slow. The clock ticks down in her head. The backward shuffle is taking too long.

To speed up, she's turned onto her stomach and, stiff armed, she pulls herself forward. She's settled into a rhythm, her hands stabbing the floor, head and chest high, legs trailing behind her. She's come to think of this stroke as her mermaid crawl.

She's about halfway down the hall when one elbow gives out, and she crashes face-first onto the wooden floor. Pain explodes through her jaw. She knows her lip is bleeding, but she's too afraid to reach up and check how bad it is. She can't afford to add blood to the sweat already running onto her hands and fingers, making her grip dangerously slippery. Her right wrist throbs, a sharp, pulsing ache that makes her grit her teeth. Now, she's down to this: shoulders, elbows, forearms, wrists, hands, fingers working together to inch her forward. It's plunge and press, claw and pull, a swimmer's butterfly stroke across the hardwood hallway floor.

Almost there. Keep going. Almost there.

She's nearly to the end of the hall, opposite of where the stairs lead down to the ground floor. She's already passed under the drop-down metal chin-up bar the occupational therapist installed to span the hallway. Set at a height of two feet, Helen is supposed to have been doing pull-ups from the laying position.

Shoulda been doin' my chin-ups, like the therapist told me. Shoulda, woulda, coulda. I'm a day late and a dollar short on that one.

She can almost touch the hinged doors that cover the clothes hamper that is the lower half of the linen closet. Despite being so very close, she cannot manage the last bit. She's so tired, and her wrist now howls with pain. She's seen this ending before. A newly hatched turtle, incapable of crawling the last few inches to the sea, is snatched up from the beach and eaten by a seagull.

I'm done in. Hell, it's just a matter of time now.

Helen lays her head against the floor and closes her eyes. Then comes the shout.

"No!" Helen hears. The voice is loud and angry and female. And it's laced with resistance. It's a bark, sharp but husky. Recognition comes to her.

It's Juanita? What the fuck? Why's she here? Fuckity-fuck. This is bad. What'll he do with her? She's a witness, a loose end that can't be left flappin' around. He's gonna kill her too!

She regrets not having shouted a warning to give Juanita a chance to flee. At least some chance. But she's also sure the masked man is a killer, through-and-through.

Even if I'd lopped off a few fingers, that wouldn't have been enough to stop him. He won't let her get away. Gotta get goin'.

Move. Move, dammit.

Helen fixes her eyes on the still unrealized cabinet doors. It starts with her shoulders, then her elbows, then her forearms, then...

Helen is absurdly giddy when she makes it. She can barely believe it herself. Somehow, her legs are now tucked inside. She focuses for a minute on her breathing. She's raggedly huffing.

Now, how do I work this goddamned gun?

Helen knows next to nothing about guns and ammo. But she recalls Ben saying that this rifle shoots twenty-two caliber bullets. He'd told her they are small bullets, meant to kill small animals. Helen wishes they were big ones, meant to kill big animals.

She knows the rifle is still strapped to her back on account of the fact that it got caught against the top of the hamper opening. Twice. She fondles her vest pocket. It feels like all three of the bullets are still in there. Awkwardly, she turns her torso to the side, and she eases the strap off of her shoulder. She swings it around to where she can point the barrel out from between the two doors of the cabinet which she's pulled mostly closed.

Can I load it? How do I load it? Will it fire? Will one small bullet do the job? Can I reload quickly enough if it doesn't? Can I kill a man? Yes, I already know that. But can I kill him?

The rush of doubts are an acid; they eat away at her confidence.

Does it have a safety? It does. Ben said so. What does the safety look like? Fuckity-fuck. I can't even see it. What does the safety feel like? How does it work? Maybe it's got some kind of thingamabob that I won't have a clue about. I'll never figure this out in the pitch black.

She slides a hand along the bottom of the rifle and caresses the circle thing on the bottom, the one with the trigger inside. She brings her hand up and feels a part sticking out. The part has a knob on the end, and she grabs it. She's able to twist it up only after having tried unsuccessfully to force it down. The lever won't go any higher and she thinks it must now go forward or backward. Her guess is correct, and it slides back with a click.

Near panic washes over her.

What next? How much time have I got?

She is, at first, frantic but she wills herself to steady her shaking arms and ignore the pain in her wrist. She remembers the special forces shows she's seen on TV. *Slow is smooth and smooth is fast,* the soldiers would say. Cautiously but intently, she reaches her hand up to the pocket in her vest containing the three bullets. She withdraws one from the pocket, careful to make sure the other two stay put.

She brings it close to her face and smells it. It's not very big, less than two inches long. She's pretty sure of which way the pointy end goes.

She lays the bullet into the chamber and her fingers explore forward and back in the trench. It's not very oily. She's worried about that. She recalls Ben sitting cross-legged on the floor back when he was alive, an old blanket spread out in front of him, the rifle disassembled. Even laying in parts, it had looked lethal. He was cleaning it before putting it back together.

He'd said gun oil is important. This rifle hasn't had any for at least ten years. It may not work at all. I wonder if a little spit would help.

She tries to summon some saliva, but her mouth is too dry. She remembers that Ben always joked about him hunting something they could eat. Something for the pot, he'd say.

I was done makin' rabbit stew—didn't wanna gut or skin nothin' no more. Now I wonder if it's me fixin' to be gutted and skinned.

Helen recalls having asked Ben.

How do I know the safety is on? How do I know it won't suddenly go off? Show me.

Ben had told her the single-shot rifle was old. Uncommonly, it had a safety that automatically reengaged after every shot. It had to be reset each time to fire.

She whispers into the dark.

Show me again, Ben. Show me again.

Helen peers through the slit, the opening made by the barrel of the rifle that tents the two cabinet doors open just a bit. She sees nothing beyond a patch of hallway but can make out feeble traces of bathroom light framing the bedroom doorway.

She hopes she's remembered Ben's words correctly. She can't risk a practice shot. He'd hear. The surprise would be gone. She pulls at some dirty clothes and tries to build them up under and around her elbow to take some of the weight of the barrel, but she can't pull enough of it from under her body to make much of a difference. She knows she's not holding the barrel still. It's a deep closet but not deep enough to allow Helen to fix the butt of the rifle to her shoulder. The butt end is, instead, pressed against the back wall of the cabinet and Helen is holding it from the side, left arm out and right arm around it so that her finger can reach the trigger. It's hard to keep it from wobbling. The front of the barrel makes circles and figure eights, her arms weary and rebellious.

She's done what she can. Now she must wait.

Come on, fucker. Come now. Or don't come. You could just go away. Leave. You can do that. But you won't, will you?

Fuckity-fuck. You're coming, aren't you? Come on, then.

It's the absence—the nothingness—that threatens to shred her resolve. She wants him to come. Now. Each moment that passes with nothing seen or heard is a relief and, also, an agony. It takes all of her stamina and concentration and, most of all, her will to lay silent and wait. No matter how hard she looks, her eyes cannot penetrate the dark any further. The intense concentration saps her energy making her eyelids ache. She's afraid her stare might turn into a liability, that she'll see a mirage, or that she'll freeze up when he comes. She wants to wipe the sweat from her eyes but is afraid to move at all.

She feels more than sees something shift in the dark, something on the verge of being solid. She thinks she may be hallucinating.

No. It's him. He's comin'. Didn't even hear him come up the stairs. He must've stepped over that second stair. He's a learner, he is.

A dark blob emerges, tentatively, from the shadows. A head and monstrous face. She can see holes through which eyes and an obscenely large, round mouth are visible. As though disembodied, the head swivels left and right in a way that suggests practice. Familiarity. The head tilts up and some survival instinct tells Helen he's sniffing the air. Whether he's found her scent, she cannot tell.

The head regains its equilibrium and moves forward. The body follows, seeming to glide. His body, too, is black. Shadows seem to yield their hold on his body only reluctantly. Dark tendrils slip off as if anguished to be losing mass from the shadow's dark possession. His steps are careful, slow, rolling ones. She feels the tightly controlled intensity in his body, the energy kinetic. The movements suggest confidence but caution. Capability. Violence.

Helen trembles. Icy beads percolate on her skin and multiply and grow fat and run down her face and neck. She knows this is not entirely due to fatigue. She's panting and she tries to slow her breathing, but she cannot.

Helen had expected him to hurry, to come at her with speed. He does not. His approach is as a hunter stalking a skittish prey. His head tilts ever so slightly to one side. He's listening. Considering. Professional.

The man halts and it feels to Helen that time, too, has stopped. His eyes fix down the hall, and Helen is sure he's looking into her eyes. His eyes are telling her: I see you.

Maybe not. His head swings away, eyes no longer looking her way. Helen can't help but release the breath she hadn't realized she was holding.

As he nears the bedroom, the man presses his back against the wall and drops low. He spies around the corner of the doorway into the bedroom. He steps through the threshold, movements lubricated and quiet, his silhouette barely visible in the thin light seeping from the bathroom.

Helen counts the seconds it will take him to recheck the lift, bedroom and storage room.

This time, he'll check under the bed. He surely figures that's where I hid earlier. Then he'll come for me. Here I'll be, at the end of the line, crammed into this hidey-hole. This deer blind. The only place I could think of to make a last stand.

CHAPTER SEVEN

Bound and Gagged

*"So, every bondman in his own hand
bears the power to cancel his captivity."*

~William Shakespeare (1564–1616), English poet, playwright, actor

———— ••• ————

SHE'S AN ANIMAL CORNERED IN THE DARK, SMALL AND pitiful, frantic to flee but caught in a trap. She cannot conceive fight. Only flight.

Juanita feels kinship with the furry dead body, the roadkill she'd passed in the night barely an hour ago. She mourns it's cold, lifeless form. She regrets not stopping, penitent over her disregard for convenience's sake. She wonders whom will find her curled body.

Abuelo will be angry. He'll want answers. Alex? He'll be devastated. He won't understand. How will any of this make sense to them? It doesn't make sense to me.

She hears a popping sound from upstairs, causing her to jerk.

A gunshot? Not a very loud one. Maybe something else?

She hears the man's high-pitched laugh, and he shouts out, "Fucking cunt! I'm gonna kill you."

Helen? He must be talking to her. Must have shot her. I'm next. I'm next. Got to do something!

Juanita starts to tremble, adrenaline coursing through her veins.

A wave of frost washes over her. Goosebumps erupt like insects on her skin. Warm liquid spills from her crotch and onto her thighs and the smell of her own urine and fear spurs her to frenzy.

She throws her head back and smacks a wall she cannot see in the dark, bringing starbursts to her eyes. She feels blood run from her forehead down through one eye and her scimitar-shaped nose channels the blood into the corners of her mouth. It saturates the gag, and she can taste the iron and salt. She feels the gorge rise in her throat and her mouth fills but there's nowhere for it to go and she swallows some of it back down, heaving and bucking in desperation.

A sob erupts from her chest and snot fills her nose. The blood-soaked gag will not allow her a breath and she panics and convulses, a worm on a hook.

Her fit has brought her onto her side. Somehow, she gets her knees underneath her. She's off balance, arms secured behind her back. She surges up but cannot sustain the momentum and falls forward onto her face, smearing fluids on the floor and over her chin, neck and chest.

She tries again, this time throwing her shoulders back as far as they will go. Somehow, she staggers to her feet. She wants to run, to get away, but she can only manage small hops, each one threatening her precarious balance. She blows out through her nose, sending bits of mucus and droplets of blood splattering against the wall where she'd banged her head. She knows she will not escape bound as she is. She knows she'll die.

He'll kill her and come for me. Do something! Gotta do something!

She hops once. Then again. And again.

Her breaths are ragged and short and she feels lightheaded. Maybe from the blow. Maybe from lack of oxygen. Her dizziness makes her suspect she may pass out soon. Not much time.

She hears another bang.

Gotta be a gunshot. He's being thorough. Move!

She hops again and again and again, a sack race where the only prize is a chance at life. Ghostly dots dance across her vision. She hops and trips and starts to go down, but her shoulder hits the refrigerator door she can't see, and it arrests her fall, just barely. She recalls there's a counter around the refrigerator, and she shuffle-hops until she can feel it with her stomach. Legs trembling, she squats down. Like a berserker, impervious to the pain in her jaw and lips and teeth, she saws the gag up and down against the counter's edge.

She feels the gag give just a little and is afraid it's her imagination. She puts all of her weight against the gag and rams her head downward, adding a shredded bottom lip to her growing list of bloody injuries.

Suddenly, she can breathe through her mouth. She gulps air like a guppy, face tilted up and grateful. Only then does she register the pain around her mouth. She can still feel the gag is squeezing her face, but it's shifted. Now it's anchored by the ties to the space between her upper lip and nose. It's not going anywhere.

Breathing clears her head and some of the dizziness falls away.

This is a kitchen. That means knives. Something to cut my way loose. Where are they?

She recalls having seen a butcher block knife holder on a low counter across the room. She hops and shuffles, kicking away as she goes whatever has been spilled across the floor.

She collides with the counter, bends forward at the waist, pushes her head down, and reaches out with her tongue. She tastes wood. She chomps onto the handle, jaw shuddering with effort and she pulls, leaning back to give the long object enough room to clear the slot in the knife holder.

The knife falls from her mouth and clatters to the floor. Juanita drops to her knees and, with hands bound behind her back, she searches for the knife, keening to herself in anxiety.

A man's voice call out, "You're dead, bitch!"

She hears Helen scream something back and the man is screaming too, and there are some banging noises that trail off and end. She knows what the silence means. He's killed her. Juanita knows she's only moments left to get away.

Juanita is gasping shallow breaths when her leg kicks into the knife somewhere on the kitchen floor. One leg pins the knife in place and she's able to slide it to where she can, finally, gather it up in her bound hands. She tries to position the long blade onto the ties around her wrists, but the ties are so tight that she can't get a productive angle. What little pressure she can apply keeps sliding off the ties and, instead, she repeatedly nicks the meaty parts of her palms. Juanita is sure she has only seconds before the man will come for her.

As if on cue, Juanita hears the man. He's not hurrying. He's dragging Helen's body down the stairs. Thumps accompany each step. Juanita realizes she might be able to use the countertop to pin the knife's blade into place and maybe that will allow her to saw her way free. Fueled by adrenalin and fear, Juanita staggers precariously to her feet.

He's almost here. Seconds left. Get free or die.

CHAPTER EIGHT

It Takes Two to Strangle

"Whatever doesn't kill me better start running."

~Sarah J. Maas (1986–present), fantasy novelist, from *Queen of Shadows*

———— ••• ————

THE MAN, SILHOUETTED IN THE GENTLEST OF LIGHT, returns to the hall after checking the bedroom and bathroom. Helen can't see but, rather, senses the moment the man realizes Helen is hiding in the cabinet. Maybe he sees the cabinet doors are open a little. There's barely any light, but there's some. Maybe he sees the wobbling rifle barrel. Maybe he has found her, literally, by process of elimination.

Whatever the reason, the bogeyman now rushes. Long strides devour the distance between them so quickly that Helen has become a horrified onlooker, frozen in place. Her mind disconnects from her body as she sees but can't process or respond to the threat racing toward her down the twilight hallway.

The man is only two strides from the cabinet, hands reaching for the partially opened doors when he runs smack into the absurdly low set chin up bar secured across the hallway. He impacts the bar just below one knee and his leg buckles, causing him to fall backward onto the floor.

Helen shoots him. In the ankle. After all.

Helen doesn't recall pulling the trigger, but she must have. The man is grunting. Helen sees him reach toward his foot. The light is poor, but Helen can tell that he's looking right at her through the narrow slit between the doors.

"Fucking cunt! I'm gonna kill you," the man hisses through his teeth.

The cursing snaps Helen out of her trance.

"Fuck you!" she screams back. "You're all talk, motherfucker. Shut your fuckin' mouth and come and get me!"

She takes her finger off the trigger guard and raises it to her vest pocket. She reaches in and grabs a second bullet. She's in a hurry, and the two bullets come out of her pocket together. One bullet is safely in her fingers but the other spills somewhere in the cabinet.

Helen pushes the lever forward and down, and she hears a click. She hopes that means the leftover part of the first bullet has been cleared. She runs one finger into the groove and slides it up and down. It does not feel any different than the first time. She puts the bullet in the chamber and slides the lever forward and down again. She remembers to pull the safety release knob.

The man has stood up and is stepping gingerly over the chin-up bar, barely putting any weight on his wounded leg. Helen realizes how close he is to her.

If he jumps at me, falls even, he'll be able to just grab me.

Helen tilts the rifle up and pulls the trigger, this time on purpose. The bullet hits the man in the shoulder and the impact causes his body to spin away but not very far.

What she fears most is what the man does next. He pushes off his one good foot and throws himself forward to land, mostly outside the cabinet, but with one of his arms inside the cabinet. She cannot feel it but knows he is pawing at her leg.

Helen reaches down wishing for a miracle and it's granted. The third bullet has caught in her shirt and her fingers find it right away. She chambers the round, but the man has probably heard the sound of the rifle being reloaded again because he drags himself forward, this time pulling himself up onto her waist. His hand reaches up and gathers a fistful of her hair as he climbs the rest of the way up her body until his mouth is right next to Helen's ear.

"No quick death for you," he coos to her like a lover.

His breath is sour and Helen's stomach lurches. One hand caresses her cheek in the dark.

"Before I kill you, I'm going to hurt you. It'll all be above the waist-line. You know, the parts you can still feel, you cunt."

Vibrating with rage and quavering from adrenalin, Helen squeezes the rifle so tightly that her hands ache. She screams. She rams the rifle barrel into the gaping cloth mouth hole, thrusts it between his lips, through freshly fracturing teeth, over his tongue, and she pushes and pushes it all the way to the very back of his throat until the barrel will go no further. She hears the man gag.

She pulls the trigger.

There's a click. But the rifle does not fire. She's forgotten to pull the knob at the back.

The man gargles and retches and Helen tries to slide one hand back to release the safety so she can pull the trigger again, but his hands have seized the rifle. She feels the barrel being pulled back up and out of his throat and mouth. He rips the rifle entirely from Helen's grip and smacks the butt against her face.

"Look at me," the man lisps, tooth fragments spilling onto Helen's face, "while I bash your brains in."

Her eyes search for his in the thin light. She feels him draw back, cocking his arm, ready to smash the rifle butt into her face.

Helen lays her mouth against his and slides her lips over his cheek-bone and up to his ear. She gathers it between her teeth. She clamps down as hard as she can and grinds her teeth, flesh trapped inside. The man lets go of the rifle and slaps at her, but he's tall, and his arms are long, and this causes his hands to glance off of the top of the dirty clothes hamper and that robs the blows of most of their power.

Helen crunches for all she's worth, tongue feeling cartilage bend and crack. She can taste blood as she masticates the meat. She feels the ripping, the tearing, and she worries it back and forth like a terrier, growling all the while. She can feel now that he's picked up the rifle again, and he presses it against her jaw, trying to force her loose from his ear but maybe afraid to push too hard in his fear she will take his ear off with her.

The rifle butt pulls away and then comes back, punching into the side of her face, but not at a good angle and it mostly slides by, the blood making her face slippery.

Helen hears the man grunt, and his hands close around her neck.

He's going old school. He'll strangle me. Stop. Stop it!

Dark and light spots dance in her eyes. She cannot get a breath. She pulls at one of his wrists, but the man is much too strong.

Last chance, she thinks. She howls and extends herself, teeth pulling the ear as far up and away as she can. She chops the meat cleaver into his neck. Without enough strength to swing again, Helen puts the cleaver against his throat and saws it back and forth, grunting like a cavewoman.

Fuck you. Fuck you. Fuck you. Fuckin' die!

The man squawks, then coughs. The cough turns into a rattle that turns into a gurgle that turns into a thin keening that stops when a spew of hot blood runs out, soaking Helen's face and eyes and ears and mouth. His body shakes uncontrollably, and a high-pitched squeal escapes his throat before trailing off.

Finally, he stops moving.

Helen reaches up and pries his hands from her throat. She spits out blood. Her tongue finds something chunkier and rubbery, and she spits that out, too. She lays back and huffs in a wisp of air. Her throat is wrecked.

Calm down. Don't move. Just breathe. I won. He's dead. I'm not. Not yet. He damaged my windpipe. Can't get enough air.

She stops gulping and tries to capture air in sips, feeding herself like an invalid. She is getting air now but barely enough. She rolls her neck and looks at the man lying next to her. She pulls off the ski mask and takes in his face. Helen hugs the man tight, twists her abdomen, wriggles her shoulders, and presses her mouth to what's left of his torn, cauliflowered ear.

In a tortured, paper-thin voice she squeaks out: "Who's the cunt, now?"

CHAPTER NINE

Ding Dong! The Witch is Dead

*"Sooner or later, everyone sits down
to a banquet of consequences."*

~Robert Louis Stevenson (1850–1894), Scottish novelist,
essayist, poet, and travel writer

———————— ••• ————————

IN THE NEAR PITCH-BLACK JUANITA HEARS THE MAN shamble his way into the kitchen. Fear and frustration boil in her veins. She has regained her feet but, still, she cannot cut the zip ties around her ankles and wrists. The ties around her neck and face dig in and ratchet her top lip up and away from the rest of her mouth. What remains is locked in a toothy grimace.

And from this comes a snarl.

Down to only desperation, Juanita turns to face away from the sounds and holds the knife with her hands still secured behind her, the knife's blade pointing away from the small of her back. She summons her most warrior-like roar and charges backward toward the sound. It's a blind and awkward joust, trying to impale the man she cannot see with the knife she cannot control upon feet she cannot move more than a couple of lurching inches at a time.

Juanita trips over something unseen in the lightless kitchen and crashes onto her back, the impact sending the knife flying from her hands, skittering away in the dark. The side of her head smacks the floor and a high-pitched and echoing chime peals in and out of her ears. She realizes she has landed partly onto the attacker's body. She feels what must be an appendage. His leg? She growls, bends down and bites into the leg, but it seems to have no effect on the man underneath her. Juanita unclamps her mouth and shrieks again and again, head-butting in the dark, frenzied in her attempt to defend herself anyway she can.

Hands grab her and Juanita feels the man pull himself onto her body. She curls her knees up to her chest and she kicks out as hard as she can. She feels her heels connect with her attacker's body but, still, the man does not stop. Juanita hears panting, feels breath on her face. The man releases a raspy moan and Juanita wonders if she has hurt the man somehow.

"Stop! It's me. Helen."

The tortured sound is a woman's voice and Juanita realizes what this means. For a moment she cannot move and cannot think. Finally, she speaks.

"You're...alive!" Juanita stammers. "Thought you...were dead. Thought he...killed you."

"He tried," Helen whispers in reply. Her throat sounds raw, hurt.

"You...killed him?" Juanita asks.

"Yeah," Helen mutters.

"You sure?" Juanita asks Helen.

The word "sure" comes out of Juanita's mouth all sloppy and wet. Helen can hear that something is wrong with Juanita's voice, too. She sounds like she is talking from her nose as much as her mouth.

"Yeah."

Juanita and Helen lay intertwined, wheezing, coming down from exertion and anxiety.

"You OK?" Juanita asks.

"Yeah," Helen answers.

For no good reason at all, Juanita expects Helen will ask how she is doing, but silence still characterizes their relationship...of course.

Juanita reminds herself to give Helen the benefit of the doubt—she's likely in shock. Clinically, Juanita knows she may face PTSD herself. As if on cue, a shudder rolls through her, draining the last of her adrenaline. She's instantly cold, exhausted. Her teeth chatter, eyes well with tears. Humiliation stings. The worst part wasn't just feeling helpless—it was how close she came to hopelessness. The shudder deepens, waves of it surging through her.

Relief. Anger. Relief. Anger. Shame.

Helen feels Juanita's body tremor, and she reaches her hand down and nearly touches her, but she stays her cupped hand. It hovers just above where she thinks is Juanita's head. She decides against it.

It wouldn't be good. For either of us. He told me it was a one-time thing. He made me promise never to tell; never to involve his family. Besides, I can't pretend to be someone I'm not. Since when have I been the comfortin' type?

To touch Juanita would imply an intimacy Helen does not want. Her resolve to keep Juanita at a distance is too strong. Instead, she brings her hand to her own face. Her fingers explore her bruised cheekbone.

That rifle butt might'a got me a little better'n I thought.

Her tongue explores a molar that wiggles in its socket.

Fuckity-fuck. I think I'm gonna lose this tooth.

"Couldn't...cut...ties," Juanita hisses.
It sounds like an admission rather than a statement. When Juanita talks, her already painfully cinched upper mouth stretches even tighter. The cloth lashed to her face partly covers her nose, so she breathes mostly from her mouth. When she does talk, it is a nasally dialect of a lisping language hissed through clenched teeth.
"Tried...but..." Juanita can't think what else there is to say. She doesn't want to talk more about it. It hurts to do so, physically and otherwise.
Helen envisions how it must have happened. Juanita would've been

surprised. He'd probably grabbed her. Based on the yelping she'd heard Juanita had probably struggled and had been hit. She was obviously still bound. Sounds like she was gagged, but maybe it slipped partway off.

"Hold still," Helen mumbles. She reaches down to confirm she still has the object she now considers a talisman. Her fingers find the slick handle, wrapped in a t-shirt she'd pulled from the dirty laundry hamper—both to keep from losing it and to protect herself as she crawled down the stairs.

"Got somethin'," Helen growls. "Tried and true. First…need light. Can you…stand?"

Juanita nods and it takes her a moment to recall that Helen cannot see her in the dark. Juanita says "yes," even though a truthful answer is "maybe."

"Get candle. Lighter. On counter. By 'fridge," Helen huffs.

"Why…not…lights?" Juanita asks. "Generator is on."

"Bad idea," Helen responds.

"Why?"

"Somebody…may be…watching…us."

The words are gravel in Helen's throat.

"Watching?" Juanita asks. The word sounds more like washing. "Why?"

"Listen to me!" Helen says angrily. Immediately she regrets trying to shout. That really hurt. "He…choked me. Hurts talk," she whispers.

Juanita can hear that Helen's voice is shot. She knows that damage from strangulation can cause anoxic and hypoxic brain injury. Just because she's alive doesn't mean Helen's out of the woods, yet. Even if not life threatening, Helen's voice is a tumbledown wreck atop a foundation of three packs of cigarettes a day.

Helen puts up a finger for each thing she says next, even though she knows full well that Juanita is unable to see her do it. No matter. Helen is a believer in lists.

First finger. "Get candle."

Second finger. "Cut loose."

Third finger. "Pack up."

Fourth finger. "Go!"

Anxious and irritated, Helen says "Go" emphatically. The only things that go are Helen's hands. They fly back to and around her neck. Her fingertips pretend to apply a healing poultice, but all they can do is to tell her the pain is everywhere. Her tongue is thick and lazy and good for nothing except sneaking off to play with the loose tooth.

Juanita wobbles to her feet, Helen's arms steadying her. Shuffling toward the soft hum of the refrigerator, she steps on more crunching debris. Her forehead bumps the door—just a tap, but enough to make her wince.

She finds the counter's edge and turns, pressing her bound hands onto the surface. Sweeping cautiously, her fingers brush against something smooth and round—glass or porcelain. Pinching the jar, she drags it closer, too fast—something skitters away. A plastic lighter. Stretching until her shoulders scream, she reaches farther. Fingertips graze an object. Carefully, she hooks it closer, curling it into her palm. With one hand gripping the lighter and the other steady on the jar, she braces herself.

She pushes herself off the counter. She's energized by the prospect of being cut loose from the ties around her face. Her mouth waters, hungry for freedom. Saliva and blood mix and slosh in her mouth. She hawks and spits, but the mixture mostly runs down her chin.

She bunny hops a few times, but she realizes this is foolish. She has a glass jar pinched between two fingers and she might drop it. She goes back to her more cautious hop-shuffle to cross through still more bits on the floor.

What are they? Peanut shells?

It takes two rounds of "Marco" and "Polo" to get Juanita back to Helen's side.

Once she arrives, Helen takes the candle and lighter from Juanita's hands and sets them on the ground in front of her. She withdraws the candle from the jar, and she snaps the lighter on like the experienced smoker she is. A small flame catches and she brings the flame to the wick, and it catches, too. She eases the candle back into the glass jar and sets it down.

The light is a flickering, tenuous puddle on the kitchen floor.

From her higher vantage point, Juanita can see Helen is looking down and into the jar. Helen's head is in silhouette and Juanita can see the fringes of her short hair framed by light leaking up from the floor. Helen is rocking herself back and forth and, because of this side-to-side movement, the candle's flame is in her line of sight and then it's not. The flame hides and returns, hides and returns. It's a mesmerizing string of eclipses.

From the floor where she is sprawled on her side, Helen turns her face upward looking for Juanita's eyes. She lifts the jarred candle, raising it up as high as she can, her arm straight, a demi-Statue of Liberty.

It's hard for Helen to see all the way up as Juanita is standing and the candlelight is weak. Juanita's chin drops to better look down and Helen can see there are several zip ties ratcheted tightly across Juanita's upper lip and extending around her neck. Her face is frozen into a snarl. It looks like something Hannibal Lector might have had to wear on his way to be euthanized. It looks painful. Juanita's mouth and chin are shellacked in blood. In the ghostly light, Juanita looks like a rampaging vampire, fresh from a kill. Helen watches a drop of blood grow too full and heavy and it races down from Juanita's temple and across her check and along her nose to join the pool that has soaked the already brownish red cloth still pinned to the space just below her nose.

When Juanita squats down, her face creeps within range of the candle's glow. Helen can see more now. She can see that the bleeding is from a wound on Juanita's forehead. She has a nasty bruise on one cheek. Her bottom lip is torn and twisted, bloody and absurdly swollen. Seeing her fully in the face, she can see that Juanita's snarl is lopsided, one side of her lip being pulled higher than the other.

Helen is startled when Juanita's mouth arranges itself into a sanguinary grin.

"You look terrible," Juanita lisps at Helen.

"You're…one…to talk," Helen hisses back.

Now that their faces are only inches apart, Juanita sees that Helen looks as though she is wearing jungle camouflage except, instead of grease paint, its blood mottling her head, face and shoulders. Blood is matted onto her silver hair and caked into an ear and congealed around and into her nose and there are tracks where blood has trickled from her mouth and lips down her neck and into her shirt. There is a nasty contusion and bruising on one cheek. It might have been hard enough to damage or shatter her cheekbone. She will need to check for concussion. Later.

Juanita breaks eye contact to focus on Helen's hand, the one holding the candle. The wet, glistening hand is not steady. It shakes a little making the flame jig and Juanita's breath makes it jog so she eases her face back, afraid she'll inadvertently blow the candle out.

Helen tells Juanita to sit down, and she does so awkwardly, spilling onto her side. She is slow to sit up. Helen positions Juanita leaning back so her bound hands are close to the floor. Helen had the foresight to wipe the cleaver's blade against her shirt a time or two. It isn't clean, but at least it isn't dripping anymore.

Feeling like a battlefield surgeon amputating shredded limbs by the rocket's red glare, Helen positions the meat cleaver above the ties. She estimates distance and angle and dispatches the ties around Juanita's wrists with one good whack. The cleaver's blade rings against the tile floor underneath. Juanita's wrists are free.

Juanita insists on taking the cleaver from Helen even while her fingers are still tingling. The restored circulation makes her fingers burn and itch, but she welcomes the sensation. She cuts her own ankles loose. When she finally slices away the third and final tie that has been around her face and head, she moans a little as the pain from extreme constriction worsens now that blood flow is unrestricted.

Juanita runs her hands over her nose and lip. The pressure around her head is mostly gone, but the feel of the ties biting into her lips and nose lingers.

"Why are…you…here?" Helen grumbles out. She is careful with each word she says.

"An associate with the law firm called me. She moved up the schedule by a day. They want time to review your testimony. She said something about some new evidence. That's all I know."

Helen ponders this new development.

So. The legal eagles wanna talk to me before I testify. On account of new evidence? I call bullshit. There's only one kind of evidence that would make a difference. If they'd found it, I would've heard somethin'. It'd be on the news. I know them statutes of limitations don't expire for things like this. Still, fifty years? They couldn't prove nothin' then and they ain't gonna prove nothin' now.

I know what he wants. He wants the deed to Mama's land. Over my dead body. Mama's will is airtight. He'll never see that land.

Is it him tryin' to get even? Naw. He ain't lookin' for revenge. 'Sides, he's a coward at heart. Maybe he's gettin' squeezed. Feelin' desperate. He's always owed money. Would he resort to hirin' a sheriff's deputy for some off duty murderin'? Maybe, but probably not. That ain't his style. He's a trickster, thief, con man. Not a killer. Whoever sent the killer, I can't figure.

Juanita has been quiet, waiting, expecting Helen to ask another question or two. Helen does not.

"Does this have something to do with the trial?" Juanita queries.

Juanita receives no answer to her question. Maybe Helen doesn't know. Or won't say. Or maybe her throat hurts too much and she is saving her words. Juanita doesn't know which, just like she doesn't know exactly what has happened. She certainly doesn't know why.

She realizes she doesn't know much at all, including how Helen has come out on top in a fight with the masked man.

No doubt, he was here to kill Helen. And willing to kill me. Helen's a killer now, too. Surely it was self-defense, though. The man is big, strong as an ox. It doesn't seem possible. Helen's frail, smokes like a chimney, lives in a wheelchair. She's got to have osteoporosis, for God's sake. How did she survive a struggle to the death with that man? I don't know how, but I do know one thing. The killer has help coming. We've got to get out of here. If we still can't call 911, we'll drive to the sheriff's office. And Helen needs to go to the hospital. Probably I do, too.

Juanita spies her cell phone laying few feet away from the candle.

"Helen," Juanita says. "Would you give me my phone, please? Might still work. At least, we can use the light!" The thought of a working phone feels like salvation.

Helen hands the phone to Juanita who frowns and pushes various buttons but to no effect other than causing Juanita to grumble. She eventually gives up and slips the broken phone into her pocket.

"No good," Juanita says. "Can't even get it to power up. Okay… uh…Helen. I'm bleeding in several places. You're bleeding, too. More important, your throat may be damaged. You could still have pulmonary edema. I should get the medical kit from the ambulance but what we really need to do is go to a hospital."

"Maybe," Helen hisses. "Pack up…go. All else…later."

Juanita starts to argue, but resolution and angst pour from Helen's eyes. Juanita has a million and one questions, but she knows time is ticking and Helen is unable to talk much anyway. Answers will have to wait.

"Okay," Juanita says, "I can check you out once we get away. But you should know I heard the man talking on a radio. He told whoever he was talking to that he needed help to clean up and, well…dispose…of our bodies."

She let that sink in before adding, "But the man was angry that help isn't going to get here for another three hours. So, we have time."

"Maybe. Better safe…than sorry, Somethin'…you….should know," Helen adds. "Man…upstairs. I took off…his mask. After. Seen him…before. He's a deputy. A Nueces County…Sheriff deputy."

She let that sink in.

To Juanita, this whole thing has gone from scary to absurd and back to scary.

Why would a deputy lawman try to kill Helen? In the middle of a lightning storm? Why was he willing to kill me, too? And he wasn't wearing his uniform. He was dressed to kill, mask and all. This isn't some home robbery gone bad. It's something else. And who was the man talking to on the radio? There's more to this, but I'm damned if I know what it is. I should take the man's radio with us when we leave. Might help if we can overhear whatever they're planning.

"You're right," she tells Helen. "We can't go to sheriff's office, at least not until we know more. If we can't trust the sheriff department, we'll drive to Corpus Christi. They have their own police department."

At Helen's direction, Juanita opens one of the kitchen drawers and finds a pad of paper and a pen. She takes them to Helen who writes out a missive and numbers the tasks for Juanita.

1. Get flashlight - under bed probably, If not there, get from body
2. Get bullets - bedroom closet shelf
3. Get rifle - in hamper with body
4. Get Radio - with body
5. Bring rifle + bullets to me

The note even has a P.S. which reads: Use flashlight carefully. Carefully is underlined three times.

Taking the candle with her, Juanita climbs the stairs. Her legs feel like they're filled with lead, and she is puffing when she gets to the second-floor landing. She cannot help but look down the hall. By the pops and the shouts and the banging she'd heard, she figures the fight had happened at the far end.

Candle in hand, Juanita steps down the hall toward the door to the bedroom. The leftover light spilling out of the bathroom and through the bedroom isn't much, but between that and the candle, Juanita can just make out a pair of legs sticking out of the floor level cabinet at the end of the hall. The Wicked Witch of the East has been pinned and crushed beneath the house that the tornado has dropped upon it. The tune comes to mind.

Ding, dong! The witch is dead.

The tasks that Helen has assigned to Juanita will require her to go to the body eventually. She needs to recover the rifle and radio from the cabinet and the bullets from the closet. Helen had written sorry and that word, too, had been underlined three times but the look on Helen's face was not empathy. It was insistence. With a side of impatience.

Leaving the hall and entering the bedroom, Juanita gets down on the floor and puts the candle off to the side. She swims her way under the bed, hands searching for the flashlight. She recovers it quickly.

Once out from under the bed and on her knees, she clamps one palm over the top of the flashlight and turns it on. It makes her hand glow orange and yellow and she follows this fleshy nightlight into the walk-in closet. She pulls the door closed behind her before reaching up and finding the string. She pulls the string, and a single bulb lights up the walk-in closet. After having been in the mostly dark, the glare is jarring.

Juanita blinks while her eyes adjust. She turns off the flashlight and stows it in her pocket. She walks to the metal racks. She sees on a shelf there's a cardboard box. It's turned on its side and it's surrounded by a gaggle of bullets. She gathers the runaway bullets into the box and carries them with her. She turns out the light and waits a moment for her eyes to readjust.

Bullets rattle against each other in the box as Juanita steps through the bedroom, picks up the candle and goes back into the hall. Time to get the rifle.

Juanita tells herself there's little she hasn't seen before but she also knows this is different. This isn't a body from a random accident or drowning or stabbing or overdose or dispute that got out of hand. This is the body of a man who'd been intent on killing them both. She can still taste his hand across her mouth, feel his body's weight upon her, smell his rank breath, hear his soprano voice in her ear.

She peers down the hallway. The bent legs do not appear to have moved, but she can't swear to that. Juanita stalks the hall, the candle lighting the way. She is startled for a moment when she comes up against a metal bar at knee level, but she steps over it. Two steps later, her foot kicks into a leg.

Juanita kneels and extends the candle closer to the floor. The globe of light finds the first leg. The leg is bent, the foot twisted away. Near the foot, the black pants are still wet with blood. Juanita is certain this ankle wound is not what killed him.

Though the candlelight is sparse, Juanita can tell that the cabinet doors are askew. She opens one door wider, and she moves the candle closer. There is so much blood it is difficult to tell exactly what has happened. A cold and clinical part of Juanita wants to examine the face and body carefully, but Helen is being insistent. Time is not on their side. She's right.

Juanita runs her hand up one leg and she feels something bulky on his right hip. She grasps and slides a card deck-sized device from the holder clipped to his belt. She forces it into her own back pocket and turns her attention to the cabinet.

Something metal glints in the candlelight and Juanita can make out the end of the rifle barrel sticking up and out. Like everything else, the muzzle is slathered.

Juanita edges herself closer. She slides her knee in between the man's legs right up against the crotch. Closer now, her nose is invaded by an incense-like mix of gunpowder and iron and something sickly sweet. She knows the smell of fresh blood.

Juanita reaches in and grabs ahold of the metal barrel. It is slick against her palm. Almost reverently, she eases it out of the cabinet. Once the rifle is free and clear, the door swings partly closed. The carnage that is the top half of the man's body is consigned, again, to the dark space inside. It seems deserving.

Juanita's legs feel much less fatigued as she carries the rifle, bullets, radio and candle back down the stairs. Helen's arms are out straight, palms up, fingers motioning give me as though Juanita is carrying her child. Juanita lays the rifle in Helen's arms and puts the box of bullets in her lap.

While Juanita has been busy, so too, has Helen. She's written another list. She tears the page from the pad and gives it to Juanita. This note reads:

1. Wheelchair – bring to me
2. Medicines in bathroom
3. Sweatpants
4. Underwear
5. Hoodie
6. Socks
7. Boots
8. Raincoat

"I thought we didn't have time," Juanita says, arching a brown eyebrow.

Helen does not answer; her focus is on the rifle. She slides the bolt open, the mechanism ejecting the unused bullet. Helen reaches into the box on her lap, selects a replacement bullet, and puts it into the groove before sliding it up and home. She looks up at Juanita, winks, and nods toward the elevator.

Juanita starts back through the kitchen but stops to find two plastic baggies to fill with ice, one for her and one for Helen. A light comes on when she opens the refrigerator door.

Unbelievable. All I had to do was open the damned refrigerator door and we would have had some light. Can't believe I didn't think of that.

Juanita leaves a towel-wrapped ice bag and the candle with Helen before retracing her steps through the kitchen to the lift. Her hands find the wheelchair and she pulls it the rest of the way out of the elevator shaft. She doesn't know why a couple of pillows and a blanket are stuffed into it, but she tosses the bedding aside, spins it around, and rolls it next to Helen who is still scribbling furiously by candlelight. Without waiting for instruction or permission, Juanita puts her forearms under Helen's armpits and lifts her up. Helen's head and face loll against Juanita's chest and she mumbles something as Juanita carries her and deposits her into the wheelchair.

Helen grunts something that might be, but probably is not, a thank you. Juanita looks down at the list and off she goes.

In the upstairs bathroom, the flashlight's beam spills into the porcelain sink. The bowl of light casts shadows that crawl the ceiling. Juanita takes the small trashcan and empties its contents onto the floor. Then she positions it under the medicine cabinet. She reaches in and sweeps everything out, a pharmaceutical waterfall of who knows what, into the waste can.

Juanita carries the trashcan into the bedroom, shielding her flashlight as she rummages through drawers for Helen's clothes. She grabs hiking boots, a down coat, and the last pillow from the bed. Slipping off the pillowcase, she stuffs it with the clothes and boots, slings it over her shoulder, and heads downstairs, sack and trashcan in tow. Juanita arrives to yet another message Helen has written. It reads: green backpack. Bedroom closet. Corner.

Juanita fetches the backpack and adds it to the growing pile of items they will take with them to the ambulance. Juanita expects another written message when she returns to Helen, and she is not disillusioned.

Helen has written: Get wet towels. Clean up some.

"Once again, you said there was no time," Juanita says. Again, Helen does not answer. She only sits and stares until Juanita relents.

Juanita grabs two hand towels from the powder room, wets them, and returns to find Helen already stripped of her blood-crusted vest and tee. Handing her a towel, Juanita watches as Helen scrubs furiously, revealing deep bruises on her arms and ribs. There's already too much blood for a hand towel.

"Here, let me," she tells Helen. Juanita uses the wet towel to buff through Helen's hair, forehead, and ears and then, along her jaw, down her neck, and onto her shoulders and around a bra that was once white but now, is mostly the color of rust.

Below the waist doesn't look much better. She goes to help remove Helen's skirt, but Helen slaps dismissively at Juanita's hands. It is not a skirt but some kind of wrap, Juanita realizes. The Velcro crackles as Helen pulls it apart. Helen seizes her still mostly white underwear and she pushes it down as far as her arms can extend. The front stretches to her mid-thigh, and there it stops. The back of Helen's underwear is trapped under her sweaty buttocks and will go no further.

For a moment, Helen cannot remember how to undress herself. She looks down and sees a tuft of her own pubic hair.

What was I just doin'? Why am I half naked?

Juanita kneels down and taps Helen on the knee until she remembers Helen cannot feel her legs, so she moves her hand onto Helen's shoulder. At contact, Helen jerks and her head circles a bit before she locks eyes with Juanita.

She's confused, Juanita realizes. Concussed, maybe. In shock, for sure.

"We've got to go," Juanita says. "Right? Will you let me help?"

Helen bobs an uncertain yes. Juanita uses both hands to strip the underwear down and off of Helen's legs. Juanita smells the urine. The odor is sharp enough to cut through even the iron-infused splatter on the garments. Juanita feels semi-vindicated to know she isn't the only one to have peed her pants.

Juanita slides a clean pair of underwear up atrophied legs, but she pauses to examine Helen's thigh. There is some bleeding from bite marks. The other leg is deeply bruised around the thigh. Feeling only slightly guilty and reminding herself to put some antibiotic on it later, Juanita slips the underwear the rest of the way onto Helen. She follows that with dark sweatpants. She adds socks and stuffs the feet into the boots which she laces up.

"Too tight?" Juanita asks.

Helen laughs in spite of her sore throat. Her eyes seem clearer than they were a minute ago.

"How would...I...know?" Helen replies. "I can do...rest...myself," she says, snatching the towel back from Juanita.

Helen scrubs her hands, dragging the towel down and up between each of her fingers. Juanita sees that she is mostly pushing blood around instead of off and Helen realizes this, too, and so she tosses the towel to the floor. Juanita hands over more clothes and watches as Helen shrugs her way into the hoodie.

Juanita dabs her own wet towel against her forehead. The bleeding has stopped, but even light touching with the towel breaks open some congealed place so she abandon's her noggin. She scrapes the towel over and under her nose to where the zip ties and gag had rubbed raw the bottom of her nose and her muzzle. She stops when she touches her lips. If anything, it hurts more now. She abandons her lips and moves down and is surprised at how much blood there is on her chin and throat. Blood is slick, still, on her tongue.

"Juanita," Helen yelps. "We. Must. Go."

"Fine!" Juanita snaps at Helen as she tosses her towel away. "Guess now that you're done it's time to go."

Juanita hauls the backpack and trash can of meds to the ambulance. Spotting her Oilers cap on the floor, she shakes off the water and puts it on, ignoring the sting against her forehead wound. She nearly trips over her own backpack, slings it over her other shoulder, and pauses at the open back door. The downpour has eased to a heavy drizzle, but between the rain and darkness, visibility is poor.

Someone might be waiting only yards away and I wouldn't see them until it's too late. Well, no help for it. Ready or not, here I come.

Juanita steps into the rain. She wants to jog but forces herself to walk. Her head is on a swivel, sweeping left to right and right to left like the fan at the foot of her bed in the Summer.

She can feel the bulge of the flashlight in her pocket, but she will not turn it on. She'd rather run into a puddle than a killer's apprentice.

Juanita finds the van's bumper, feels her way to the side, and quietly slides open the door. The cabin light flickers on, making her tense. She quickly sets her bundles in the rear, then eases the door nearly shut to kill the light. Crouching, holding the handle and her breath, she listens—only rain.

She goes back for Helen. As she's wheeling her out the back door, Helen suddenly asks her to stop. Unable to write in the rain, she motions for Juanita to come closer, then leans in and presses her mouth to Juanita's ear.

"Get cigarettes," she croaks out. Juanita looks Helen in the eyes.

"No way," Juanita says. "I'm not going back for that."

Helen clacks and squawks and for the first time Juanita is glad Helen can barely talk.

Juanita initially tries to lever the wheelchair through the rain-soaked sand with Helen in it, but the wheels keep sinking. Helen squeaks and huffs, hurt throat and all, when Juanita gives up on that and carries her to the ambulance and puts her into the fixed backseat. Despite the whore's bath, Juanita sees that Helen is still speckled with blood. Juanita goes back for the wheelchair, collapses it and stores it in the van as well. It is a relief when the sliding door closes, and the cabin light winks off.

Inside the ambulance Helen coughs and Juanita turns to look over her shoulder back at her. Helen pushes something into Juanita's hands. It's the handle of a meat cleaver. Helen follows up with a note. It reads: *You might need this. And, next time, don't pick a bread knife.*

Juanita starts the vehicle but does not turn on the headlights. She eases the van down the incline and over the bridge and goes right at the fork and down the sloppy road to the access road where she, again, turns right. She drives for several minutes, for as long as she dares, without headlights. Reluctantly, she turns them on. Then, also, the windshield wipers.

Juanita reaches up and tilts the rearview mirror down, but she cannot make eye contact with Helen in the backseat.

Here we are. Again. Helen the passenger. Me the driver. Nothing to say. She's gonna have to come clean. I need to know what's going on and why. If we aren't killed first, I'll have the truth from her.

Juanita smashes her foot down and the ambulance hydroplanes, skews and slews sideways, but the tires hold on just long enough for Juanita to speed away into a, still, stormy morning that is pierced only by a pair of headlights that appear feeble and tired.

CHAPTER TEN

A Mad Dash

*"I know well what I am fleeing from,
but not what I am in search of."*

~Michel de Montaigne (1533–1592), Lord, essayist, statesman,
philosopher of the French Renaissance

———— ••• ————

ALL IS CARBON BLACK WHEN JUANITA AND HELEN DRIVE away. The obscurity is a gift.

Juanita is glad for the dark and for the rain. This night is a cloak, this rainfall is a hood and, together, they might conceal her and Helen and the ambulance long enough for them to get away. Barring something unforeseen, Juanita figures she needs less than an hour to get off the island and onto the mainland. Juanita envisions getting over the bridge is like getting over the Berlin Wall.

Just get over it. Safety on the other side.

The ferries will not be running during the storm. When Juanita announced her decision to make for the JFK Causeway Bridge to Corpus Christi instead of opting for the shorter drive to Port Aransas, Helen didn't argue. Port Aransas is within the Nueces County Sheriff Department's jurisdiction. Given the dead man in Helen's Casita is a Nueces County deputy, they've ruled that out. Corpus Christi, with a population of over three hundred thousand, has its own independent municipal police department.

Juanita looks through the rain plastered windshield, eyes searching for any evidence of dawn. She cannot yet see the horizon. The rain has slackened a bit and she can occasionally hear a wave crash against the shore off to her left, but the sound is so faint that it might be her imagination. The sky is still inky, but that will soon change. Sunrise in December will come at about six thirty in the morning. With Juanita's phone broken and the clock on her dashboard showing the grossly inaccurate time of nearly high noon—or midnight, take your pick—Juanita guesses the current time to be about four in the morning. If they're going to escape in the dark, they only have a couple of hours left to do it.

In the seat behind Juanita, Helen frets over her damaged throat. It's a curse, one more handicap she must bear. Admittedly, though, it's also convenient. If not for that, Juanita would be asking a lot of questions. Questions she doesn't want to answer.

"Plan B to Ringo. Do you copy?"

The metallic voice that erupts from the dead man's handheld radio is a shock, a suddenly materialized poltergeist. Hearing it, both Juanita and Helen jump in their seats. Even though the radio's sound is mechanical and laced with static, it's unmistakably the voice of a young man.

The silence that follows is unnerving.

Helen starts to growl out a word—maybe a question—but the radio squawks again. It's the same message, repeated. Someone called Plan B is trying to reach someone called Ringo. Ringo, whoever that is, remains silent.

Helen pieces it together.

Ringo isn't answerin'. 'Cause he's dead. 'Cause I killed him.

When she'd first realized she'd won, when she'd felt him stop breathing, when he finally was still, his legs no longer drumming the floor, she was too spent to care about anything except the fear that was blossoming into panic. She'd known she was not getting enough oxygen through her damaged throat. It felt like she was drowning. She was deep down in the dark and cold water. She was much too far below the surface, and what little she could see of the sky above was out of reach. She would never make it.

She'd closed her eyes and put her hands to her throat, reexperiencing the moments right after the man's death. Her viscous fingertips had left divots behind as they'd dragged through the ichor on her face and throat. She'd thought she might just go to sleep. Rest. It sounded good. If she could only drift away, her throat would stop hurting, her face would stop aching, and she would stop being afraid and angry at everybody and everything. Including herself.

She'd refused her body's invitation to drowse.

Rather than suck in air, she'd expelled every last bit from her lungs and throat and mouth until it had felt like every molecule had been squeezed out of her shriveled body. Only then did she refill. She'd drawn breath as deeply as she could, but she did it slowly and over the urgent objections of her air starved lungs. She'd pretended she was young and fully able. She was expelling bubbles while she was swimming underwater from one end of the swimming pool to the other. She knew she could and would wait to touch the far wall at the far end of the pool before she would come up and take a well-earned breath.

She swam these laps in her mind again and again, reminding herself to touch the wall first and breath second. At some point, she'd realized she was breathing without her having to will her body to do so. A dizziness, one that she didn't even know was there, dissipated. For the first time, she thought she might live.

Then, she was euphoric.

She'd let her anger off the leash, and with it came a sense of victory. Had she not been so tired, crammed into the dirty clothes hamper with a dead man, she might have raised her arms and clasped them together over her head. Had her throat not been so hurt, she might have howled in triumph. Much of that feeling had ebbed away since. But not all. Especially the anger.

Her meandering thoughts are interrupted again.

"Plan B to Ringo. Do you copy?"

Silence.

"Uh, look. If you can hear me, my, uh, ETA is ten minutes. Plan B will rendezvous at premises in ten minutes. Do you copy? Over?"

Helen thinks that over.

Plan B? Sounds like hastily organized help. It's not a very shrewd pick of call signs. Maybe that's why Plan B, whomever he is, is, well, Plan B. He's the backup to the backup. Maybe he's the only one they could get on short notice. Where was he recruited from? Day care? Whomever planned to kill me is not all powerful. They have asset issues.

"Shit!" Juanita says, adding to the tension. Juanita is angry at herself and at the circumstances that are spiraling out of control.

We left the Casita less than fifteen minutes ago. This Plan B character, whoever he is, will soon arrive at the Casita. He'll discover a dead body. He'll know that Helen is gone. They're not going to think she rolled herself into hiding somewhere on her lonesome. They'll figure out someone helped her. If they're any good at all, they'll figure it out pretty quickly.

Juanita had already been regretting not having followed her initial instincts. Now, her regret grows exponentially. She's on the verge of pounding her fist against steering wheel, but she refrains. The ambulance's steering wheel isn't at fault.

It's her fault. But it's my fault, too. We should've left earlier. I thought we had three hours. It hasn't even been one hour since I heard the man talking on the radio. They found help close by? We should've left. Right away. No clothes. No backpack. No cleanup. No rifle and bullets. Well, maybe the rifle and bullets. But not the rest. Given another half hour of lead time, we'd likely already be on the mainland. There, we could easily hide. We could drive straight to the nearest police station or fire station or parks and recreation department, for that matter. Go someplace where there are people that have nothing to do with the county Sheriff's Department. This can't be some kind of worldwide conspiracy. Whatever is happening, there has to be a limit to the number of people in on it. Doesn't there?

Juanita knows Mustang Island pretty well. It's not a large island. Only 18 miles long, the island is just 3 miles wide where it's fat, and not much more than half a mile wide where it's skinny. Given the relative flatness, there are few natural hiding places. There are quite a few tall sand dunes and Juanita briefly considers whether she can drive off the road and hide among them. She realizes they would surely get stuck in deep sand and would be found in no time. Given they are close to the nature reserve and there are no residences nearby, she dismisses that option.

Rounding a bend, Juanita sees headlights coming their way. It's another vehicle, a sedan, traveling in the opposite direction. Even in the dark and rain, Juanita can tell the car barreling toward her is going too fast on the rain-slicked road.

Window to window, the two vehicles pass each other. Juanita can't help but peer into the passing car. She gets a glimpse of the driver. It's a man and he's holding something in front of his face. Juanita fears it's a gun and she almost jerks the steering wheel to the right but before she can do so, the car has gone by. She holds her breath. The car keeps going, water-colored red taillights growing smaller in her rearview mirror. Juanita exhales a sigh of relief, the tension easing as she finally lets go of the breath she'd been holding.

In that split second, it hits her—the vehicle has a light bar on the roof, similar to the one on her own ambulance.

Speeding as it was, why weren't the blue and red emergency lights on? If it's a first responder rushing to some emergency, why is the siren not helping clear the way? And what the hell was the driver holding in front of his face?

The radio squawks again.

"Top Hat to Plan B. Do you copy?"

This is a new voice, one that is considerably deeper than that of Plan B's. It dawns on Juanita that this new voice is likely coming from the man in the car they have just passed.

The thing held in front of his face? Not a gun. It's another radio.

"Plan B copies," the young man's voice replies.

"Give me a sit-rep," the deep voice commands.

"Well, uh, the situation is, uh, well…Ringo is dead. There's a lot of blood. In a closet. Upstairs. A lot of blood. He's dead. I can't believe he's dead."

Helen remembers. Yeah. A lot of blood.

"Calm down Plan B. What's the status of the target?" It's the deep-voiced man. Clearly, Top Hat is in charge.

"She's…well…she's not here. Uh, I mean, target is not on the premises. Clarence's body is here, though. My God. Looks like it was a struggle. Up close. I think I'm going to throw up."

"Stay off the radio unless I call you, Plan B. Wait for me. Do not touch anything. Do you copy?"

"Copy that, Top Hat."

The silence that follows is weighty.

Juanita says to Helen: "Plan B and Top Hat? What's going on here, Helen? Who are these people?"

"Don't…know," Helen forces out. "Honest," she adds. Juanita twists in her seat to look into the back seat. Helen is leaning forward as far as she can, holding up three fingers. Scout's honor. *As if*, Juanita thinks.

Almost immediately the radio comes back to life. "Top Hat to Bam Bam. Do you copy?"

"Go for Bam Bam," a new, Spanish accented voice answers. More characters are joining the auditory cast. Juanita's head is swirling. It's like a James Bond movie. Bad guys are everywhere.

"Did you monitor the exchange with Plan B?"

"Affirmative, Top Hat."

"Well, you know, then. The bird is in the wind. Lock down those goddam bridges. Nobody gets off the island. Tell people you're concerned about the bridges' structural integrity. Tell 'em it's due to the storm. Whatever. Stop all vehicles. Make sure our guys are among the crews. Whatever it takes, dispatch the target. That's imperative. Do you copy?"

"Roger, Top Hat," Bam Bam responds. "Distribute teams to both bridges. All vehicles stopped. Confirm order to dispatch target."

Dispatch target? Juanita is sure what it must mean. It means kill. Both bridges will be blocked. Her plan to escape onto the mainland has now gone up in smoke.

"Top Hat to Bam Bam," the radio squawks again.

"Go for Bam Bam."

"Another thing. I passed an ambulance. Just a few minutes ago. It's the only other vehicle I've seen. I haven't heard any emergency calls come in. Check it out."

"Roger that, Top Hat. Eyes out for ambulance. Will update ASAP."

Immediately after, they hear the man in the sedan, once again, raise Plan B on the radio.

"Top Hat to Plan B."

"Plan B, here," the young voice answers.

"What's status of Ringo's radio?"

"I'm, uh, I don't know. I don't see it. Where should I look?" the young voice asks.

"On the body. In a holster on his belt, idiot! Find it."

Two minutes go by before the radio crackles again.

"Plan B to Top Hat. Do you copy?"

"Go for Top Hat."

"There's no radio with the body. Should I case the premises?"

"Negative," says Top Hat.

There are a few seconds of silence before the radio squawks again.

"All teams, all teams," Top Hat says. "Switch to first alternate channel. Now."

The radio falls mostly silent but, still, there's a whisper of static. Helen does not know why she feels this way, but she is convinced that Top Hat is still on this frequency, listening. Her sense of paranoia turns out to be justified.

Top Hat's next words over the radio are measured and precise:

"To the driver of the ambulance," Top Hat says, "I'm talking to you. You're hearing me, aren't you? Pull over. You will not be harmed. You have my word. Your passenger has something in her possession, something I want back."

Helen and Juanita are wide-eyed but remain silent.

"If you're determined to run, there's nowhere to go that we won't find you. You know that, right?"

The static dissipates and the radio falls silent. The threat is a chilling. Juanita's skin tingles, and her scalp itches under her Oilers hat.

"Fuck," Juanita says.

"Didn't know…you could… curse," Helen warbles.

Juanita feels no inclination to answer. Instead, she replays in her mind what she's just heard.

The light bar on top? That was a patrol car. Sheriff's department, likely. No one else could have gotten here that fast. The teams, whoever they are, are blockading exits from the island. The bird on the wing is surely Helen. And now they know to be on the lookout for an ambulance. Out of the frying pan…

There are almost no places on the small, relatively flat island to hide an ambulance where it will not be seen. They can't possibly get to town before being stopped and killed on a dark roadside. Given the stormy weather, there won't be people about even if they've sheltered in place. There are only two bridges to the mainland, and both are closed and manned.

Swim? How long would I last in the cold winter gulf water, swim-

ming and pulling Helen after me? Not very long.

Juanita is convinced Top Hat will have turned his car around as fast as he can. He will have put two and two together. He will chase them down. Juanita has faith in her ambulance, but she knows its limitations. She will not outrun pursuit.

It's too dark for Juanita to see Helen in the rearview mirror. She looks anyway. Juanita can feel Helen's eyes searching for hers.

"You...can't..." Helen begins to croak.

"Shut up," Juanita tells Helen. Juanita is sure that Helen is alarmed at the volume and tone. An admittedly distasteful part of her enjoys her discomfort.

"I'm thinking," Juanita finally says.

Helen is in purgatory, unsure of what Juanita might do. Helen drops one hand to the rifle she carries in her lap, unsure of why she does so. Finally, Juanita breaks the silence.

"I have an idea," Juanita says. "We're going to take a detour. I think I know somewhere we can go. Unless I want to do as the man says and just give you up and run away. It's the only thing I can think of. It's literally, my way or the highway."

Juanita's eyes search the right-hand side of the road. She's afraid she's already passed it by. If so, she'll have to turn around to find it. That doesn't seem like a very good idea. Then she sees the sign. *Wilson's Cut.* She slows down but she's also afraid to go too slow. The car chasing her might crest the small hill she's just come down at any moment.

Even though she's focused on nothing else, she nearly passes it by. Without breaking, she wrenches the van into a sudden right-hand turn. The ambulance tilts on two wheels but falls back onto all four tires. The ambulance rattles and slides but Juanita knows not to use the brakes. She keeps her foot on the gas and the ambulance responds to her commands and straightens back into the middle of the sandy road that is little more than a narrow pathway.

Immediately she knows the surface on which she's driving is different. Her tires make the sand crunch, and she can feel the vibrations in her hands on the steering wheel. Once again, she's grateful for the rain. The sand is harder because of it. She hopes it's enough. This is not a road that's well-maintained. Wilson's Cut is an old, manmade oilfield channel cut into the Corpus Christi Bay side of Mustang Island. With the exception of ocean kayakers who occasionally launch at Wilson's Cut, the little road that runs alongside it is mostly forgotten.

Juanita switches off the headlights, brake lights and running lights. Independent control of all lights, even while driving, is a feature absent among new vehicles. It's something she never imagined would be an advantage. She knows her pursuer would easily see the van's lights as they cut across to the other side of the island. For now, stealth is more important than speed.

"Where…?" Helen begins to ask.

"Quiet," Juanita interrupts. "I need to concentrate."

The surrealness of their circumstance envelopes Juanita in a mind-numbing blanket.

Just an hour ago I was just doing my job, driving, picking up a client, taking her to Houston. Now, a man is dead. Someone wants Helen dead. Let's just face it, me dead, too. When did I step into the pages of a cheap paperback book?

"Where…we…go?" Helen manages to ask.

"Well," Juanita says, "desperate times call for desperate measures."

CHAPTER ELEVEN

Dive All Dive

"If I'm free, it's because I'm always running."

~Jimi Hendrix (1942–1970), American guitarist, songwriter, singer

———— ••• ————

THE ABSENCE OF LIGHT AND OVERABUNDANCE OF RAIN combine to make Juanita feel as though she's piloting a submarine. She wishes it were true. She wants to dive beneath the surface, lay low in the briny deep, and hide from the deadly destroyer that's hunting them.

Stealth is her choice. Being able to see is not worth the risk of being seen.

Normally, there'd be lights in the distance, across the bay, along the mainland shoreline. Not tonight.

Power's out everywhere. It's still a no-light night.

Headlights off, she guides the ambulance by sound and intuition. Whenever she feels vegetation slapping one side of the van or the other, she corrects, hoping this keeps her on the narrow path. She frequently checks the rearview mirror, looking for signs of pursuit. Her eyes don't linger before they dart back to the front windshield. There, she fears calamity from what she cannot see but, even so, must avoid.

Juanita lowers her driver's side window and does likewise with the front passenger's window. She needs to be fully awake and decides a jolt of cold air will keep her alert and, also, prove she's not in the midst of hallucinating.

How could this be happening? Is this really happening? Am I going to wake up to find it's a nightmare?

She wants the cold and the wetness and one thing more. She wants to better hear.

Rain sluices in through the partly open window and splashes her arm. She cups her hand, fills it with rainwater, and wipes it across her face and neck. The cold dribbles feel good on her swollen lip and the few cool droplets are a balm to her throat.

The downpour masks most sounds, so she listens for something... different. The sound of hissing rain is pierced by a rumble and followed by shushing. Juanita risks everything to turn on her headlights.

Instantly, Juanita recognizes it might already be too late.

She brakes hard and hears Helen's "Oh" as both of them are arrested and yanked back by their seat belts. Headlights illuminate advancing lines of curling seawater that swell, fall and spit white foam that surges toward them up the sand. Looking out the window, Juanita can tell her front tires are engulfed by the incoming wave that races by and around the vehicle.

"Oh," Helen squeaks again from the back seat.

Helen doesn't know where they are. Or where they're going. Or why the smell of the sea fills her nose so strongly now. Or why there's wind and some bits of water blowing in her face. She's confused and momentarily sure that Juanita is going to simply drive straight into the ocean. She wonders how long she might tread ocean water without the use of scissoring legs.

Ocean water is salty. Maybe I'll float better.

Juanita extinguishes the lights and puts the van in reverse. She's grateful that there is just enough traction for her to back up. Then, she turns left and begins driving on the beach, running parallel to the ocean itself.

"The tide is coming in," she says over her shoulder to Helen.

"Oh," Helen warbles again.

It's Helen's third "oh" in a row. The three chirps sound like a smoke detector whose battery has run low. Juanita can't help but grin at the thought and, given Helen's smoking habit, she's sure there's witty irony to be found in there if she had time to stop and think about it. Which she doesn't.

The grin drifts away and Juanita feels some guilt. Truth is, Juanita is concerned. The bruising around Helen's neck is pronounced. The little sounds she's making are evidence of thyroid cartilage damage. As an experienced EMT, she knows it's not unusual for strangulation victims to suffer emesis and inhale vomitus into lungs desperate to be filled. Pneumonia is often a result. Juanita knows that seemingly recovered victims of strangulation sometimes die from untreated damage and complications even after having been discharged from a hospital.

I need to examine Helen properly. As soon as we aren't in immediate danger. Which had better be soon.

Juanita hopes she still has enough time to exit the beach before the rising water swamps the ambulance to trap them in no man's land. At the same time, she offers a prayer of thanks for the ocean that will smooth over and hide the tracks her tires carve into the sand. They must be off this beach before the tide is fully in or they will never get off the beach at all.

She quickly does the math. If she maintains a speed of ten miles per hour, that means she'll have gone one sixth of a mile in ten minutes. She estimates the turnoff is a quarter mile away. That means it should take about fifteen minutes.

Waves wash onto the shore every eight seconds, give or take. She uses this as a crude stopwatch. Fifteen minutes is nine hundred seconds divided by eight suggests she'll arrive at the ramp in one hundred and twelve waves. Approximately. She knows there's a wide margin for error.

She counts down the waves. Her voice is no louder than when she prays, rosary beads in hand.

Eighty-five. Eighty-four. Eighty-three. Eighty-two...

Juanita feels like she's counting down to a rocket launch. More like a bomb. She isn't sure which. She realizes that sometimes the waves come a little faster and sometimes a little slower and that makes her worry she's gotten everything wrong.

Forty-eight. Forty-seven. Forty-six...

She takes a moment to mentally double task.

"Helen, make sure you're using the ice," Juanita admonishes. "Five minutes on, five minutes off."

Forty-four. Forty-three. Forty-two...

Shaken from her fugue state, Helen puts the towel-wrapped baggie of ice to her throat. Ice doesn't numb the pain much. Forgetting to care? That seems to work.

Don't like the ice. Makes my neck cold and my hand cold and I've been holdin' it here a long time. Five minutes on, five minutes off. How long is five minutes? I can't remember. Is it five minutes now?

Juanita is refocused on the countdown.

Twenty-nine. Twenty-eight. Twenty-seven...

Her hand opens and closes, a carpal metronome in time with each wave.

Juanita's flat-voiced countdown has a hypnotic effect on Helen. It makes her sleepy. She keeps forgetting where she is and why. Her hands relax, and the rifle starts to slip, triggering panic, which makes her retighten her grip until, again, she drifts into forgetfulness. Helen doesn't recall ever having felt so weak, so numb, so unable to summon the strength to care. The not caring, at least, is an anesthetic. It occurs to her that she is, literally, just along for the ride.

The ride. In her muddled state, fear has left Helen. The ride is soothing, not frightening. It agrees with her, this plunging devil-may-care movement in the dark. It feels familiar. Like she's done this before.

Am I supposed to be afraid? I ain't. Let's go. Go down the tunnel. No lights. No fear. How long is the ride? How long is five minutes?

Helen's eyelids feel heavy. She's tempted to close them but she's desperate to see everything even though, in the dark, there's nothing to see. No matter. She feels oath-bound to ride the tunnel to the end. She doesn't want to miss anything, even if just to prove to herself there's nothing to see. More than that, she fears sleep because she fears her dreams. She's sure she'll dream of the man in the mask, his voice, his smell.

He'll be with me in the deep, cold water. We'll drown together, hands around each other's throats.

Juanita knows she should be thinking only of counting waves, but her attention keeps drifting to Helen. Helen sits behind saying nothing, not even piqued enough to ask Juanita where they're going. Even though Helen may be saving her voice for obvious reasons, Juanita knows it's more than that. She's aware that Helen isn't just silent. She is listless. Lack of oxygen, for as little as ten seconds, can lead to brain damage. Juanita wonders how long Helen was choked.

The prowling ambulance begins to tilt. The beach is sloped higher on the inland side than the beach side. The tilt worsens.

Juanita smells the ocean water but also silt, sand and grasses. From the mixture of these smells and the sound of undulating water, she can tell the beach is shrinking. Waves herd them inland. Juanita fights the urge to overcorrect and steers a bit more to the left, calculating a path between two dangers, the rising water on one side and the deeper sand on the other flank. Too much in either direction will leave them stuck. Dead in their tracks.

Five. Four. Three…

When the beach suddenly evens out, Juanita sighs in relief. She knows the feel of driving over cross-channeled concrete. She's come to the boat launch ramp. She eases the ambulance through a turn and climbs the modest incline. Juanita hopes it's still in good enough order to use.

As she crests the humble hill, Juanita's eyes are drawn to scant light. A generator must be on. A metal shrouded lamp shines high up on a post. It looks like a lantern held forth in a giant's fist. Whether the light is a welcoming or a warning, Juanita cannot decide.

Juanita's gaze is expectant as the ambulance crawls forward and, sure enough, the wooden sign under the lamp materializes out of the gloom. In flowing red script are the words: *Los Desperados.*

There is lore about Los Desperados. The name was bestowed upon a small cabin built in the 1930s, a brothel that once offered up its services to fishermen, oil roughnecks and ranch hands billeted on the island. Juanita shudders.

Any pool soul wretched enough to have sex in that place must've been desperate, indeed.

Underneath the Los Desperados sign is another, larger, sign but it's not legible in the meager light cast by the metal hooded lamp. Nevertheless, Juanita knows what is written on the second sign. It will read: & Oriental Emporium.

Juanita pauses her forward roll and lets the ambulance idle in the rain. She's eager to see Sam but, also, afraid of the danger their presence might bring. She racks her brain to think of any other option. Juanita does not wish to involve the man who's the kindest person she's ever met.

He's, well, he's much more than that. Much more. Especially after Papa died.

Her father's sudden death via heart attack caused Juanita to quit college and come home to take care of her mentally handicapped brother and aging grandfather. She resumed her ambulance driver role, something she knows well after having worked for her Papa ever since she'd gotten a commercial driver's license when she'd turned eighteen. Soon after, she'd received her EMT certification. But that wasn't her passion. She'd saved her pay for college. Real college, not community college. She'd loved her classes, meeting other students and, for the first time, felt she was going her own way, planning her own future. Papa's death changed all that.

She contemplates the man she's come to ask for help. Chan Sam, owner of Los Desperados & Oriental Emporium, could never fill the void her father left, but he had helped her carry the weight of loss. She had endured her mother's death in childbirth. The passing of both her abuelo and father, barely a year apart, had only deepened the loss. Yet Sam had reminded her that suffering was part of life's natural path—not a punishment—and that even loss could lead to wisdom and strength.

At first glance, Sam could easily be mistaken for a young boy were it not for the wrinkles upon wrinkles and the many teeth missing from his perpetual grin. Juanita does not know how old he is and, according to Sam, neither does he.

The first time Juanita met Sam several years ago, when she first visited Los Desperados, the little man scurried his way into her path as she emerged from the vehicle. He was dressed in a baggy shirt, droopy high-water-length trousers that exposed matchstick-thin legs, and miniature feet nestled into child-sized sandals. The man bowed low and then straightened, a smiling face underneath a glistening bald head. His hands were clasped before him as though in prayer, his fingertips lightly touching his mouth.

"Choom rep soor," he'd said, offering up what Juanita came to learn is the traditional Theravada Buddhist greeting. His sing song voice is heavily accented, and Juanita had initially thought he was Vietnamese though she later learned he is Cambodian.

A friend who works at the Immigration and Naturalization Service told her that Sam had come to the United States in the late 1970s. Sam had once been married with three children. In a hushed voice the INS agent shared that Sam's family had been executed in front of him, one by one, by members of the brutal regime of Pol Pot. Juanita recalled having seen the movie *The Killing Fields*, and that the Khmer Rouge had massacred between one and two million men, women and children in a country that had only six million people. She had no idea how Sam had survived and found his way to the Texas coast.

In the many times Juanita had talked with Sam, he'd never spoken of his personal tragedies. Eventually, Juanita got up the courage to ask Sam if what she'd heard was true. Juanita had thought she'd seen a ripple hurry from his eyes to his mouth, but it had happened so quickly that Juanita couldn't be sure if Sam had reacted at all.

As is Sam's nature, he'd thought for a few seconds before responding. Sam replied only that he chanted each day for the strength and wisdom to forgive any who may have harmed him, and any he may have harmed and, even, forgiveness for himself. Juanita can hardly imagine Sam ever having harmed anyone or anything. Sam not only reveres all living things, but he also says all natural objects possess unique consciousness.

He says prayers for the fish that he catches from his rowboat and prayers for the bait he gathers and sells and prayers for locals and tourists alike. He practically charms his customers into accepting a free cup of not-too-hot green tea. Juanita's fingers flex, an involuntary response to the memory. She reaches into the console to touch the paper cup containing months old green tea residue.

Since Sam had bought the Los Desperados property, he'd added to the grounds creating a compound. The original two room bordello serves as his residence. Sam built a small grocery, bait supply and trinket store in front. At the rear of the property, near the short pier and rowboat he used, he'd built a woodworking shop and warehouse. Rectangular in shape, the tin roofed building has rollup doors on both the eastern and western sides. Inside this warehouse is a collection of Asian furniture, statues, and assorted housewares that he's collected over the years. Sam rescues damaged and discarded pieces and restores them. He'll sometimes sell them but only if he's convinced the buyers will treat the refurbished items with reverence. There's a tall, many-drawered apothecary chest in the Emporium that Juanita has long thought she'd like to buy one day.

Will there be one day? After today?

The van's stillness, the fact that they are not moving, worries Helen. The rattling rain is the only thing that keeps her from feeling like she's in a sensory deprivation tank. She can move—above the waist only, of course—but only slowly. Like her movements, her thoughts are slow. It's difficult to concentrate. Helen, too, has seen the sign: Los Desperados. The name is vaguely familiar, but her recollection is too addled.

Is this a bar? Oh. A drink would be nice.

Chastising herself for losing focus, Helen slides opens the rifle's chamber and looks for the box of bullets so she can load the rifle, but she remembers it's already loaded. She slides the bolt back into place. The metallic clacking draws Juanita's attention.

"We won't need that right now," Juanita tells Helen. "Do you want to give it to me?"

"No." Helen grunts, cradling Ben's rifle against her chest. Now that they are idling, no longer moving forward, Helen's anxiety grows. She doesn't understand why Juanita seems to have let down her guard. She doesn't share Juanita's seeming calm.

Move. Move, dammit! We're sittin' ducks here.

Finally, the van drifts forward. Helen exhales and relaxes her fists. Juanita drives past the little store and around the backside of the Emporium. She stops and turns off the ignition.

"Helen?" she says. "I'm going to see if we can get some help. Will you be okay by yourself for a few minutes?"

"Yes," Helen grunts. "No choice."

The ambulance's interior cabin lights come on briefly when Juanita exits. The lights come back on, again, when Juanita climbs through the sliding side door into the space next to Helen's fixed seat. For several seconds Juanita and Helen simply look at each other with blinking eyes.

"Hold still," Juanita says. She reaches out, placing her hands on either side of Helen's face, gently turning her head this way and that. With her thumbs, she pulls down the skin beneath her eyes, then lifts her chin to study her throat. Even in the poor light, signs of petechiae are visible, with more small red spots clustered across both cheeks. Her lips, thin and colorless under normal circumstances, are now swollen and bluish. Juanita lays a palm on Helen's brow, then checks her pulse.

Releasing her wrist, she whispers, "I won't be long." She closes the door. The cabin lights go out, and she fades into the night.

Helen, frustrated by being able to see so little, scrunches herself deeper into her chair, leans forward, and cranes her neck and head sideways to look through the window from as low an angle as she can manage. She sees that it's not completely dark. There's a mild glow, a place where the sign's thin light spills over the roofline.

Good. There's some light. Maybe it's enough to where I can see

*them when they come for me. I'm ready. Gotta be ready. Gotta stay
ready.*

Her hands caress the rifle lying in her lap as though it's a living,
feeling animal. She's never had much use for pets. She's never wanted
the responsibility of caring for an animal in her home, dealing with
the feeding and pooping and hair. But now, sitting alone in the dark,
she understands why someone might want a watchdog—something
that sees, hears, and smells danger before it arrives. Something that
can bark. And bite.

Helen lays her head back against the headrest, eyes open wide. She
tells herself to stay vigilant. She recalls having learned from some TV
show that movement is best detected with peripheral vision. So, she
wills her eyes to relax as she pans back and forth. She's sure she can
stay vigilant. She will stay vigilant.

Instead, she falls asleep.

Juanita stands outside the door to Los Desperados, hesitating. She
takes a deep breath, a mix of trepidation and fear filling her chest.
Her hands rise nervously to her face, wiping away the rain—and
maybe the doubt and darkness, too.

*Is this right? Am I putting him in danger? I don't know what else
to do. Where else to go. God, please don't make me regret this.*

She knocks and waits. The door creaks open. Humble light leaks
out. A small figure stands in the doorway.

CHAPTER TWELVE

Knockin' on Heaven's Door

*"The smallest act of kindness is
worth more than the grandest intention."*

~Oscar Wilde (1854-1900), Irish poet and playwright

———— ••• ————

I'M HERE. AGAIN. I'M HERE IN THE DARK, COLD WATER *where there's no air to breathe and there's never enough time to get to the surface. Like all the times before, the good air has run out. I spit out the last, the final bit of the used-up air. I gulp down water that's so cold it forces me to come awake, sputterin' and pawin' at my bed. It's always the same, every time. The same. Every time.*

This time, though, it's different.

The water I drink is not cold but warm, almost hot. There's somethin' in the water here with me. Whatever it is, it's burnin'. What can burn underwater? The burnin' thing won't let me sleep. It tickles and nudges. It teases me into swimmin' upward, even though I've already admitted defeat and filled my lungs and belly with water. The burnin' smell is alive. It twists and turns like a snake, circling its way upward, and the movement lures me, so I drift upward, too. Up I go. Up to the singin'. The song's pitch is constant, a melody of only one note. The song's lyrics repeat and run together and are unrecognizable. The words go on and on. It's not quite a hum, but maybe somethin' similar. I feel tiny vibrations in my bones.

This is what I can hear. And what I can smell. What can I see?

Helen's eyes flutter open. For so long, she's expected only the dark of nothingness. This is not that. She's cocooned in soft light.

Tentatively, she reaches out toward the gauzy light that fills the entirety of all she can see. Her fingertips graze the light itself and, to her astonishment, the light bends and creases. It feels substantial. Real.

She has no sense of time—five minutes, maybe?—so she doesn't know how long it takes before she realizes the light is filtering through what must be a veil.

It's a funeral shroud. I think. Am I dead?

Helen is fearful but, still, she pinches the substrate and drags it away from her face.

A brilliant pillar of light is visible. An intense shaft of silvered white light pours down through a rupture in the heavens. The sky that surrounds the puncture deepens into shades of purple, blue, and black.

Helen does not believe in heaven or hell or anything in between and, so, she's surprised that afterlife comes with a window.

Free of the fabric, her mouth and nose pull at the air around her and she breathes it all in, including some of the burning smell. She feels the air come in and it streams down her throat and into her lungs which swell and become bellows that send vessels scurrying away to deliver oxygen to the far reaches of her flesh. All the parts of her body that can feel anything quiver in gratitude.

She revels in a full, second breath, aware that the claustrophobic fear of it being her last is slowly fading away. She wonders how she could have ever taken breathing for granted.

She coughs, a tiny one. Her throat hurts and this is confusing. She thinks she might have had a dream where something thick, a boa constrictor maybe, was squeezing her neck.

A face emerges between her and the window. The brilliant light coming in from the window, frames a crookedly smiling face beneath a bald head that's shiny and haloed. Small eyes peer through wire framed glasses.

Is this God?

The face has a mouth, and it sings more of the song to her. She can't understand the words, but the rhythm and tone are soothing.

Is he speaking to me? I don't understand. I don't know God's language? He must be so disappointed.

"Helen," the smiling figure says. "You feel better. Yes?"

It's a man. I think. Not a god. Am I sure? No. Yes. Maybe?

Helen puts one hand on her throat.
"I'm...ahem...I...um...where am I?"
"You are here," the man says, throwing his small arms wide. "With me."
"Who are you?"
"I am Sam," the smile answers.
For a moment it feels like she has fallen into a purgatory edition of a Dr. Seuss book. *I am Sam? Who is Sam? Sam I am?*
"I help you," the small man adds. "I help you. Make tea. Your throat is better, yes?"
Helen nods. Remembrance returns to her in bits and pieces and out of sequence. She recalls that time was so very important, but she can't summon the reason.

Somethin' about five minutes. What was it?

Details begin to emerge. Images shoulder their way into her consciousness. She remembers being scared. Hurt. And time still feels important.

"How long have I been out?" she asks. "How many days?"

The little man's face scrunches and then, transforms back into a smile.

"No days. Only hours," he says, turning to point at the window. "Dawn is here." He faces her again. "And so are you."

She can vaguely remember her body floating, cold water falling onto her face.

Did someone carry me?

She remembers drinking something warm. It had made her sleepy. Sleepier than she'd already been.

"Where am I?" she asks again.

"You safe," the man says, his smile broad. He lays his palm across her forehead. "You in my home. Los Desperados. Fever gone. You better now."

"I'm better? Better than what? Hammered dog shit?" Helen says. "I feel like hammered dog shit."

The small man looks at her, head tilted like a hound, saying nothing at first. Then, he asks, "this is joke?"

Surprising herself Helen begins to smile back but she catches herself.

The guy seems harmless. But...what if he isn't? What the hell is goin' on?

Like the bow of a Viking ship emerging from fog, gathered memories assault her. The masked man. The closet. All the blood. Running away. The ambulance. Juanita.

"Where's Juanita?"

The words irritate her throat but, still, it feels much better than when she was in the ambulance where the thickness of her tongue sometimes gagged her and she'd had to fight hard not to panic with worry that she was suffocating, bit by bit.

"I get her. One moment," he says. The little man shuffles across the room and returns with a steaming cup.

"You drink," he says.

"What? You some kind of Chinese witch doctor? How do I know it isn't poison?"

Sam does the sideways head thing again. He smiles.

"Oh. This joke. You very good at joke."

This time Helen can't help but chortle, though she disguises it as a throat clearing.

"This tea different tea," Sam says. "Not sleepy tea. It good for you."

Helen crosses her arms to think it over. She doesn't want to be knocked out and she's still unsure whether the man is being truthful.

"You think you can heal me?" Helen asks.

She'd intended her question to be sarcastic. Despite her intent, it hadn't come out that way. It had sounded plaintive, needy. She's embarrassed at the tone.

The smile fades from the little man's face. He extends his arms toward her, and, for a minute, Helen thinks he'll touch her, but he does not. Rather, he brings together his palms like he's praying. He peeks at her over his fingers and doesn't answer.

He doesn't know. Or doesn't want to say. Or maybe there's somethin' else wrong with me? More damage? What else is broken?

"Oh, no. I no heal you. You heal yourself," Sam says. "You need heal body, but need heal mind, too. I help you. This tea very good tea for you."

Heal myself? That ain't happenin'. Been broken too long. Can't hear when my body whispers. Can't even hear it when it screams.

"Helen?" Sam says. Helen, lost in thought, doesn't answer. Getting no answer, Sam tries another path.

"Okay I touch?" the little man asks.

Surprising herself, Helen nods yes. She cannot believe she's given him permission. She does not like to be touched. Sam's fingertips dance around her throat and along her breastbones. They are as feint as butterflies that settle briefly before flitting away.

"Yes," he says. "This tea. Good for you now. I invite you drink."

If those are doctor's orders, they are the nicest doctor's orders Helen has ever received. She smells, considers, and finally relents to sip the tea. She can taste ginger but also other things she cannot identify. It doesn't taste good. It doesn't taste bad. Like the burning smell, no fair comparison comes to mind. The warmth is nice.

"Wait," Sam says. "I get Juanita."

When Sam leaves the room, Helen sits up in the bed. Low to the ground, it's more pallet than bed. She starts to pull herself onto the floor and sloshes some of the tea from her cup so she, instead, settles down to sip and scan around her.

Her eyes go back to the window. White curtains hang on either side. The bright light in the sky has diminished, the beam now thinner, weaker.

The room is sparsely furnished. Against one wall is a very long, narrow table. A small lamp casts a circle of vanilla light onto the table-top. On the table is a burning stick. The incense aroma is now familiar but, like the tea, it's indescribable. Also on the table, facing the window, is a statue, a Buddha sitting cross legged, hands folded in his lap, eyes open but only a little.

A sleepy Buddha?

There are two wooden chairs pushed up under a small table across the room. There's a deeply indented bamboo mat on the floor by her bedside. She realizes Sam has been using this mat.

It wasn't a song. It was a chant. It was him, on his knees, probably. I think it went on for a long time. A long time to chant. For me. For someone he doesn't even know.

Helen has never liked having anyone hover over her. Peculiarly, though, she does not feel smothered. To her own surprise, she feels calmed. She sips more tea and almost spills, again, when she hears feet shuffling back to the room.

Sam, the diminutive probably-just-a-man-and-not-God, clops back into the room with Juanita right on his heels. Sam resumes his spot in front of the window and Juanita joins him, rubbernecking her tilted head to gaze at her sideways. Their heads practically touch as they scan Helen.

"Hi, Helen," Juanita says in a voice that somehow matches her haggard, spent face. Blue, yellow and purple bruising mottles her face.

"Your color is much better." Juanita observes. "You had me worried. How are you feeling?"

"Erm, better. I guess. Why are you here? I mean, why here now? You were supposed to come Thursday morning. Why did you come early?"

Juanita retells Helen about the phone call from the law firm instructing her to bring Helen to their offices in Houston a day early so they can review her upcoming testimony.

"I already told you this. Do you not remember?"

"That must be it," Helen says. "Someone doesn't want me on the stand."

"But why?" Juanita asks. "I was under the impression that your testimony was routine. That you'd confirm what you said before. Isn't that true? What's changed?"

"Don't know," Helen says. "Can't imagine any other reason."

"It might be important, but it doesn't change things," Juanita says. "We don't have any good choices. You heard what they said on the radio. They've closed the bridges. We'd never make it across. We can't just stay here either. They'll find us. Eventually. The island's too small. The ambulance, it sticks out like a sore thumb."

Silence follows Juanita's summation. Sam is the one to finally interrupt it.

"I have idea," says Sam. "Hide ambulance. In Emporium. I go for help."

"Sam, you don't even have a car," Juanita replies.

"I have bike," Sam smilingly says.

Juanita considers this.

The Emporium is large enough. There are garage-like roll up doors on each end. It's crazy. But it might work.

"Okay. Sam, can you help me clear a path? We'll have to move stuff out of the way, drive the ambulance inside. We can stack stuff around it so it's hidden. It won't stand up to a thorough search but maybe it won't be seen if someone comes looking for us."

"Yes. We do this," Sam says while shuffling around the bed to rearrange the sheet over Helen and to replenish her tea before the two of them leave again.

Given the rain has tapered off, Helen can hear the clanking metal garage door being rolled up. Fifteen or so minutes later she hears the ambulance start and the sound fades. Juanita must be driving the ambulance into the Emporium. Minutes later, she hears the door being rolled back down again.

Soon after, Juanita comes back into the room. This time, she's pushing Helen's wheelchair.

"Sam might be able to get through," Juanita shares with Helen. "Sam tells me he can. He says he knows the paths and, if he has to, he'll walk his bike into the dunes and go around any traffic stops. Plus, if they do stop him? He's harmless. No one would think twice about him."

Juanita's voice trails off as Sam bursts back into the room.

"You hide!" he shrieks. "Car come here. Now. You hide. Now!"

"Where?" Juanita replies, exasperated.

Sam thinks.

"You hide. In Emporium. Hide like soldier in Troy. No time. Please hurry. Must go now!"

Juanita lifts Helen up from the pallet and practically dumps her in the wheelchair.

Before Juanita can wheel her around, Helen takes another look through the window. All she can see is gloomy gray. The bright light has gone.

CHAPTER THIRTEEN

The Trojan Elephant

"We are all collateral damage for someone's beautiful ideology, all of us inanimate in the face of the onslaught."

~Benjamin Alire Saenz (1954-present), American poet,
novelist, writer of children's books

———— ••• ————

THE LUSTROUS STERLING SILVERED DAYBREAK HAS GIVEN way to a stained and tarnished iron morning. Juanita feels the wind gusts at her back. The invisible forces of nature push and shove. Though they're unpredictable, they aren't unappreciated. They hasten Juanita's own pushes and shoves. They encourage Helen's grabs and pulls. They chaperone and usher Juanita and Helen toward a place of hiding.

Reaching the side door of the Emporium, Juanita manages to prop the heavy metal door open with her hip so she can drag Helen and the wheelchair inside. As soon as they're in, Juanita closes the door and slots home the deadbolt. Being out of sight is a fleeting but, even so, welcome relief to Juanita.

With any luck, a locked door will discourage a search. Don't count on it. This hasn't exactly been our lucky day.

This is Helen's first look inside of the Emporium. It's a dark, chaotic jumble of indistinguishable objects and inhospitable shadows. Dust motes, awakened from their winter hibernations, swarm like tiny moths drawn to the salt and pepper light coming in through the small window in the door. Helen sneezes. She's overwrought with worry, a premonition that she'll have to fight off a sneeze at exactly the wrong moment.

Juanita, having driven the ambulance inside less than an hour ago, still must reorient herself to the chock-a-block congestion. To move at all is to navigate an obstacle course.

Since she knows what to look for, it doesn't take long for Juanita's eyes to find the ambulance's bulk. It's mostly hidden behind an ornate bookcase and is draped with a tarp. Juanita and Sam have done their best to camouflage it, adding an Asian privacy screen on one side and the tall, multi-drawered apothecary chest Juanita covets on the other side. In the pale, weak light from the door's window, Juanita judges the ambulance to be nearly invisible. Whether the ambulance is found depends on if the emporium is searched, for how long and how thoroughly. Juanita hopes the search, if any, is short and haphazard.

"What now?" Helen asks.

"Gimme a sec," Juanita responds.

Juanita moves deeper into the outbuilding toward the end opposite of where she'd driven the ambulance into the Emporium.

What did Sam mean? Hide like the soldiers of Troy? What the hell's that supposed to mean?

Juanita's shuffling feet bump up against an immovable object. Her hands reach out and she rests her palms against a large, smooth, curved mass. She steps back, considering. Her eyes, adjusting to the dim indirect window light, finally convey that this is a looming, hulking mass of wood that blocks her way deeper into the Emporium.

She slides her hands up the obstacle until her arms are at head height. Her wrists find a rounded top. Forearms ski down the sloped side until fingers caress what feels like a large, carved leaf. Exploring further, hands find twin somethings that jut out and up. Palms cup and travel over these two curved, smooth cylinders that taper off to rounded points. She probes further and there it is. It's thick, rounded, long. It feels like a ribbed, muscular python.

Juanita recalls Sam having shared with her the story of the blind men and the elephant. It's a story, Sam said, first written down during the lifetime of the first Buddha, from when he'd lived and breathed and walked the Earth.

The parable. Sam's parable. The blind men and the elephant. Each blind man thought the creature to be something different based on what part they'd touched. What was the moral of the story? Something about the nature of one's truth. How hard it is to see the whole truth?

Damn. So tired. Hard to think straight.

Recollecting that Helen's life, and hers, won't save themselves by prayer alone, she shakes herself out of the fatigue-induced pause.

A series of soft knocks and respondent dull echoes confirm her suspicion. The brute is hollow. Back to the midsection, her hands slide down and under and, like a midwife aiding birth, she locates the center of its generous tummy. There's a hole. A pretty big opening.

Understanding blossoms.

Hide like soldier in Troy? Yes! Inside. It's a Trojan elephant.

Retracing her steps, Juanita goes back to where Helen is waiting in her wheelchair.

"There's a good place to hide. It might be cramped but I think it'll work," Juanita says. "I'm gonna have to carry you. Can't get the wheelchair there."

Not waiting for agreement, Juanita gathers Helen into her arms and lifts her out of the wheelchair. Helen isn't heavy but the path through a mishmash of sofas, tables and chairs causes her to slide sideways and she nearly trips over something in the murkiness. She's grateful when her knee bumps against the side of the mammoth.

"It's a grand old wooden elephant," Juanita tells Helen. "It's hollow inside. There's a way in, on the bottom. I'm gonna help you, but you'll have to pull your way inside. Can you do it?"

"I reckon," Helen answers. "Ain't got much choice, do I?"

Grunting whispered curses, Helen climbs her way up into the belly of the beast. Juanita's hands shove on her bottom helping pack her useless legs in as well. It's pitch-black, cramped and scary as hell, but at least she's in.

"I'll be right back," Juanita whispers, her voice disembodied in the gloom.

Juanita returns to the wheelchair and considers. She pushes the wheelchair against one wall. She spies a tapestry and yanks it off the wall, hoping she hasn't damaged it beyond repair. She lays this across the wheelchair. Spotting a waist-high concrete statue, she picks it up and puts it onto the chair. Good enough, she hopes.

She's about to return to the side door but notices something laying across a small side table. Her hands close around what feels like a thick stick. The handle is wood and there's irregular metal on the top. It's solid, heavy.

Maybe a scepter of some kind? It's perfect. You know. Just in case.

Shambling back to the side door, Juanita cautiously raises her head and peeks out the small window. The encouragingly bright morning light has retreated. All that's left is ashen. She can make out some of Sam's store and a bit of the parking lot. She's about to leave and join Helen when she notices movement.

A hulking man steps into view. He's walking toward the Emporium. Before she can turn away to join Helen in their beastly hideaway, Juanita sees Sam emerge from the store. Hands full, Sam trots toward the man. Once he reaches him, Sam extends whatever he's holding with both hands. There's a pause before the unknown man sharply sweeps an arm down, knocking to the ground whatever Sam had offered up.

Now Sam is saying something to the man. Juanita cannot hear so she concentrates on his face.

Maybe I can read his lips. Understand what he's saying. I can't tell. Can't tell what he's saying.

Whatever it is Sam is saying, the man has clearly decided to disregard it. He brushes away Sam's arm and resumes his march toward the emporium.

What happens next shocks Juanita.

Sam throws himself onto the man, wrapping his arms around the man's legs. The man staggers a bit but finds his footing. It's difficult to be sure but it appears as though the man is hitting Sam, throwing punches at his head and shoulders. Sam falls away but he quickly scrambles back to his feet and reattaches himself to the man's legs. This time it's clear, the man is hitting Sam but not dislodging him. The man reaches to his side, pulls something out and he clubs Sam on the head. Juanita is pretty sure it's a pistol. Sam collapses in a heap. He no longer moves.

Juanita's arms shake. Her grip tightens around the shaft she is holding. Rage scurries through her veins. She seizes the deadbolt and snaps it open. The metal door is heavy and the wind rails against it, but it gives. She transfers the weight from her shoulder to her hip so she's ready to burst out.

Go help Sam? I should go. But the man's got a gun. I'll never reach him before he shoots me. Is Sam dead? Can I get to him before it's too late? Is it already too late?

Okay. First, open the door, nice and steady. Let him see me. Look relieved but not hysterical. Second, walk toward him. Not too fast. Not too slow. Tell him I need his help. Tell him Helen is crazy. Tell him I've been kidnapped and I'm so glad he's come to rescue me. All he has to do is let his guard down. For one moment. That's all I need.

How? Okay, hide the stick. Hide it behind my back until I get close enough. I can do it. I'll keep talking and walking and talking and walking. Just like the masked man coming down the stairs. I'll walk right up to him like I'm walking and talking in the dark and I'll clobber him. I will.

If he kills me? So be it!

"Juanita?" Helen calls out from the dark. "Are you coming? What's happening?"

She grinds her teeth, the tension sending sharp pain through her jaw. It blends with the throbbing ache in her chin, lips, nose—and heart.

"Juanita! What's happening?"

Still, she ignores her.

I'm going…I will go…I can go…I should go. But then there's Helen to think about, too. What if I can't surprise him? What then?

Juanita watches the man lean over Sam and then straighten up. He now has Sam's keys in his hands.

So much for a locked door keeping him out. She reengages the deadbolt anyway.

Helen calls again: "Juanita?"

Anguished, Juanita turns away from the door and scrambles through the maze back to the elephant.

"Quiet! Don't say anything," Juanita says as she pulls herself up through the underbelly of the wooden monolith. "He's gonna be here any second."

No sooner does Juanita get her legs inside than they hear the side door handle rattle. They hear jingling as the man tries a few keys, finds the right one, and opens the door. Heavy footsteps clump against the concrete flooring. She hears snapping sounds and figures the man is trying to turn on the lights. When Sam told her the Emporium's lights weren't hooked up to the generator, he'd said so apologetically, as though he should've anticipated Juanita's need of light.

Even now, a killer is coming through the door. Even now, Juanita struggles to think of anything but Sam.

It looked bad. Sam. He was hit hard. Maybe I'm wrong. God, I hope I'm wrong. Please God let me be wrong?

Why didn't I go help him? Why? To save Helen? Save her? She's not worth it. That's a bad trade. That's the truth. She's not worth more than him. She's not.

Inside the hollow elephant, Helen is smooshed face down, butt up, and onto one shoulder. Any and all the aches that might have eased under Sam's care and tea have come roaring back. Juanita lies partly on top of her making it hard to breathe. Helen concentrates on trying to slow her inhaling and exhaling. She can recall no other day in her life when she's thought as much about breathing as she has today.

Breathe. Swim the pool. You can make it.

Though the teak elephant is solidly built, seams run between its curving panels. Through these slim gaps, Helen catches stabs of light being jerked around the room. The flashlight's beam forms a glittering cone, with dust particles swirling and reflecting light like embers stirred from a dying fire. The narrow end shows her where the man holding the flashlight is, while the wide end reveals what he's looking at.

Helen watches because it's mesmerizing. As tired as she is, she can't look away. It's as hypnotic as it is horrible.

I can see the flight of the light. It's a lightsaber—wider on the sides, thinner in the middle. Less dense, Juanita would say. Still, it's a lightsaber. Is he the bad Jedi?

Juanita, on the other hand, can see nothing. She's bent the other way. Eyes closed, she's listening as hard as she can. She's heard him shuffle deeper into the Emporium. She's heard him kick and hurl things out of his way. Soon, the bangs and bashes are replaced by plunks and clunks and then, by slams and bams. She knows what this means.

He's found the ambulance. He's searching it. What didn't we take out? The registration papers. He'll know who I am. Shit! The gun. And the bullets. Shit and more shit! Our backpacks. Helen's back-pack. The one with the computer. Double shit!

Oh, and my hat.

"Hello," the man calls out. "There's no need to hide. I'm here to help. We think you might have been assaulted. I've been charged with facilitating your safety. Look, we don't know who the dead guy is, but it looks like it was a case of self-defense. You can come out. It's safe. I promise."

Neither of the women fall for the obvious falsity. Helen's heard the like before.

The tone of his voice. The words he chooses. His pretendin' to be a good guy. The bullshit he spins. He sounds just like the other guy, the masked man, the deputy that's lyin' dead and cold in my closet.

The next fifteen minutes are a terror. The man searches the Empo-rium and by the sounds, is not shy about destroying things as he goes. Several times items are hurled through the dark to thud against the wooden elephant causing them both to wince.

Eventually the sounds wind down. The man returns to the approxi-mate center which happens to be very near the elephant. Helen fights the instinct to hold her breath and, instead, sips at the air. She feels as though she's back in the clothes hamper. Barely able to breathe. Covered in blood. Asking for Ben's help.

"Fuck!" The sound echoes off the metal walls and ceiling.

The man speaks again, this time not as loudly but clearly.

"Plan B to Top Hat. I have an update."

"Go for Top Hat."

"I'm at Los Desperados. Had no trouble finding it. The sign out front is lit up like a Christmas tree. Anyway, you were right about the ambulance. It's stashed in the big building in back. No sign of the birds, though. I searched the house, store, and this place. They got to be somewhere close, though. Can't imagine hauling a cripple around would let them get too far."

"Copy. What else?"

"According to the vehicle registration papers the owner of the ambulance is Juanita Maria Jiménez, aged 36. Got a home address in Baytown; it's 3863 Loreal Avenue. I also saw traces of blood in the ambulance. At least one of 'em is hurt. There's a rifle in there, too. Old single shot twenty-two. Figure it's the same one Clarence was shot with. I didn't touch it or any other stuff until you decide what we should do with it. Didn't want my fingerprints on anything in case you need it for whatever cover story you decide."

"Good thinking," Top Hat replies. "Okay, stay put. I'll send someone to that Baytown address. I'm coming to you. We'll find them hiding somewhere nearby. I'll be there ASAP."

"Uh, one more thing," the man says, voice echoing slightly within the metal structure. "I had resistance from a third party. That Chinese guy that owns this place. Had to deal with him. Permanent like."

Juanita gasps and one hand flies to her mouth. She's sure the man has heard her. The silence that follows is brittle and about to break. She's relieved when the radio conversation continues.

"Did you use your weapon?" the man on the radio asks.

"Affirmative. I used my weapon, but no shots fired. Had to club him."

"Good. Don't leave unnecessary forensic evidence. Get the body out of sight. I'll arrange a better long-term disposal. We'll search together when I arrive. Oh, and turn off that sign and any lights. There's nobody on the roads but, just in case, I don't want anyone to think the place is open for business."

"Copy that. There's a couple of dumpsters on the far side. I'll use one of those for now."

"Do it. My ETA is, now, fifteen minutes."

Footsteps retreat followed by the sound of the side door of the emporium opening and closing. Juanita thinks on all she's just heard.

"We can't stay here," she says to Helen. "If they search this place again, and it sounds like that's what they're going to do, they'll find us."

"Where?" Helen asks, "How? What do we do? Just sail away?"

Juanita thinks for a moment.

"Yeah. That's exactly what we're going to do."

CHAPTER FOURTEEN

Madcap Mayhem

"Freedom is just chaos, with better lighting."

~Alan Dean Foster (1946-present), American writer of fantasy and science fiction

———— ••• ————

SPRINKLES FALL LIKE TEARS FROM AN OYSTER SKY. Juanita, still carrying the metal-capped rod, makes her way back to the side door. She peeks through the window, keeping her head as low as possible. Moderate rain has resumed, and the window is splashed with droplets that distort the view like a fun house mirror. Without the fun. In the ghostly gray light, she sees a man in long coat over jeans tucked into boots. There's a holstered pistol at his hip. He's staring down. At Sam's body.

Despair grips her.

Oh God. This can't be happening. Why did I come here? Why did I put Sam at risk?

Her grip retightens around the club. Her hand trembles. Tears blur her vision. She blinks them away.

I want to bash him. Crush his head. God. No. Not Sam!

The man, not tall but muscular and broad, easily hefts Sam's body onto his shoulder. Adjusting his grip, he starts trudging around the building, disappearing from view. Juanita remembers the dumpsters are on the other side of the property near the road.

He should be out of sight, for a few minutes, anyway. Five minutes or so? Enough? No, not enough. We'll never make it.

"Wait," she says aloud, slapping her forehead and wincing as fingers come away tacky from the still sticky wound. "What did the Top Hat guy say?"

He told the man to turn off the sign and all the lights. He may not know where the switches are. That means the generator. He'll probably find and turn off the generator. It's on the backside of the shop. That's still too close but maybe he'll waste some time figuring out where it is. Maybe it'll be enough time.

Racing back to the elephant, Juanita grabs hold of Helen's legs and pulls her out of the hole, speaking softly all the while.

"I'm gonna carry you. We'll go fast. Hold this for me and hang on as tight as you can and try not to make any sound," Juanita whispers, thrusting the wooden baton into Helen's arms. She lifts Helen, feeling a tweak in one knee but pushing through the discomfort.

With Helen cradled in her arms, Juanita risks one more look out the window before she shoulders her way outside. Unsteadily, she hustles around the far corner of the Emporium.

"Okay, here's where it gets dicey," she tells Helen. "We need to cover some open ground and hope he doesn't see us. Pray he's slow. And stupid."

She plots her path. The fastest way will take them right by where Sam was struck down. It's their only hope.

Cradling Helen, Juanita quickens the pace. Approaching the spot where Sam was killed, Juanita spies a bloodstain that's already thinning and melting away in the drizzle. Next to it is a paper cup. The green tea it held has long since been diluted by the rain.

She cannot contain a sob. Just one. That's all she can afford now.

Bearing fear, urgency and Helen's body, she hurries, knees pumping high. Helen's body bounces in her arms. Rainfall drenches them. With just one near stumble, she reaches a little fence. She jogs around it toward a wooden pier.

Helen hears Juanita's footsteps slapping against wet, packed sand. She lets her head fall back and down to see where they're headed. She gets it.

Girl's got smarts. Seems like I always underestimate her.

Helen relaxes her grip around Juanita's neck but, in doing so, she drops the baton which thuds onto the sand just before they reach the dock.

Leaning over the edge of the wooden slats, Juanita deposits Helen into a small wood rowboat that rocks, irritated by the suddenly added weight. Juanita's eyes search for the baton, but she can't find it in the boat. She retraces her steps looking around for where it fell from Helen's arms. That's when they hear the sound of footsteps pounding.

"Run, Juanita!" Helen says in a whispered voice. "You can get away."

Juanita sinks to a crouch and crabwalks to the other side of the little wooden fence. She's no sooner hidden than she hears the man's boots hammering the dock.

The man slows his run, drawing his pistol as he nears. He sees Helen sprawled in the bottom of the boat. She's on her back, legs splayed obscenely apart on the boat's bench. His gaze does not linger on her. He immediately begins looking elsewhere.

"So," Helen says mostly to herself. "You ain't slow after all. That's too bad. Bet you're stupid, though."

The man ignores Helen's opening salvo. His head pivots deliberately, scanning the surrounding area. He's a bit overweight, a beer belly pushing at the buttons of his orange-colored shirt. She can't see his eyes under the Gilligan-like bucket hat that sits on his head. What she cannot miss, though, is the long, wicked scar on one cheek. It carves a nasty path through the black, thick beard that covers most of his face.

"Where is she?" the man finally asks, eyes peering into the distance.

"Who's that?" answers Helen.

"The other girl. The Mexican girl." He recalls the name. "Jiménez. Where's Jiménez?"

Helen doesn't respond.

"Where is she?" he barks again, louder.

"Hey fuckhead," Helen replies. "She's gone. Left me here a long time ago. Told me good luck. Took off runnin'. She's long gone by now, dipshit."

Unable to stop herself, Helen's eyes dart to the side, searching for where she last saw Juanita. Realizing that might give her away, she quickly shifts her gaze back to the man, relieved to find him focused elsewhere.

"A complication if true," the man answers. "But I don't think so. You couldn't have gotten yourself here without help. Admittedly, I didn't look too closely the first time, but I did notice the boat. And it was empty. You couldn't have gotten yourself into the boat that fast on your own. You think I'm stupid?"

"Come to think of it, yeah, I do," Helen spits back. "You're the stupidest motherfucker of all time. She's gone."

"No. No she's not. You've got one chance to tell me where she is. If not, well, you know," the man says, waving his pistol. "You'll talk. I promise."

As though summoned by these threatening words, the wind picks up, and the rain returns with renewed force. Helen blinks rapidly to clear the swiftly falling rainwater from her eyes. She's already reconciled herself to being taken prisoner. To being killed. But Juanita? She might still get away.

It's not her fault. None of it. I've got to give her a chance. I need to distract him.

"Fuck you cocksucker!" she yells. "Think you scare me? I ain't scared of you, you piece of shit."

The man doesn't respond. Instead, he takes several steps toward the small fence behind which, Helen guesses, Juanita is hiding. So, Helen raises her voice to a shout.

"You wanna make me talk? Come over here and do it. I'll do for you what I did to your friend. I've got a knife right here waitin' for you. I'll cut your throat just like I did his."

The man tenses and growls. It suddenly hits her.

"Come to think of it, he looked like you. A lot like you. I'm gonna make an educated guess here. I'm thinkin' he was your brother. 'Cept for that pretty little scar, you look just like him."

"Shut up," the man says fixing his eyes on Helen's. She has his full attention now.

"Clarence! That's his name, isn't it? Well Clarence was a pussy!" she screams. "You hear me? He's the cunt. He squealed when he died. Did you know that? Pathetic. You hear me? Pathetic. He squealed like a little piggie when I sliced open his throat!"

Bellowing, the man rushes and jumps onto the boat, his added weight lurching it from side to side. The man leans down and uses his free hand to slap her full in the face. The blow twists her head sideways. Helen comes up laughing through bloodied teeth.

"That all you got? You're a bigger cunt than your brother. Didn't think that was possible. You're the biggest cunt of all. Squeal piggie. Squeal!"

The man shudders while staring intently at Helen. He growls, a full-throated war cry.

"You bitch! I'm gonna…"

He never finishes. Instead, he rocks violently to one side.

Aided by the renewed rain, Juanita has crept unheard and unseen from behind him. She smashes his hand sending the gun flying off to hit the edge of the boat before plunging into the water. Enraged, the man faces Juanita in time to ward off a second whack with his shoulder, sending his hat spinning off into the water. The blow and his reaction cause the boat to rock more violently and the man falls forward onto Helen. He straight-arms Helen's chest and launches himself up, howling. The sound ends abruptly when Juanita brings the stick down a third time, to the side of his head. The man collapses.

Still, he won't stay down. He raises his head, again. Juanita puts her full weight behind one more swing and she brains him on the top of his head. The metal end bites into and lodges in his skull. The man jerks and staggers up, still refusing to die. He reaches up and pries the bloody metal-topped baton from his head. It makes a sucking sound when he pulls it out. He looks at it in disbelief and then at Juanita. His eyeballs roll in circles, and the baton falls from his fingers into the boat as he tips over the side and lands half on the sand and half into the water. That Helen is eagle spread in the bottom of the boat is the only thing that keeps her from spilling over as well.

Bent over, one hand on her knee, Juanita watches wind-stirred waves slap against his legs in the water, his torso at the waterline. He isn't moving and she can see pink where his head rests in the shallow water.

"Damn," Helen says. "That was a helluva whack-a-mole job. 'Less I got it figured wrong, this here guy is Plan B. And Ringo? The man in the closet. That was his brother. This thing is turnin' into an episode of Family Feud."

Her breathing still quick and shallow, Juanita is too numb to answer. Finally, she does.

"I think I killed him," Juanita says mostly to herself. "I should check for a pulse."

"Fuck that," Helen replies. "I hope he's dead. He oughta be dead. That's the second man who's tried to kill us. Between us, we're two for two. Whoever their mama is, she ain't goin' to like us."

"Where did you get a knife?" Juanita asks, raising herself to full height. "You told him you'd had one. Said you'd cut his throat."

"I lied," admits Helen. "Hey. Not my first rodeo. Not my first lie, either."

Hands on hips, Juanita looks out into the water. The wind is really picking up now, causing the waves just beyond this inlet to show whitecapped crests.

"We've got to get out of here," Juanita declares.

"Wait!" Helen says. "We need the rifle. And the backpack. I put it in the cooler in the ambulance. He didn't tell that feller on the phone that he'd found it. I don't think he did. We need 'em."

"Are you crazy? That Top Hat guy? He's on his way here," she replies. "We gotta get out of here. Now."

"Juanita, listen to me. The backpack. What's inside. It's important."

Juanita looks anything but sure. Helen looks anything but trustworthy.

"Look," Helen continues. "Remember when the Top Hat feller said on the radio that I got somethin' he wants back? What else is it gonna be but my computer? It's in the backpack. If we're gonna understand what's happenin', we need it."

Juanita hesitates at a time when she knows she can't afford to. In the end, it's being able to retrieve her ball cap that makes the difference.

After one long look at the man's unmoving body, Juanita dashes back into the Emporium and practically dives into the rear compartment of the ambulance. She releases the buckles on the built-in cooler and finds the green backpack within. Dropping to her knees she reaches under the bench seat in the back and finds the rifle. She cannot locate the box of bullets, however. After seconds of frantic searching and pocketing a few more things, she gives up, worrying that she's already taken too long.

Last, and certainly not least, she snags her ball cap and pulls it tight onto her head.

Partly hunched over, she runs back to the dock. She tosses the backpack into the boat, hands the rifle to Helen and clamors in. It takes a moment for her to find an oar. She'd hoped there would be two of them, ones she might fit into oarlocks, a faster and more reliable way to paddle and steer. Still, one is better than none.

After untying the boat from the bow and stern cleats, Juanita uses the paddle to push away from the pier. On her knees she paddles, two strokes on one side before switching over for two strokes on the other.

An inexperienced paddler, she's finding it difficult to move against the rain and wind that wants to push her back to shore. With excruciating slowness, she finally gets the boat out of the little inlet and out of sight from the dock.

Juanita thinks about the two bodies she's leaving behind: Sam, the father figure she's grown to love, and the man she's killed—a man she doesn't know but has come to hate. Tears run down Juanita's face, but they are indistinguishable in the rain.

She struggles to make headway paddling away from Los Desperados and toward what well may be more death. Probably their own.

CHAPTER FIFTEEN

Sittin' on the Dock of the Bay

"The clouds are scudding across the moon,
A misty light is on the sea;
The wind in the Shrouds has a wintry tune
And the foam is flying free."

~Bayard Taylor (1825–1878), American poet, literary critic, translator, travel author, and diplomat

———— ••• ————

OVERHEAD, THE LAST OF CAULIFLOWER-WHITE CLOUDS swirl in confusion. Like a school of greenback fish sensing threat, the thinnest of the celestial nimbus flees. Chasing the white clouds away is a veil of darkness. The cloudscape is being invaded by purple and black, the colors matching Juanita's face and Helen's neck. A chill of both temperature and dismay washes over them.

As though summoned to further thwart their escape, the wind kicks back up. Whitecaps appear on the crests of emergent waves. The bay water begins to simmer then churn; seethe, then boil.

The wood boat is bulky, ponderous at best in calm waters. It's nearly uncontrollable in stormy ones. Initially, Juanita had made encouraging headway. No longer.

Straining with one oar, still trying to paddle twice on one side and twice on the other, Juanita is mostly going in circles. She realizes she cannot make enough headway to row across Corpus Christi Bay to the mainland. If they continue floundering, they'll capsize. If that were to happen Juanita might survive but Helen surely would not.

The boat is, now, less than a couple of miles away from Los Desperados. A search will undoubtedly find them.

We can't stay on the water. Where to go? How to get there? Can Helen survive the rain and wind? Damn, it's cold. When did it get so cold?

Juanita resolves they'll have to land, somehow hide the boat, and figure out a place to hole up. Aware that most, if not all, of the island's residents will have evacuated in advance of the storm, she racks her brain to think of somewhere they might shelter. The nearest cluster of houses is ten miles or more away, and they all line the main road. She'll never get anywhere near them without being spotted. She knows she doesn't have the strength left to carry Helen that far.

What about the Wild Horse? It's old, but it's built like a bomb shelter. How far away? A mile? A mile and a half? And what about Betsy? She might be there. She told me she'd ridden out many a storm there. If she's there, is that better or worse? I can't handle another dead friend on our account.

Getting the boat to the shore is hard enough. Getting Helen off the boat nearly causes them both to spill into the water. Juanita returns to the boat and snags the backpack, rifle and a tarp Sam kept tucked under the boat seat. She wraps Helen in the tarp, hoping it'll offer at least a little warmth, even though she's already sopping wet. Juanita can see Helen's teeth clacking as she shivers from the cold.

There's not enough vegetation to hide the boat. No big rocks or anything to sink it with. If I just let it go, they might see it. Maybe that's best. They might think we fell over. Might think we drowned. Let's pray they think we've drowned.

Juanita grabs the baton before using the oar to push the boat away from the shore. The wind and waves send it spinning, roiling away. She's grateful for the wind. After considering whether to keep the oar as a weapon, she hurls it into the water, deciding instead to keep the baton—the same one she'd, literally, brained the scarred man with.

"We can't stay here," Juanita calls to Helen. "Need to put some distance between us and Los Desperados. Pretty soon, we're going to need shelter. Food and water would be nice, too. I'm thinking we'll make for the Wild Horse Lodge. It's on the other side of the island so well have to cut across. You agree?"

Helen shrugs her shoulders.

"I got nothin' better," she says.

For the first quarter mile, Juanita carries Helen over the uneven, wind-whipped terrain, cradling her as if she were an oversized sack of groceries. She grips Helen one handedly, the other holding onto the baton. Her fingers sometimes slip on the slick, wet tarp in which she's wrapped Helen. Despite Helen's relatively modest weight, the strain on Juanita's arms is immediate and relentless. The muscles in her upper arms and shoulders begin to protest after just a few hundred yards. She adjusts her hold, shifting Helen's body slightly, but the effort soon becomes unbearable. The added weight of the tarp, rifle, baton and backpack, coupled with the unevenness of the ground, forces her to stumble more than once. Each step feels like it takes more energy than the last, each breath more labored.

She knows time is running out. The search for them could have already begun, and they can't afford to be slow. Her heart races not just from physical exertion, but from the fear gnawing at her gut. If they're spotted, everything they've done so far, including her having killed a man, will be for nothing.

"We gotta reposition," Juanita says. She lowers Helen to the ground and shakes out her arms and shoulders, numb from fatigue. She bends over, hands on knees, drawing in breaths.

Helen looks up at Juanita, noting her exhaustion.

She's dead tired. It's too much for her to carry me the whole way. I know what an unbearable burden looks like. Been one most of my life. She needs to leave me. Get away. At least one of us might live.

Helen holds her arms up, palms flat toward Juanita. It's the universal stop sign.

"Leave me," Helen says. "On your own you might make it. Go. You might get away. You keep tryin' to carry me? They'll catch up to us."

As though she's been waiting for just this very thing, Juanita answers at once.

"Not happening."

Before Helen can protest again, Juanita shrugs on the backpack. She picks up the rifle and considers.

"Sorry, but I couldn't find your meat cleaver in the ambulance. Also, I didn't have time to find more bullets," she tells Helen. "It's got just the one bullet chambered. Maybe we should lighten the load and leave it."

"Please. No. One bullet's better'n none. 'Sides, it's…it's Ben's. If I don't…um…I'd rather have it in my arms. Come what may."

"Never known you to be sentimental," Juanita says through a grin. "Figures you'd get all misty eyed over a gun."

Helen thinks but does not say it out loud.

I won't let 'em take me. I'll use it on myself if it comes to that. No. Fuck that. If I go down, I'm takin' one of 'em with me.

Juanita's mind clicks into gear as she recalls her training on how to conserve energy when carrying a load over long distances.

This isn't going to be easy. I'm already worn down and Helen can't stand up. This is going to be uncomfortable. For both of us. But it's the only way.

She squats, puts her forearms under Helen's armpits and stands her up. Helen dangles in her arms like a jointed puppet whose strings have been cut. She slides one arm down and under Helen's legs, curling it around her thighs. She lifts, twists, and pulls her body high onto her shoulders where, now, Helen lays sideways. Helen's head extends out over Juanita's left shoulder and her legs over the right.

Juanita grunts while she squat presses up. Her legs shake but obey and she stands. Helen's abdomen rests on the top of the backpack Juanita wears. The backpack helps, somewhat, to distribute Helen's weight but it also makes the straps dig even more cruelly into her shoulders.

The first few steps are the hardest. Her body adjusts to the slightly lopsided burden of Helen's body. Juanita's knees rise high to clear the damp, uneven sand, each step deliberate since her center of gravity is, now, so high. Helen bounces just a bit with each stride, and she hears an "oh" pop out of Helen's mouth with each bounce. Though the discomfort is mutual, there's no time to complain; there's only time to move.

The fireman's carry forces Juanita to lean forward and down to counterbalance the weight and keep from toppling backward. It makes it easier to look at the ground but almost impossible to look anywhere else. Still, she pushes on, every step more exhausting than the last, knowing that this carry will be their best chance of reaching safety.

She tries not to count footsteps. Unlike counting down the waves, she has no idea how many steps she'll need to take. Dwelling on the fact that she has no sense of the distance left is a recipe for defeat. She shakes her head, dispelling the thought and shooing away the blackfly that keeps buzzing around her face and threatening to take a bite out of her ear.

Trudging through sand, Juanita imagines she's been transported back in time, to when Romans ruled the Middle East. She's a Christian who's been condemned for rebellion, and her sentence includes carrying a staggeringly heavy wooden cross up a hill to where her crucifixion awaits.

Shaking off the morbid thoughts, Juanita forces herself to focus on the ground in front of her, looking for the most navigable path. Her instincts urge her to stay close to the low, wet ground, anything that might help obscure their tracks. She moves left, then right, zigging and zagging in an attempt to throw off any potential pursuit. But the sand is unforgiving, and even with her best efforts, every step she takes seems to leave a footprint. She spins in a half pirouette, hoping to check her trail, and though she's relieved to see that the prints are quickly being swallowed up by the rain-sodden earth, it's not enough to quell her rising anxiety. She can't shake the feeling that time is slipping through her fingers.

Her legs burn, her knees rising higher than usual to clear the dense sand and thorny vegetation. But despite the exhaustion settling deep into her bones, she knows she can't stop. The longer they stay exposed, the greater the risk.

Minutes stretch into what feels like hours, and after what seems like an eternity, Juanita's endurance gives out.

Juanita drops to her knees and Helen's body teeter-totters precariously on her shoulders. She tries to be gentle, but she mostly drops Helen onto the ground. She's so tired she can't stop herself from collapsing as well. She lands face first on the ground. Her first gulp of air comes with a mouthful of wet sand.

"That...was...tough," Juanita wheezes. "I need one minute to rest. Maybe two minutes."

"You earned it," Helen replies. "You might be the toughest mule I've ever rode."

Helen sits up and brushes sand from her face and arms. She looks around, hoping to see a landmark she'll recognize. There was a time when she'd traipsed every inch of the wild parts of the island and she would've always known exactly where she was, landmarks or no. But Mustang Island is always changing, surf, wind, storms seeing to it. Even so, Helen thinks she knows about where they are.

"I know you're beyond tired," Helen says to Juanita. "I ain't sure how you've got us this far. I think the Wild Horse is right over those dunes."

Too tired to stand, Juanita crawls the face of the dune blocking their view. There sits The Wild Horse Lodge and Roadhouse, the only vestige of civilization in the immediate area. She doesn't have the luxury of relief, though. Her mind is still focused on the danger at hand.

Huh…closer than I thought. Is that good or bad? Good, I guess, since I can't carry Helen much further.

Sliding back down the dune to where Helen waits, Juanita tells her they've found it. She arranges part of the tarp to be under Helen, the other half over. Helen is the meat in the tarp taco.

"I need to go ahead alone," Juanita says. "Make sure it's safe. See if we can even get in."

"You go," Helen replies. "Leave me the gun. You should go. And keep goin'."

Juanita helps arrange Helen into a fetal position.

"I want you to promise me you'll hang on," Juanita asserts. "One way or the other, I'll be back for you. Soon as I can."

Helen watches Juanita's back get smaller and smaller as she moves away at a crouch. Waves of uncontrollable tremors cascade over her body as she reacts to the coldness that seems to have worsened now that Juanita has left. She pulls her head inside the tarp.

For the first time since Ben's death Helen cries. A lifetime of secrets, lies and stoicism crumbles away, eroded by fatigue and guilt.

CHAPTER SIXTEEN

Things You Can't Unsee

*"You know the saying, bad things
don't happen to good people? That's a lie."*

~Tori Amos (1963–present), American singer-songwriter and pianist

———— ••• ————

LOW AND HEAVY RAIN CLOUDS SPIT DRIZZLE FROM A monochromatic gray sky. Hunkered low to the sandy ground, Juanita pauses and studies the motel from a distance.

The motel's name, Wild Horse Lodge and Roadhouse, is braggadocio given it's just a dozen cheaply outfitted rooms plus the small manager's office and lobby. There's nothing much lodge-like about it other than the many horse paintings that adorn the walls of the rooms and a no longer used hitching post out front.

Though she cannot see it from the backside of the motel, Juanita knows there's a freestanding, cinder block, garage-like building that is occasionally rented out as a bar and band stage, given it's wired for electricity and plumbed for running water. Add in a large circular concrete patio, the indoor-outdoor combination is generously—and sarcastically—a self-styled roadhouse. The ocean-facing property features a rugged beach and a small wooden pier that juts out into the water.

For hundreds of years Mustang Island was known as *Isla de Caballos Salvajes*: Island of Wild Horses. Untamed horses, descendants of Spanish steeds who'd survived shipwrecks to swim ashore, found themselves lords of a predator-free island with plenty of grasses. The only horses still on the island today are owned by a rent-a-ride operation open only in the Summer. The motel, like the island, invokes an unbridled equine saga that is long gone.

Wouldn't that be great? Lasso us up a couple of stallions and ride away. Where's Abuelo when we need him? Grandpa could do it, lickety-split.

While Juanita weighs the risks of braving the exposed distance to the motel, a moth alights on the back of her hand. It's a large moth, nearly eight inches wide with iridescent purple and pink coloring that looks almost electric against the colorless surroundings. Green and orange dotted wings open and close several times. The normally nocturnal moth rests for a heartbeat or two, surely tired from skirmishing with the wind. Then it lifts off and flutters in the direction of the motel.

Taking it as a sign, Juanita throws caution to the blustery wind and follows, despite knowing that Black Witch moths are associated with misfortune.

And death.

Juanita's exhaustion makes her lope a listless one. Her concentration is slipping, her thoughts undisciplined.

She knows Betsy lives in the room connected to the office. Juanita imagines how cramped it must be, not just having only the one motel room to call home but, also, having raised two children in it as well. She recalls the children, a daughter and a son, are now both young adults and no longer live in the motel.

Is she there? Is it fair to get her involved? No, but what else can I do?

Juanita respects Betsy for her smarts and toughness. She runs the motel single-handedly except for some help in the busiest months. She keeps the books. She does a lot of the repairs herself including fixing backed up toilets and leaky roofs. She has an uncanny recall of names, dates, and numbers. As for faces, her brain has some kind of facial recognition software that Juanita knows she, herself, lacks. Betsy appears to never forget anyone.

Still, Juanita has shied away from being a closer friend to Betsy. She told herself that's due to the inconvenient distance between their homes, but now, she finds herself admitting it's mostly because Betsy is a non-stop talker and gossipmonger which, to Juanita, is a real turn-off.

Is talking her superpower? Maybe her words are like sonar: ping, ping, ping. Might be a slick way to pick up on things that others might miss. Half the time she's talking, it's to retell me stuff she's already told me, but I've forgotten. She's always so determined to bring me up to speed on the newest addition to her gossipy block-chain.

Shaking off the stupor, Juanita brings her attention back to the motel that is now only a few yards away.

Juanita's approach is from the backside of the motel, away from the windows that line only the front. Having visited Betsy a few times, she recalls there is a backdoor to the office. She edges past it and partly around the side so she can see the parking lot in front. There is one car visible in the mist, a green Chevy Malibu, which Juanita knows belongs to Betsy. She sees no movement other than windblown fronds of two sago palm trees on either side of the sidewalk leading to the registration office.

Retracing her steps, Juanita raps lightly on the back door. When there's no answer, she knocks again, more firmly this time. Juanita is about to try the handle when the door whisks open. Betsy, dressed in blue jeans and turtlenecked sweater, red hair flapping in the breeze, looks wide-eyed out the door.

"What are you…?" Betsy says, looking past Juanita, eyes scanning beyond. "Come in. Quick!"

Betsy pulls Juanita through the back door but halts her just a few feet inside.

"You can't be here!" Betsy says. "It's not safe."

"I need help!" Juanita pleads.

"I know. Or figured, at least," Betsy says. "A deputy, Bill Fecto, came by here about two hours ago. Told me they were looking for you. Said you are dangerous."

"Do I look dangerous?"

Betsy hesitates before answering. Her eyes take in Juanita's bruised face, swollen lips and shirt streaked with dried blood and wet sand. A flicker of concern crosses Betsy's face.

"Yes. Kind of. Well, no. Just…wet and dirty. Tired, too, by the look of you. What's going on? Why is the sheriff looking for you?"

"Not just me," Juanita replies. "Last night a man tried to kill Helen in her home. She survived. He didn't. We escaped as far as Los Desperados. Then, another man came looking for us. He killed Sam. We managed to escape but we're running out of places to hide."

"Oh my God. You're talking about Helen Chesterfield, aren't you? Owns Mustang Manor? She's the one who rents the place to Georgi Kask. Why does Mustang Manor keep coming up?"

Juanita leans toward Betsy.

"What do you mean 'keeps coming up'?"

Betsy begins to reply, but Juanita interrupts her.

"Helen. I left her out there. We've got to get her out of this weather. She's been injured. She needs medical attention. Can you put us up in a room?"

"No," Betsy sighs. "Deputy Fecto said he'd be back to check on me. Last time, he checked every room. I expect he'll do it again. Might be he was lying, but I don't think so. What's going on?"

Juanita downloads to Betsy a consolidated version of what's happened in the last dozen hours. Betsy interrupts Juanita's account of the arrival of the man at Los Desperados and is clearly agitated.

"The man. Bearded but he's got a scar? Big potbelly?" Betsy asks.

"Yes, and he won't be a prob…"

Juanita stops mid thought.

"Wait. Betsy, how do you know what this guy looks like?"

To Juanita's surprise, Betsy starts crying.

"Because…because I've met him."

"How? When?" Juanita asks.

"He paid me a visit. About three weeks ago. I've had nightmares ever since."

"What do you mean 'paid you a visit'? What for?"

Betsy's chin drops to her chest, and she busies herself wiping away tears with the back of her hands.

"To blackmail me," she tells Juanita, eyes still downcast.

"Blackmail you? Why? How?"

"The man with the scar took over the motel completely. He forced me to shut down the Wild Horse to all other guests. I had to cancel every reservation—some from families who've been coming here for their winter vacations for decades. People were furious, but I had no choice.

"There's a group of Mexicans—five of them—who arrived a week ago. They were dropped off at the pier by a boat that appeared out of nowhere. I'm almost certain they're part of a drug cartel. They're tatted up, armed, and move like men who know violence. They keep to themselves during the day, staying out of sight, but when night falls, a van shows up. They pile in, disappear for hours, and return just before dawn. I don't know what they're up to, but they've got shovels and picks. When they come back they're pretty dirty; it's takes some doing to keep up with the laundry.

"You're lucky they're not here now. The storm forced them away for a couple of days, but it won't keep them gone forever."

Juanita's head spins trying to make sense of Betsy's story.

"Whatever they're doing," Betsy adds, "It's almost done."

"How do you know that?"

"Two days ago, they backed the van they use up to the roadhouse. I saw some men unloading two heavy-duty storage containers. I haven't let on I speak Spanish and, most of the time, I haven't been near enough to hear what they were saying. But the night before last

I was bringing fresh towels and they didn't see me. I heard one of the men, El Jefe, say they'd come back for the rest of it."

"Rest of what?" Juanita asked.

"I don't know. But then the other man asked: Es ese el último del tesoro?"

"El Tesoro? Treasure? The last of the treasure? What treasure?"

"I don't know."

"Where are these men now?"

"Gone, for the time being," Betsy clarifies. "They left early yesterday morning in the van. But they're coming back after the storm passes. Get this. I heard El Jefe say 'cuando regresan El Ruso y sus hijos.' When the Russian and his sons return. They've got to be talking about Georgi Kask and his sons, Dimitri and Andrei. They're due back mañana, too. And that brings us back to Mustang Manor.

Juanita pauses to think that over.

Kask and sons working with a Mexican cartel? Why? What are they doing here? And, what's in the roadhouse?

"With no one here, why don't you leave? Go to the police?"

"I was told, in no uncertain terms, that if I tried to contact the sheriff or any police, they would know. If I told anyone— anyone—they would know. They took my car keys and cell phone. They cut the lodge's phone lines. He told me...he told me he would kill me if I did. Clearly, they have someone inside the sheriff's department. Could be the whole department, for all I know."

Betsy pauses before adding: "If that weren't enough, they've got a video they say they'll post on social media if I don't do what they want."

"Video? What kind of video?"

"A video of Danny," Betsy says after a pause.

Betsy tells Juanita about her having been visited by the man with the scarred face. He'd sat her down and forced her to watch a video on his iPad. In the video, her son was the center of sexual attention from several other men. He warned her that the video would be made public if she didn't cooperate. And that, he said, was just the beginning. He claimed to know where her children lived and threatened to track them down and hurt them if she refused to comply.

"Splattering that video across the internet? I can't imagine what that would do to Danny," Betsy whimpers. "He's…well…prone to depression. It got really bad starting about a year ago. Now I know why. I'm pretty sure that's when it happened. His behavior worsened overnight. It's killing me. I need to get him professional help. I know that. But I can't do that until these people leave."

"Tell me about the video," Juanita says.

"The video was from just one camera. It had a…you know…light mounted on it. It was handheld because the picture was jerky, bouncing around. When I saw the video, I couldn't take my eyes off of Danny. It…it was all I could do not to throw up. Whoever was shooting the video was careful not to show anyone else's face. But I can tell you, Danny's expression was distant. His eyes didn't look right. I'm sure he was drugged up. He tried to say something a few times, but his words were slurred."

"Oh my God. That must've been horrible to see," Juanita says.

"It was," Betsy answers. "Both times."

"Both times?"

Betsy had surprised the scarred man standing in her motel's office by demanding he play the video a second time. She insisted she didn't believe it was her son and needed to see it again to be sure.

"The second time I watched the video, I looked everywhere other than at Danny. A few times I could just make out things in the background. There were lamps on somewhere. There wasn't much light but there was some. And I saw…legs."

"Legs?"

"Yeah. There was an audience. Some people sitting in chairs. Watching. Bunch of sick fucks. I only saw shoes and pant legs, but they were there."

Juanita takes a half step toward Betsy to wrap her in a hug only to find herself stiff-armed away. Betsy draws in a ragged breath before continuing.

"There's more," Betsy says, her voice dropping to a whisper. "At the very end, the person holding the camera let it hang down. I don't think he realized the video was still going. It was only a couple of seconds, and the image was sideways, but I'm sure of what I saw. It wasn't a blur or some trick of the light. It was clear as day. There was a bull's head, horns and all."

"A bull's head? Are you sure?"

"Yes. I've thought about it. Not only am I sure of what I saw, I'm sure where the video was shot."

"What do you mean?"

"It was a mechanical bull. What I saw in the video, I mean. I remember seeing it before, when it was loaded on a flatbed truck that drove right past the motel. Until traffic could be redirected, it was parked on the road right next to the motel for over an hour. I talked to the driver who'd pulled over to get a drink from the vending machine. He told me where it was headed."

"And? Where was it headed?"

"He said it was to be installed in a basement turned party room. The basement where the video was shot. The basement where my son was raped."

Juanita can't summon the words to express her shock.

"I suspect something else," Betsy adds between sobs. "I don't think Danny is the only person they've made videos about. There were others too, I think."

"Why do you say that?"

"Because the scarred man said something he probably shouldn't have. He told me I'd better toe the line like all the rest. Like all the rest. I think they've got more videos. People in all kinds of compromising situations. If that's the case, I have no idea who to trust. Involved or blackmailed…it could be anyone."

Juanita gathers herself to ask one more question.

"Where is this mechanical bull?"

Betsy hesitates, takes a deep breath, and answers.

"It's in the basement of Mustang Manor."

Juanita is stunned. It's as if the weight of what she's just heard has stolen her ability to speak. Her mind races, desperately trying to make sense of it all, while struggling to figure out how to tell Helen what is really happening at the Manor.

CHAPTER SEVENTEEN

The Least Likely Place

"Death is a delightful hiding place for weary men."

~Herodotus (484-425 BC), Greek historian and geographer

———— ••• ————

PEARLED HEAVENS LOOM OVER JUANITA AS SHE SLIDES OUT the back door of the Wild Horse Lodge's office. While still fearful of being seen, the shock of what she's heard from Betsy has scrambled her thoughts. The cold adds physicality to that emotional numbness. Even with a light drizzle wetting her face, she now feels as dirty on the inside as she noticeably is on the outside.

Betsy's description of the video and what had happened to her son, Danny, has made her nauseous. She'd asked Betsy to leave—begged, even. Told her to walk if she had to. But Betsy said she'd thought about it, and in the end, it came down to fear—not for herself, but for her children.

"If I'm not here when they return tomorrow, they'll know I've run," Betsy pointed out. "They know where Danny and Angela live. I can't take that chance."

Betsy's decision is final. And hard to accept. Even as Juanita yields to Betsy's resolve to protect her children no matter what the cost, she can't help but feel as though she's abandoning her. It's an emotional departure. But there's no time for sulking.

She's a really good person. A good mother. A good friend. Please, God, watch over her.

The implications of what she's learned are making her head swim.

There's more to this than murder. It's a full-blown conspiracy. What other reason would someone have to record people in sexual circumstances? It's blackmail. And coercion. Who's been compromised? How far does this go?

Juanita's thoughts turn toward Helen who, she knows, is alone and probably growing frantic. She'd talked with Betsy much longer than she'd intended. Her need to collect Helen and find a dry, warm place to hide is achingly urgent.

She's a tough bird, but still, she's got to be scared. She's not fully recovered from being strangled, despite the care Sam gave her.

Thinking of Sam makes her eyes water, her own throat swell. Her fists shake with fury as she slogs her way through dunes to where she's left Helen huddled under the tarp. Juanita is relieved to quickly find the black puddle of plastic that marks the spot. She sees no movement, which is reassuring. But the lack of movement makes her anxious, too, as she peels back the tarp.

Helen's green eyes blink open, flooding Juanita with relief.

"Fuckity-fuck, you scared me! Put a bell on you. Get in under here," Helen directs, pushing the tarp higher to make room. Juanita is shivering such that she doesn't argue. She slides inside.

The two women face each other in the stingy light. Helen peers into Juanita's eyes, and she returns the gaze. It's as though each is fearful of what the other might say. Helen knows that when the news is bad and options are worse, words don't come easy. Rather than wait, Helen speaks up.

"Glad you're back," Helen says. "Feels like I been wet and cold in the dark so long I got mushrooms sproutin' on me."

Juanita laughs. She needed that.

"I've got lots to tell you but the short of it is, we don't get to have a relaxing vacation at the Wild Horse like we hoped. They've searched the place already and I expect they'll do it again."

She anticipates Helen will be crushed. If she is, Helen doesn't act like it.

"Figured as much. No way they ain't gonna be watchin' that place. So, I been thinkin' 'bout what else we might could do."

"I'm all ears," Juanita says. "Unless they've fallen off. It's so cold I wouldn't be surprised. I can't feel them. Or my nose."

"If'n yer nose had fell off, you probably woulda tripped over it."

Juanita snorts in reply, confirming her nose is, indeed, still attached.

"No offense, but you stink," Juanita says.

"Takes one to know one. I don't need a honker of a nose to smell you, either."

Juanita lays it out to Helen; the videos, the Mexicans, and something about treasure that she still doesn't understand. She tells Helen they have two options. First, stay where they are, huddled under the tarp, and hope they survive the weather and aren't found before people return to the island once weather allows. Then, maybe, they can find a phone or transport, some kind of help. Or, second, go someplace else, though Juanita has no idea where.

"I'm tired of decidin' between two shades of shit," Helen says. "So, I been thinkin' 'bout that. Where's the least likely place they'd look for us?"

"I don't know. Where?"

"In their own backyard. The grounds of Mustang Manor, of course. There's a kayak shed near the Casita. You can't see it from the Casita 'cause it's small, so they might've overlooked it. It ain't much, but it's gotta be better than bein' out in the open like this."

"I don't have a better idea," Juanita replies. "In fact, I don't have any other ideas."

"Let's rest a spell longer," Helen suggests. "You gotta be dog tired."

"I am," Juanita admits.

Helen turns away from Juanita to think through her plan. She knows Juanita will think it crazy—suicidal, even. But she's tired of running, tired of reacting. Just plain tired. And still angry.

Juanita moves closer, wrapping her arms around Helen, spooning herself against Helen's back. They are both cold so they exchange, instinctively, what little body warmth they can generate. Despite their shared anxiety, they fall asleep to the sound of moderate rain tapping on the tarp.

Helen is the first to awaken. For a few moments she forgets where she is. She's surprised to discover Juanita's arms around her are a comfort. Touch isn't her love language. Not since Ben died. She reflects on what she's gone through. On what they've gone through, together.

For the first time in a long while, Helen feels grateful. Grateful for Juanita's stubborn unwillingness to give up on her. Given how she's treated Juanita, she's been harboring a fear she'll be left to her fate, a fate she deserves.

The gratefulness outweighs her sense of unworthiness. She realizes she hasn't felt this way in a very long time.

She coulda run. Shoulda run. She didn't. She killed for me. Might die with me. Why? All I ever done is treat her like shit. It's time I told her. I owe her the truth.

She squirms herself onto her back and shakes Juanita's shoulder, waking her up.

"Are you okay?" Helen asks.

"A little better, yeah."

"Make sure you're all the way awake," Helen tells Juanita. "There's somethin' I've got to tell you.

CHAPTER EIGHTEEN

When the Dam Breaks

*"The grave soul keeps its own secrets
and takes its own punishment in silence."*

~Dorothy Dix (1861-1951), American journalist and columnist

———————— ••• ————————

IN THE SCANT, OLIVE-GREEN LIGHT TRAPPED UNDER THE tarp, it's difficult to see. Helen is thankful for that. She can't say what she needs to say if she has to look Juanita in the eyes. She hangs her head, focusing her eyes on useless legs.

"What do you want to tell me?" Juanita asks.

Good God. What now? As if there's room for more bad news. And judging from the tone of her voice, this isn't good.

"Not want to. Need to. The reason I been rude to you? Mean, sometimes? It's on account of somethin' I did. Somethin' that might've hurt you, if you knew. I didn't want to get close to you. Didn't want to risk slippin'. Lettin' the secret out. And to be honest, I was jealous. It hurt to be around you. You were a reminder of somethin' I couldn't forget, couldn't have, couldn't let go."

Juanita hears the gravity in Helen's voice. She knows this is something meaningful.

"What are you talking about?"

"You gotta understand. After the crash…I got depressed. What did I have to live for? Ben was dead. My legs were dead. My heart felt dead, too. I was cooped up in my house. White trash were livin' in the

Manor, lordin' themselves over me. I considered suicide. Was still thinkin' maybe that was the way to go. Then, I met a man in the clinic waiting room. Handsome. Kind. You could tell he was a good man. That was the first time we talked. Long story short, I had an affair with him. His wife was sick. She had dementia. Didn't recognize him anymore. So, he knew what it felt like to be left behind. Sorta. But still…"

As Helen's words trail off, a tingle snakes up Juanita's spine. A dawning.

Wait. A married man. A wife with dementia. Can't be. Can it?

"Tell me," Juanita directs. She fears she already knows the answer.
"It was Horacio. Your grandfather."
The silence that follows is thick. Juanita is stupefied. She pants, her breaths shallow.

Abuelo? And Helen? That's…ridiculous. How? How could he? No, really, how could they in her condition? Can she even have sex? Can she even feel anything?

Envisioning her grandfather and Helen coupling, picturing variations on the mechanics of it all, leaves Juanita flabbergasted. She's sure nothing like that happened in real life. No way.

Before Juanita can conjure questions, Helen resumes, words tripping over themselves to get free.

"I don't think he ever really wanted me that way. As a lover. I wasn't sure we could even…do it…you know? I begged him. Wore him down. Played the victim card. I know it for what it was. Pity fuck or no, it was a one-time thing. After, I asked to see him again. He refused. He said it was the wrong thing, even if it was for the right reasons. He didn't want to hurt his wife—his family. Especially…you and Alex."

Juanita can't get her head around this. A teenaged illegal immigrant, Horacio had walked, ridden and hitched rides all the way from Patagonia to Texas to find work. He got hired to muck stalls because he'd grown up around horses in Argentina and had a way with them. He literally wrangled a promotion to ranch hand and, later, trail boss. Eventually, he'd started his own business finding and returning stolen stock.

Juanita's grandfather had always been wrapped in mystery and legend. The image of her cowboy grandpa rescuing cattle and bringing horse rustlers to justice filled her with pride. Growing up, she'd often looked at—but never touched—the twin six shooters holstered and draped over the headboard in the bedroom he shared with Abuela. That the guns were there made her feel scared. That her grandfather knew how to use them made her feel safe.

She recalls her grandmother. Mariposa had taken on the roles of both grandmother and mother after Juanita's mother died giving birth to Alex. Juanita had been very young at the time, and her memories of her mother are faint and fleeting. Her grandmother, however, stands out in vibrant, touching detail. Abuela Mari was always singing, no matter what task she had at hand. She made the most delicious homemade tamales, selling the extras to laborers to help make ends meet. She cherished attending mass on Sundays and Wednesdays, and, unless someone in the family was ill, would herd them all into St. Joseph Catholic Church in Baytown with the same whip-cracking determination Horacio used when rounding up stolen horses and cattle.

Best of all, she'd made her grandfather happy for a very long time—but not forever. First, Alzheimer's stole Mariposa's memories. Then it took her life. She remembers her grandfather's tears; it was the first time she'd ever seen him cry. The second, and last, was less than a year later when Juanita's father died, leaving her with her grieving brother and grandfather as her only surviving family. A house that once seemed too small now feels impossibly big. Haunted spaces are everywhere.

Who is Helen? Really? She's a cheater. A sinner. A liar. She's a would-be homewrecker. Who'd ever have thought Abuelo would have had anything to do with a woman like her?

"Did he say why he did it? Don't tell me he said he loved you. He wouldn't," Juanita says.

"He never said he loved me," she whispers. "It was the opposite. He told me he loved his wife. And his family. Your family."

A memory bubbles up to Juanita's conscience: it was the day Abuelo had agreed to be her show-and-tell at school. The rope trickery and lasso display he'd put on made her the envy of her schoolmates.

"I don't know what to say," Juanita finally manages. "Why tell me? Why now? We're up to our elbows in alligators and you decide now's a good time to dump all this on me? What's wrong with you? What am I supposed to do with all this?"

"Before you say anything, there's somethin' else," Helen continues. "And, hard as it might be for you to believe...it's worse."

The dam has burst. The resulting flood hurls long-denied lies, hidden secrets and long-harbored guilt tumbling down to overrun the riverbanks of Helen's mind.

Tell her. Do it. You need to. Got to. Someone needs to know. Before it's too late.

"The masked man in the Casita? He weren't the first man I killed. Long time ago I killed 'nother man. Buried his body on my land. Never told a soul."

When Helen had told Juanita that the second piece of news was worse, she hadn't believed it. Now she does.

"Who? Who did you kill?"

"He weren't a good man. He didn't give a shit about anyone other than himself. He...," Helen trails off, takes a breath, and continues. "It don't matter who he was. I ain't askin' for no forgiveness. I ain't even askin' for your understandin'. I just needed to...I guess...I needed to say it. To someone. Say it out loud. Before somethin' more happens. To us."

Juanita wants to get up. Walk away. Yell at Helen. Instead, she nods.

"Why tell me this now?" Juanita asks.

Helen shrugs her shoulders and answers.

"You and me, we both know we ain't likely to get through this. Alive, I mean. Bein' honest, I been holdin' on to some lies since, well, since my whole life. Far back as I can remember. I was born into lies, I guess. Them secrets. Them lies? I'm gonna lay 'em down.

"Even if, by some miracle, we live through this? For me, it won't be long. You know how many years a brand-new paraplegic will live? On average? It's twenty years. Already been ten years since the accident. That puts me halfway to the grave. Now, what if it's a woman in her sixties? Subtract another six years. Add in a lifetime of smokin'? Take off another four years.

"Do the math. No matter what number you come up with, I'm on my final stretch. I'm on borrowed time. Somethin' happens to me? Big deal. I ain't livin' much longer anyway. But you? You got a whole life in front of you. Before we take any more risks, you need to think about that."

Juanita does just that; she thinks about it.

Dad, Alex, and I were all heartbroken, but it was especially hard on Abuelo. I know how much he loved Abuela Mari. He understood it was the disease—it wasn't her fault. It wasn't just that she didn't remember him; it was how she couldn't bear to see him. She thought he was someone else, someone she didn't want near her. Sometimes, just to be close, he'd stand for hours in the shadows where she couldn't see him. He'd softly sing her songs from his vaquero days, letting her believe the melodies came from someone else. He loved her. Fiercely. Devotedly. But I could see the pain in his eyes—the pain of being forgotten. It's the closest thing to losing a loved one while they're still alive. I can see now what he and Helen had in common. I understand why she wanted him. And I can almost understand why he gave in.

Surfacing from her thoughts, Juanita is surprised Helen hadn't broken the silence. She'd waited. She's not trying to explain; she's not trying to justify. She's content to let Juanita sit with the hush-hushes she's told her. She's already pled guilty. Now, she awaits Juanita's sentence.

"Maybe you are near the end of the line," Juanita says. "But you're here. You're not across that line today. You're alive—now. That still means something, at least to me. The thing with Abuelo? I'll try to understand. Someday, maybe I'll even accept it. The other thing—the man you killed? I don't know who, how, or why. Whatever those things are, they don't mean the rest of your life doesn't have value. You need to think about that."

Helen raises her head to make eye contact with Juanita.

"I knew you'd say somethin' like that," she says. "You make a gal feel like it might be true. Maybe there is somethin' valuable I can do before the end."

CHAPTER NINETEEN

Any Port in the Storm

"There are no shortcuts to any place worth going."

~Beverly Sills (1929-2007), American operatic soprano

———— ••• ————

HELEN SQUINTS WHILE LOOKING UP. THE SUN, ARCING toward day's end, is trying to burn a hole through the clouds. Ringlets of vapor writhe at the flaming orb's edges, curling and coiling, on the verge of winning through. But they lose the fight. The watery sun looks distressed. Fatigued.

We get you Mister Sun. We know just how you feel. Especially Juanita.

Helen speaks, her voice rough.

"I know you're tired, but we oughta get goin' before they stumble onto us," she warns, her eyes scanning the horizon. "We ain't even a half mile or so from the shed, as the crow flies anyway. Can you get us there?"

Juanita doesn't answer. Rather, she slides her palms up and down her thighs and calves. The self-massage is an absent-minded one that does little to coax her lazy legs into submission. The rest she's had feels little more than a cruel illusion. Her body is running on fumes.

Betsy's disclosures combined with Helen's admissions seem to have robbed Juanita of whatever reserves, mentally and physically, she had left. She finds herself staring, slack-eyed, into the distance. She tells herself it's time to go, she knows it's time to go, it's just that she cannot seem to get up and go.

"Honest," Helen says. "It's not too far. It won't be too bad. We're close."

Close? Close to what? The end?

"Juanita," Helen tries again. "Let's get to the kayak shed. It'll be warmer. Drier. You'll see."

"Yeah. Let's go," Juanita mutters, her voice flat and drained, devoid of any enthusiasm. The words feel hollow even to her, but she forces herself to nod and pull herself together.

Juanita knows they shouldn't delay. Some part of her is shocked that Top Hat and his codenamed minions haven't caught up to them already. Maybe the empty rowboat, the drowning ploy, did the trick. With a sigh, she shrugs off the mind-numbing exhaustion. She starts by rolling up the tarp with the rifle inside, securing them as best she can. She prepares to hoist the pack onto her shoulders again, but Helen interrupts.

In a voice seemingly stronger and more practical than she's used to hearing from her, Helen says: "Let's do this another way. I'll wear the backpack. That way you can piggyback me. Not sure I can bear bein' carried sideways on your shoulders again. More important, I can see to give you directions. The shed ain't that easy to spot. Plus, you can set me down easier if'n you need to."

Juanita doesn't argue. She doesn't even respond verbally, showing no discomfort over shifting leadership roles. She pulls her cap onto her head and shrugs the backpack off and helps Helen put it on.

She squats next to Helen who climbs onto her back. Juanita picks up the rolled-up tarp, rifle inside, and reaches it back for Helen to tuck between her chest and Juanita's back. Lastly, she snares the baton and squat presses to her feet.

Helen's paralyzed legs are unable to wrap themselves around her waist, so they dangle, her locked hands around Juanita's neck, an albatross of dead weight. Juanita bows forward causing Helen's legs to swing forward as well. Juanita grabs one foot in one hand and does the same with her other hand, all the while trying not to fumble the baton to the ground. She hops to bounce Helen higher on her back and readjusts her grip onto Helen's calves and, finally, behind her knees.

Juanita's not sure whether it's because she's growing used to the exhaustion or because her body has simply resigned itself to the weight, but she moves with more purpose now, though the strain on her body is evident with every step.

The only sounds accompanying their journey are the rhythmic squelching of feet in wet sand and the occasional whisper from Helen, guiding her left or right. There's no talk of anything else, no distractions. Every step is a struggle, each stride a small victory.

The scarred face of the man she's almost certainly killed still lurks in her mind. She hasn't been able to shake the memory of striking him. More, it's hard for her to admit to herself that she wanted to do it. After seeing him club and kill Sam, it's what she wanted more than anything. She's horrified by her own blood lust. She knows it was self-defense—she had no choice—but the image haunts her still, the grotesque noise of skull bone cracking and blood sheeting when she'd embedded the baton into the top of his head and the squelching, sucking sound when he'd pulled it out. Most disturbing, it felt good to beat him to death, to avenge Sam. And, she knows, that's not what Sam would have wanted for her.

She looks more closely at the baton, tight in her hand, still holding Helen's knee. Remnants of the struggle are still visible—traces of blood stained on its surface. She stops, releases her hold on the knee, and hurls the baton, sending it spinning end over end to land halfway up a dune. She's done with it.

Helen, seeing what Juanita has done, tries to speak to her, but Juanita doesn't hear the words, lost in her thoughts. Helen is worried Juanita has lost sight of where they're going and why.

Juanita is flagging. What can I say? What would Ben tell me I should say? He would say tell her she's a survivor. Tell her you're grateful she saved your life. Tell her you're sorry Sam died and for putting her in a position where she had to kill a man to save me. And for staying alive. For not abandoning me.

Abruptly, Juanita resumes her lurching walk. She doesn't look from side to side, only ahead. The ground she's approaching looks just like the ground she's already covered. She feels like she's in a desert of sameness, one with no beginning and no end. Step after step after step.

Helen tries to keep track of how much time has gone by. For sure, it's more than five minutes. She reckons it's closer to twenty.

Only after several tries does Juanita realize Helen is talking to her, the fingers of her interlocked hands tapping at her throat.

"Over there," Helen says, her voice finally breaking through Juanita's fugue state. "See that stand of oak motte? The shed is nestled under 'em."

Juanita nods, her gaze shifting to the distant cluster of trees. Her exhaustion, while overwhelming, now carries with it a spark of hope. They're close.

She spots a dune slack, the lowest point between a group of twenty-foot-high sand dunes. She squats down. Helen releases her chokehold and slides off her back, hitting the ground with a distinct "oomph."

"She nails the dismount!" Helen calls out with an amplified cheer. "A score of ten for the duo of Jiménez and Chesterfield."

Juanita looks at Helen's smiling face and smiles herself.

"A score of five from the Russian judge," Juanita contributes.

Both take to laughing with gusto, hardy and long, well beyond what their shared witticisms merit.

Juanita takes off her ball cap and tilts her face skyward. She opens her mouth to capture some of the rain that falls from the heavens. She says a prayer of gratitude. She returns her gaze to Helen and puts her cap back onto its rightful place.

"I'm going to check it out. See if it's safe. If, for any reason I don't come back, unroll the tarp and shelter under it. I won't tell them where you are. I'll say you fell out of the boat. Drowned. They might buy it."

"Given how waterlogged I am, it's close to the truth," Helen replies. "And Juanita...please be careful."

Juanita crawls her way up the dune on hands and knees. She peeks over the top, keeping her head low, making it harder to be seen. She watches, waits, and, finally, log-rolls herself down the other side. It reminds her of the hallway, rolling to and from a spot where she could overhear what the masked man was saying on the radio. She swears she can still feel the zip ties.

Crouched low, she weaves a path toward the trees, and sighs with relief once she reaches them. After a few more tense minutes of waiting, she creeps up on the shed to check it out. She touches one side of the prefabricated metal shed. Her fingers trail against the ribbed aluminum and around to the water-facing front on the marsh bank. The structure is three-sided, long and skinny, with a sloped roof. No need for a front door given there's no front at all. The shed might be standing but doesn't look inviting and certainly not cozy.

Inside, the kayak shed is a jumble of paddling, fishing and miscellaneous sporting gear, much of it haphazardly thrown around. Juanita figures the shed has been searched given how stuff has been tossed this way and that. Or maybe that's how Ben rolled.

Battling her fear that they'll be discovered if the grounds are searched again, she fetches Helen and carries her into the shed, but not before dangling her body into a half-crouch so Helen can pee. Once inside, she unrolls the tarp and retrieves the rifle. She makes a bed out of cold, moist life preservers, positions Helen on them, and lays the tarp over her.

She'd hoped there might be rain gear or coats or a dry blanket. Gloves, even. No such luck.

Temperature-wise, the shed may be no warmer than outside. However, with walls to keep the wind away and a roof to keep the rain away, the wind chill is considerably less. Still, it's cold, dark and, given there's no front, not very defensible if it comes to that.

"Not quite The Ritz-Carlton is it?" Helen says. "It's warmer in here, at least. I'm already feelin' better. But when the sun goes down we're liable to be miserable. Well, more miserable than we already are. If'n that's possible."

Juanita barks, a response that's more shiver than word. She's been thinking about their lack of water and food as much as lack of warmth and dryness. Other than Sam's tea, neither have had any sustenance. She regrets not having thought to pack food and water when they'd fled the Casita. She's irritated with herself; she'd intended to get, at least, something for her and Helen to eat and drink from Betsy. She was so stunned by what she'd heard she'd left empty handed.

Stupid. Stupid. Stupid. We're both dehydrated. We need calories. How could I have been so stupid? Time for the last thing in the larder.

"I've got a room service dinner for you," Juanita says, smiling. She pulls two energy bars from one of the zipped pockets in her jacket. "Rescued them from the ambulance. Best news? You don't have to tip the server."

Helen's been told she eats like a bird. She wants to eat like one, assuming that bird is a pterodactyl. Her face and throat still hurt, forcing her to take small bites. Plus, she knows, one energy bar each is all they have. Still, it's marvelous. She feels strength returning with every tiny swallow.

"I don't suppose there's any more food or water squirreled away in here, is there?" Juanita asks, taking the last hurried bite of her energy bar. She barely registers the taste before it's gone. The sun is trending toward dusk. Juanita squints in the fading light, fingers exploring hopefully through the detritus.

"Doubt it," Helen manages through her still munching mouth.

After a few minutes of digging through mildewed gear, coils of nylon rope and plastic-bladed oars, Juanita gives up. She'd found a thermos and was momentarily giddy until she screwed off the cap to find it empty. She put both cap and bottle outside to collect rainwater. She'd been hopeful, too, when she found a square, hard plastic case. When she'd opened it, she discovered it was a headlamp camera with a hand-held monitor. She was optimistic this would give them another light source other than the one small flashlight she'd grabbed from the Casita.

Disappointingly, however, when she pressed the power button on the hands-free, lighted camera, it didn't work. After popping off the back plates on the two devices, she saw that they were both missing batteries. With a sigh, she had set them aside.

Most of what she finds in the shed, including two skateboards of all things, appears old or dilapidated or both. She does find a folding camper's stool with a partially torn canvas seat. She gambles that it isn't too old, worn and shredded to hold her weight. She unfolds the stool next to Helen's makeshift bed and sits down. Her thighs and lower back moan with relief.

Feeling somewhat discouraged, Juanita takes a deep breath and gathers herself. She gently takes one of Helen's hands in hers. Sliding fingers down to her wrist, she checks Helen's pulse. Not bad but not good either. Helen's shivering has stopped. Her lips are less blue. She and Helen, both, are doing better due to the shelter. However, she knows that could change. She wonders how long their improved health will last if they're still here when night comes on.

She regrets deciding not to bring her own backpack when she'd carted supplies from the ambulance in the Emporium to the boat. The thought of a change of clothes or simply putting on layers to get warm sounds blissful. Still, even though her backpack wasn't particularly heavy, she thinks that one more thing might have been the straw that broke the camel's back. Her back.

The calories from the energy bar are helping. Shelter from the wind and rain even more so. Still, I can't see how we can stay here. Nighttime will be a lot colder. If that weren't enough, they could decide to search this place. At any moment. We'd never even see them coming. It's not like there's a door to at least give us a shot at defending ourselves. They could see right in. They'll take us out like the metal duck shooting gallery at the county fair. Rather than a stuffed teddy bear, they'll get the computer as their prize.

A thought occurs to Juanita.

Maybe we can make the front of the shed more defensible. Use the tarp to cover the front? Cut a couple of murder holes into it? That way we could shoot them if they find us. Well, shoot one of them, at least.

She steps over to where she sees some tools. Hanging on a nail is a chainsaw. She takes it down and notices the cord and plug—it's electric. She doesn't relish the idea of reenacting the *Texas Chainsaw Massacre*, but it's better than nothing. Unfortunately, it needs to be charged first.

Is the power back on?

Juanita looks for an outlet. She finds one but it's already occupied. A plastic device of some kind is plugged into the top socket. She unplugs and opens the container to discover two sets of rechargeable batteries.

Wait. Even if power's been out for a day, these batteries might've been fully charged before it went out.

She puts one set of batteries into the wearable camera-light device and the other into the handheld monitor. Holding her breath, she turns them on. A green light on the monitor blinks to life first, followed by the light above the small lens. She pans the device around the shed. Video shows up on the monitor.

"Should I smile?" Helen asks. "Am I on Candid Camera?"

Juanita looks confused.

"Candid Camera? What's Candid Camera?," Juanita asks.

"Never mind," Helen says. "Guess you had to be there."

Juanita raises her clenched fists above her head and marches in a circle, making noises like a cheering crowd celebrating her victory.

Finally! Something's going our way.

"Well," she tells the wide-eyed Helen. "At least we have another light source besides just the flashlight. I'm not sure how valuable that is, but it's something."

"Ben would be glad we found it," Helen says. "He loved wearin' that headstrap thing when he went kayakin'. Sometimes he'd play back his trip for me on that monitor. It records, too. Maybe it's somethin' we can use. Gotta figure out how."

This small win has buoyed Juanita's spirits. But it doesn't fix their bigger problems.

Maslow's hierarchy of needs: Food. Water. Shelter. Safety. The big four come first. Self-actualization, reaching your highest potential? That's a bit lofty for us. Hard to reach your potential if you're dead.

"You know, I wonder whether anyone is watching your Casita," Juanita says. "Is there a chance I might be able to sneak in and find us some food and water? Some blankets, maybe?"

"Don't reckon we should risk it," Helen answers. "Goin' back to the scene of the crime? Sounds kinda obvious, don'tcha think?"

"You're probably right," Juanita says. She returns to her little stool to think.

There's got to be something else we can do. Hunkering down here might feel like the safest thing. But that'll change. I'm sure of it.

"I gotta pee," Juanita squeaks. "Something more serious, too." She'd noticed a saturated roll of paper towels and considers using them as toilet paper. On closer look, however, she sees mildew has taken root, so she dismisses that.

A rainwater bidet it is, then.

It dawns on her she can't recall urinating since—well, since she peed her pants in the Casita kitchen. It's another sign that she, too, is dehydrated. After telling Helen she'd be right back, Juanita steals outside and makes a latrine in the sand. Squatting, she looks toward the Casita she cannot see. She finishes up, covers the hole and scrubs her hands with sand, then, holds them up, letting the rain rinse them. She sees the blood caked under her fingernails. It's stubborn and impossible to wash off.

Driven by sudden impulse, Juanita climbs her way out of the low ground where the shed sits, to the higher surrounding terrain. She slinks from spot to spot, telling herself to move slowly, not quickly, to reduce the chance of being seen. Soon, she reaches a vantage point where she can see the Casita. She's on the verge of chancing it when her eyes register the slightest of movements. Partly sheltered from the rain by a small grouping of peppertrees stands a man in cowboy hat and long trench coat, his back to her. He's clearly watching the Casita. Juanita shakes off the fright from her near-deadly mistake.

Stupid. Of course someone would be watching the place, staying hidden like that. Sheer luck I spotted him. That was a close call.

She retraces her path back to the shed. She stops on the way in and drinks from the metal cup now filled with rainwater. She gives the half-full thermos to Helen and manages to convince her to drink it all.

After confirming the Casita is being watched, Helen doesn't waste the opportunity to give Juanita a smug "I told you so."

Hoping Helen might have forgotten an energy bar, bottle of water, bag of peanuts or, even, a mint, she drags Helen's backpack over and zips it open. The front pocket contains a bulging envelope.

"What's in this envelope?" Juanita asks.

"They're my important papers. My birth certificate. Ben's, too. There's our trust, Ben's and mine. It's just a copy, mind you. There's a copy of Mama's will, the one leavin' me the parcel of land and house I grew up in. I still pay taxes on it every year. There's an older will in there, too, the one where my grandma left the land and house to my mama. That one might be an original. There's the deed when my grandpa, Richard Holcomb, bought the land. That's for sure an original. It's dated back in the late eighteen hundreds.

"My grandpa's daddy—Samuel Holcomb was his name—he was a Union soldier come down from Iowa. He'd come to Texas to fight against the rebs durin' the Civil War. Guess he liked it here 'cause he stayed. Don't know how he got rich, but he was."

"Can't see how there's anything in there that someone would want," Juanita says as she puts the envelope back into the front pocket.

Inside the larger, padded compartment of the backpack is the laptop computer, a charging cable and, disappointingly, nothing else. Eyeing the laptop, Juanita agrees with Helen's guess. This must be what these killers want to get their hands on.

"What's on this computer?" Juanita asks. "They're keen to get it. Why?"

"Don't know."

"When we left the Casita, you made sure we brought it with us. You must know why?"

"It has everything on it. Bank and tax stuff. Pictures. Medical records. Ben didn't keep a lot of paper files. He scanned documents and uploaded them onto his desktop."

"Think," Juanita says. "There's something here they want. A document? A picture? An email? Have you noticed anything strange? Anything...unexpected?"

"Lemme see," Helen replies, struggling to sit up. Juanita tilts her up and lays the computer onto Helen's thighs, the laptop earning its nickname. Helen presses the power up button. Nothing happens.

"Don't you keep this thing charged?" Juanita asks with more than a little exasperation in her voice.

"Sorry," Helen replies. "It wasn't plugged in 'cause I was using it in my bedroom. I sorta forgot about it and just put it in the backpack when the power went out."

"What's the last thing you did with it?"

"Well, I decided to clean out Ben's old desktop computer. Day before yesterday was the tenth-year anniversary of his death. I been puttin' it off but finally got around to transferrin' his old files over to my new laptop. I used that thing, uh, FireWire, to do it. It took longer than I'd figured. Must've run the battery down."

"Did you see anything that seemed, like, strange? Off?" inquires Juanita.

"No. Well, uh, except for that old porn."

"What do you mean, old porn?" Juanita asks.

"There was an old email with instructions on how to view a video. The email had a link, and when I clicked, it took me to somethin' called *The Onion*, but I didn't know what that was. There were instructions to copy a website address, so I did that. Anyway, it took me to a page with three links on it. I clicked on one of 'em. It was disturbin' stuff. They were dark, like, whadaya call it? You know...dungeon stuff. Camera wavin' around. Grunts and moans. Creeped me out, to tell the truth.

"I'd forgotten I'd seen this same email a long time ago. Back when I found it, I got mad at Ben. He denied knowin' anythin' about it. Come to think of it, Ben was sent that email the day before the car crash. I remember 'cause I was plumb vexed at him and wouldn't talk to him on the drive. Last minutes of his life, and I spent it givin' him the silent treatment. Me callin' him a liar. It was the last thing I said to him. How's that for partin' words?"

Helen wipes some moisture from her eyes while Juanita pretends not to notice.

"Did you keep them? The pornos? If we can get your laptop powered up, can you show me?"

"No," Helen says after a tense moment. "I didn't copy 'em over. They wigged me out. I just deleted the email." A chill leaks into Juanita's bones, one that has nothing to do with the cold.

They're connected! The video links in Ben's email and the video the scarred man showed Betsy. Creepy sex. S&M-like stuff. The way Helen remembers it, it sounds a lot like what Betsy described. That's how come they want the computer. What was viewed that made them want to steal the laptop? Kill for it?

"I think when you viewed that porn on Ben's computer, something changed. It triggered all this. You ever heard of tracking notifications? If someone clicks on certain links on a website, the site can send a notification to whoever's tracking it. Maybe if someone were to visit a specific site and watch a particular video, for example? Even if those videos were ten years old, that function might still be active. In fact, if it's still being used at all, it's surely active."

This thought steers Juanita to her next question.

"Helen, what made you open that email? The one with the videos?"

"Best I can recollect, it was on account of the email bein' sent by Andrei Kask. We'd gotten emails from him before—stuff about the house, mostly, like paperwork and updates. I remember he needed a receipt or somethin' for tax purposes, but nothing out of the ordinary. But I don't think we'd heard from him in a long time."

Andrei Kask sent the email. Why? To make a point? That doesn't make sense. Was Ben, somehow, in on it? I can't see Ben being involved in something like that. An error? Maybe he sent them by mistake. When Helen opened those videos, maybe they thought something long buried had come to light. It meant they couldn't take the chance that Helen might realize what the videos were—what they truly meant. That's why they made the decision to kill her, to bury the truth before it could surface.

"Here's what I think happened. Ben was sent that email on accident. He was never meant to see the videos. Ten years ago, Ben opened that email. What happened next? The hit and run crash. Ten years later, you open the same email. What happens? A man comes to kill you and steal your laptop computer. That can't be coincidence."

Helen is stunned into deathly silence. Tears pour from her eyes, carving visible tracks into her dirt coated cheeks. She no longer cares about hiding her tears from Juanita.

"Those motherfuckers!" Helen hisses through closed teeth. "They killed Ben. They killed him. I always said the accident wasn't an accident. As bad as I come to believe them Kasks are, they're worse. They're murderers! Monsters! They're gonna pay. I swear it. I'm gonna stop 'em, if it's the last thing I do."

"I know you want revenge," Juanita replies. "I understand. But how are we going to do that? You remember what Betsy told me? They're out of town now, but she said they're coming back tomorrow. She heard the Mexican say the Kasks are leaving again soon. Maybe permanently."

Anger-laced quiet follows. Helen breaks the silence.

"We got one chance. One chance to prove our innocence. We need proof. That proof is in there," she says, pointing in the direction of Mustang Manor.

"No way," Juanita says. "The Manor might be empty now, but that's not the only potential problem. I've only seen the grounds once before, but it was guarded by a big Russian man. I talked to him, years ago. Well, maybe talked isn't the best description. More like exchanged sign language. I didn't get his name, but I've come to think of him as Igor. Anyway, if Igor's here, and there's no reason to think he isn't, how would we get by him? And, even if we can somehow slip by, how would we get in? That place looks like a fortress to me."

After a pause, Helen replies.

"You forget. I know the place better'n them. I know how to get in."

CHAPTER TWENTY

Rooms with a View

*"And his eyes have all the seeming
of a demon's that is dreaming"*

~Edgar Allen Poe (1909-1949), American writer, poet, editor, and literary critic

———— ••• ————

THE CAMERA LIGHT STRAPPED TO HELEN'S FOREHEAD slices through the pitch-black boiler room, dazzling as it swings wildly from side to side. Its eerie glow disorients her, making her dizzy whenever she moves too quickly. Like a game of Red Light, Green Light, each object caught in the beam appears frozen in stark, lifeless detail, as if trapped in time. But the moment the light shifts, they seem to inch closer, creeping toward her unseen. The crisp, unforgiving clarity reminds her of that lightning flash on the aluminum bridge—the brief, blinding moment when it illuminated the masked man, his presence burned into her memory.

This dang light is so powerful, it's damn near overkill. Least Juanita won't have no trouble seein' what I'm seein'. Guess I oughta be grateful I got the light at all—woulda been a real mess tryin' to paddle one-handed while holdin' our only flashlight.

Her rolling platform is a jury-rigged one. She'd found a random sheet of metal and lain it across the two skateboards. She'd fallen off half a dozen times before she figured out how to balance herself atop the tin, skateboards lined up underneath. It wobbles to and fro with each paddle, but it works. She's never surfed but imagines it might be something like this, paddling out to catch a wave that will carry her to shore. After trundling down several dead ends, she finally spots the delivery doors that, when open to the outside, will allow Juanita to enter.

Finding the delivery doors in the vast, gaping maw of the boiler room had felt like a victory. Failing to get them open had been a crushing defeat. She'd strained against the heavy doors, trying to force them open for Juanita, but they refused to budge. An iron pipe she'd found became her tool of desperation—hammering, prying, jamming—but the thick chain and rusted lock held firm. The racket echoed through the emptiness, and she was relieved no one was around to hear the clamor.

Certain that Juanita has seen the failure on her device's video screen, Helen wiggles her fingers in front of the camera and points forward, figuring Juanita will understand her intent. She's decided to go on and look for another way to let Juanita into Mustang Manor.

She paddles around a series of three immense metal buckets. The bottom one is nearly empty, just traces of coal dust remain. Resting on a hinge above it is another, identically sized bucket—this one still full of stoker coal. Helen cannot see that high but assumes the third, even higher hinged bucket, is also full of coal that has been crushed into pieces small enough to be shoveled into a furnace. She grabs the iron chain hanging down and gives it a little tug. The middle bucket rocks to and fro, as though excited to have been called to duty after such a long layoff.

Helen resumes surfing her way past the huge doors to the furnace itself, the incendiary heart of the boiler. Decades ago, the manor was fitted with a modern electrical central air and heat system. The old coal-fired beast is no longer needed and has been left to rust.

Helen knows what that feels like.

After bumping into and dodging around a barrel of what must be rusted and no-longer-used metal parts, she finds herself at the door she knows connects to the rest of the basement. She pauses to readjust her makeshift rolling platform. The skateboards under the metal sheet she's laying on don't like staying put. Helen frequently has to stop and wedge them back into place.

Once through the doorway out of the boiler room, what she sees is not what she expects. Clearly, rooms have been built on both sides of this section of the basement. Rather than open space, there's now a hallway. There are two doors on each side of the newly constructed aisle.

Contorting herself on her improvised rolling platform, Helen opens the first door, half expecting the door will be locked. It isn't. Given the garish light, it takes some time for her to understand what she's seeing.

A mirrored wall reflects the brow-borne spotlight onto a large metal bed. It's bolted to the floor, a bare mattress on top. The next two rooms are identically appointed.

Don't take no genius to figure out what these rooms are for. They're fuckin' studios. Betcha a dollar to a donut those mirrors are the see-through kind. Video cameras on the other side. These murderers are some fucked up pieces of shit.

Paddling to the fourth door, she finds it locked. She isn't going to let that stop her.

One for the money. Two for the show. Three to get ready. Four to...well...to go ahead and kiss my ass!

Using a two-handed grip, she hammers the doorknob again and again. Finally, the knob pops, listing to one side. The door swings inward. Even before the door fully opens, Helen can hear an electric hum. Paddling through, she sees green blinking lights on shelves installed along one wall.

Fuckity-fuck. Computers. It's a data center. This is where they record the action. This ain't no small potatoes operation.

She imagines the three cable-connected laptop computers store hundreds, maybe thousands, of illicit videos. A wave of fury washes over her.

Someone's gotta stop these bastards. It's my lucky day. Today, that's me.

Seizing ahold of cables that drop down to a large, shared power strip, she yanks all three laptop computers down onto the floor one by one. Not a computer tech wizard, Helen wishes she knew how to erase the videos.

She decides on the barbarian solution. She bends the screens backward until they break off with a satisfying crack. She smashes them with the pipe. Screens break, plastic skin dents, and some keypad pieces fly away.

Motherfuckers! Motherfuckers! Motherfuckers!

The repeated obscenities echo around the room. She's feverish with destructive energy. Sweat breaks out on her forehead making the skin under her headband itch. It's a chant, but a curse-laden one.

The chanting reminds her of Sam's singsong voice.

The chanting reminds her of Juanita's repeated blows to the head of the scar-faced man.

The chanting reminds her of the ragged death rattle bubbling up from the masked man's throat as she'd sawed into his neck.

Even after she no longer has the strength to swing the pipe, she chants and chants more. Finally, her voice trails off into silence. She's lightheaded from the hysterical effort.

Though cathartic, Helen realizes she's probably not hurting the laptop's hard drives or the data on them. Now that the madness of the tantrum has left her, she realizes it's fortunate she hasn't destroyed them entirely. The videos on these computers are evidence. Rather than destroy them, she needs to preserve them. Hide them.

Discarding the pipe, Helen gathers up the bottom halves of all three computers. The nastiness of her idea makes her cackle. She retraces her wheel tracks back into the boiler room. One by one she tosses the hard-drive halves of the laptop computers into the stoker coal container that's nearly empty. With relish, she pulls the iron chain attached to the higher bucket. That container rocks and protests so Helen pulls harder and, finally, the bucket obeys and tips to pour black rock down and into its twin below, burying the laptop computers under thousands of pounds of coal.

Ta da! Take that! Won't that be a nice surprise for them bastards. They'll never find 'em.

She rests for a few minutes. Her frenzied hammering on the computers, yanking on chains, and paddling her skateboarded platform around has taxed her arms. She wipes her face but only after does she realize her hands are thickly coated in coal dust. She sneezes, wipes her nose, and laughs to herself. She can't seem to stop forgetting that every time she touches her face, it only makes it blacker and blacker. She doesn't care. It matches her mood.

Now what? Get while the gettin's good? No way I can pull myself all the way back up that coal chute. 'Sides. I ain't done. So...let's see what else they've done with the place.

Helen pivots her trolley around, readjusts the skateboards underneath, and heads back to the hallway, a smile plastered on her face.

She's so intent on the next stage of discovery and demolition she doesn't notice the man waiting for her to the side of the doorway.

The last thing she sees is an explosion of stars. After, all is black.

CHAPTER TWENTY ONE

Once More Unto the Breach

"A mouse never entrusts his life to one hole"

~Rubellus Plautus (33–62 AD), Roman noble and a political rival of Emperor Nero

———— ••• ————

TRACES OF BLUE LIGHT PULSE FROM THE SCREEN IN Juanita's hands. The instrument Juanita found in the shed had been synced with the wireless video camera strapped to Helen's head. For the first few minutes, Juanita had been able to follow Helen's progress on the video screen. No longer.

Using nylon rope sourced from the shed, she'd lowered Helen down the chute into what she'd said was the boiler room, a place no longer in use since central air conditioning and heating was added. As per their plan, Helen had crawled forward, dragging the two skateboards after her. She'd used one of the many tin sheets stacked inside the boiler room as a platform which she'd placed on top of the two skateboards. Once balanced on her makeshift trolley, Helen had begun paddling her way deeper into the cavernous basement. All of this Juanita has seen on the monitor screen.

Soon after that, however, the video image disintegrated. Now, the center of the screen is filled only by a spinning, hurricane-like graphic that serves as a constant and worrying reminder that the device is no longer receiving transmissions from Helen's video camera.

The Manor's stonework is too thick. Or the distance is too much. Or the batteries in the camera have run out of juice. Take your pick. I'm blind to what's going on.

Watching the digital cyclone on her screen, praying that live video will resume is like seeing a horror movie. Juanita finds herself anticipating the jump scene where a ghoul bursts out of the dark. A monstrous creature of the night wouldn't be the first shock since Helen went down the chute.

Discovering the dead body in the oven was.

And finding it has changed everything.

Juanita had been waiting at their agreed-upon lookout post, the high-walled outdoor dining room. From her position, she'd seen the Russian guard, the man she thinks of as Igor, make a circuit around the estate grounds. Each lap seemed to include what appeared to be a smoke break—based on the smells carried to her on the wind—and she estimated each circuit took about twenty minutes.

While keeping one eye out for Igor, she kept her other eye on the large double service doors that Helen was supposed to open from the inside.

That was the plan, anyway. But the doors remain closed. Where in the Manor Helen has now gone is a mystery. Juanita has, half a dozen times, crept close and put her ear to the metal doors and tried unsuccessfully to open them herself. She's heard and seen nothing for over an hour.

Still carrying the monitoring device, backpack and rifle with her, Juanita had decided to plan for the worst.

We might need a place to hide, a place big enough for both of us. Worse comes to worse, we could both squeeze in there to hide. I think.

Those thoughts brought the oven to mind. She'd dropped to a crouch and duck walked to stay below the counter height of the bar and into the kitchen. Even at a distance the oven looked massive. A set of double doors with pull handles were at waist height across the front.

She'd walked heel to toe over to the oven doors. After a few quiet seconds spent listening for any signs she might have been seen, she'd grasped the handles, opening the doors on nearly silent hinges.

Juanita had turned on her flashlight and targeted it inside. Immediately she'd seen the oven was occupied. Something was lying sideways filling about half the space. It was slick, shiny and black.

Fabric? Plastic? What is this?

Juanita had leaned in and swept the flashlight's beam from right to left. Whatever the bag held, it was long. She'd retraced the light's path, this time from toe to head, confirming her suspicion.

Holy shit. I know a body bag when I see one.

She'd retreated from the body's evil aura, duckwalking back to her post. The awareness that the body of the masked man who'd bound her, terrorized her, threatened to kill her might be just a few feet away was horrifying. And arousing. As though any sense of self-preservation had no voice in the matter, she'd gone right back to the oven doors and opened them again.

This time she'd reached in, her hands sliding over the rubberish material. The body bag was slightly damp. There was only a little water pooled into the pan beneath the rack onto which the body bag had been lain. She'd rolled the bag a bit onto its side until she found the zipper. It sighed as she slid it open.

She'd turned the flashlight on again, keeping it carefully shielded within the oven. The light gave the interior an eerie glow, like a science fiction movie, one where the cryogenic tube had failed, and the astronaut inside had perished.

The body was clad in black fatigues, mask removed. She lifted the flashlight's beam to his face. Partly turned away, his skin bore the telltale pallor of death—unmistakable to her practiced eye. His throat had been cut; the gash thin but deep. One ear was shredded, the lobe entirely gone. Blood matted his shoulder, the mark of a bullet's path. Her fingers slid down his stiffening arm to his ice-cold hands. Around the bones of his fingers, the smaller muscles had begun to seize—the first signs of rigor mortis setting in.

Juanita hadn't gotten the specific details of how Helen had killed the masked man other than assuming Helen had shot him. She'd heard two shots, but she'd seen no visible sign of a second entry point.

Those injuries to the neck aren't consistent with a bullet wound. She must have finished him off with that meat cleaver she cut my ties with. She's a lot fiercer than I've given her credit for.

Juanita rocked back onto her heels. Whatever had happened, Juanita envisioned it had been a ghastly thing. She zipped the body bag shut and eased herself back into a squat, closing the doors.

No vacancy in that inn. It's been, what, twelve hours at most? Not much water on or under the cadaver pouch. That means the body was probably moved when it wasn't raining very hard. It's been raining non-stop until recently. The body was moved here sometime within the last three hours. Someone, more likely more than one person, fetched the body from Helen's Casita and stashed it in the oven.

The implications hit Juanita like a runaway train. Given what she's just discovered, Juanita realizes she, too, must go down into that black hole, despite her acute fear of confined spaces.

Whoever did this, they're here! They're probably inside the Manor. And Helen doesn't know. I've got to find her. Warn her. Get her out.

Those thoughts had led her back to the coal chute.

Juanita takes one more hopeful but disappointing glance at the spiraling screen and puts the device into her back pocket. Her eyes pan the yard, looking for Igor.

Igor should still be on the back nine if he sticks with his established patrol pattern. He's proven to be a creature of habit. I'm pretty sure he's about to start his smoke break. If I'm gonna go, I've got to do it now.

She hoists the pack onto her back, cradles the rifle in her hands, and walks as quickly as she can to the doors covering the coal chute. She'd debated whether to leave the backpack in the outdoor kitchen, but she didn't see a spot where she might stash it that wouldn't potentially be found.

After furtive glimpses left and right, she opens the chute doors. To Juanita, this yawning black hole is dreadful. She's claustrophobic.

Her eyes measure the width of the coal chute. Her shoulders are wider. Her hips are wider, too. Her eyes measure the height of the coal chute. The sum of her buttocks and thighs are higher. Her stomach might be higher, too.

Just because Helen got down doesn't mean I can. I must weigh nearly twice as much. Once in there, how will I push my way down? If I get stuck, what then? Plus, Helen had me holding the rope. I would have pulled her back up if it was too tight. Me? I got no one. If I get stuck, I just might die there.

Unlike Helen's descent, Juanita cannot imagine going in face first. The thought of getting trapped face down, squirming and praying and taking a long time to die is among her worst nightmares. Hiding in the cramped wooden elephant in the emporium had been bad enough. This is worse.

If it comes to that, at least, let me die looking up at the light, not down into the dark.

She takes off the backpack and loops the straps around one ankle. She cradles the butt of the rifle between her knees, the trigger guard pressed against her crotch, the barrel against her stomach. She hugs it tight, like a lover. She scoots herself to the lip of the opening and slides inside, deep enough to grab the edge of the doors and pull them shut.

She cranes her head and looks up at the closed doors. She bids what she prays isn't a final goodbye to the thin slashes of twilight that leak in from where the old metal doors have warped and no longer fit tightly. She turns away, refocusing on the darkness beneath her feet. Counting down three, two, one, she bucks her hips, pushes with her hands and begins to move away from the last bit of daylight above her head.

She worms her way down. Hands above her head, pushing off the ceiling and sides. She digs her heels into the floor, arching her back each time. Her progress is measured in inches and, so, she feels like an inchworm. Twice she gets stuck and twice she has to fight off panic. The second time she gets stuck she realizes the butt of the rifle is catching on the seams of the metal plates that had been welded to form the chute. Once she remembers to keep the butt of the rifle up and away, she makes agonizingly slow but undeniable progress. She's trembling, dripping sweat and thanking God for answering her prayers when she finally tumbles roughly into a metal trough at the base of the chute.

Clamoring out she can feel the coal soot and filth coating her fingers. She plays the flashlight around, unsuccessfully looking for something with which she can clean herself.

Dirt, coal dust, rat droppings and who knows what. No chance I'd find anything down here to wipe my hands with anyway. Time to cowgirl up.

Redirecting the flashlight, Juanita can see streaks in the grime on the concrete floor where Helen had crawled away. She follows these deeper until she finds a wider swatch of smears. From there, the marks suggest where Helen pulled herself onto the sheeting atop the skateboards and began paddling herself across the floor. The regularly spaced wheel tracks lead off into the darkness. Juanita figures this is about where the video signal had cut out.

Juanita spies a barrel overflowing with rusted, forgotten tools. She buries the laptop-filled backpack beneath the heap. Face and hands blackened like a ninja, she slots the flashlight into her armpit, grips the rifle tightly, and follows the wheel tracks etched into the grime-coated floor.

CHAPTER TWENTY TWO

Three May Keep a Secret…

*"The bitterest tears shed over graves
are for words left unsaid and deeds left undone."*

~Harriet Beecher Stowe (1811–1896), American author and abolitionist

———————— ••• ————————

THE YELLOWISH CANDLELIGHT, EVEN SUBDUED AS IT IS, hurts her blinking eyes. Her stomach churns. Her head is a drum and it's being pounded, pounded, pounded. She sits up just in time to vomit. Saliva mixed with bile trickles down her chin. Her hands feel clumsy, shaky as she wipes the spew from her face. She reaches up to find a tacky bump the size of a walnut on her head.

"There she is," a Russian accented voice calls out. "What an entrance! You're a sight for…what do they say? Sore eyes! Yes, sore eyes."

"Fuck me," Helen utters. "Fuck you, too."

Battling nausea, Helen forces her own sore eyes wider. She finds herself laid out on a sheet atop a sofa. The sheet is smeared with soot, grease and now, vomit.

"I hope you don't take offense that we covered the couch. Fact is, you're a dirty, dirty girl. Couldn't have you staining the furniture, could we?"

Looking up, she finds herself surrounded by men. Georgi Kask lounges in one chair, a wolfish grin on his face, while his son Dmitri occupies another. A pistol rests on the table between them. Standing nearby is Andrei, Georgi's other son. The fourth man, his head wrapped in a blood-stained bandage, bears an unmistakable facial scar.

"Hey you! Scarface!" Helen calls out. "You're that feller from Los Desperados. Reckon we got somethin' in common. Both of us got our brains scrambled. I was hopin' you was dead. You ain't. That's disappointin'."

She hadn't expected anyone to be home, let alone lazing around the cavernous, cold Manor den. She'd thought her only worry was the outdoor guard. What had brought them home early, Helen had no clue.

"Surprised to see us?" Georgi says. "I can promise you, not as surprised as we were to find you crawling around in our basement. Have to admit, didn't see that coming. But, since you've delivered yourself to us, I'd say this is a nice surprise."

"If you're gonna do it, do it," Helen goads Georgi. "Go ahead and fuckin' kill me. Listenin' to any shit you feel like you got to say ain't how I'd like to spend my last moments."

"Really?" Georgi says. "And how would you rather spend your last moments?"

"Killin' you, of course," she says.

He chuckles.

"I do love your directness, Mrs. Chesterfield," he says. "Or may I call you Helen? We should be on first name basis by now, don't you think?"

"No," Helen replies.

"It's decided then, We'll go with Helen."

"You can kiss my ass, you murderin' motherfucker. What? You a coward? Gotta have someone do it for you? Like that cunt you sent. Don't wanna get dirt under your nails, do you? Lost your nerve, haven't you? Do it cocksucker! Take a donkey kick up your ass why don't you? Go ahead and fuckin' kill me!"

"My, Helen, don't you just ooze charm? You really do seem to be in a hurry to die, don't you?" Georgi says. "Or is it that you want to get it over with for another reason? Well, everything in due course. Now, it's time for adult conversation. How about this? I ask a question. You answer truthfully. Then it'll be your turn. If you're honest with me,

I'll be honest with you."

Helen goes to respond but Georgi interrupts her with: "tut, tut, tut. The first question is mine."

Georgi leans forward in his chair, his moist, bare forehead glistening through combed over strands of slicked back hair. Thick lenses magnify black eyes that dance in the candlelight.

"First order of business," he says, raising one finger. "Where is it?"

Helen feigns ignorance. "What are you talkin' about?"

"Your computer. The one you used to view our videos. And the three others from the basement. Don't play dumb, Helen. You know exactly what I mean."

Helen's thoughts go to the backpack she's left in Juanita's care and the computers she's buried under a pile of coal.

Fuckity-fuck. I can't tell him where they are. Play dumb. I'm good at that.

"I got no idea what you're talkin' about. I ain't got no videos or whatever else you say I got."

"Oh, but you do," Georgi insists. "We've searched your house. We found the old desktop computer. Made sure it's wiped clean. But your laptop computer is gone. I'm certain you took it with you. Will says your friend must have gone back to the ambulance for the rifle—but also, for the backpack. So, you know it's important. Let me guess, you left the backpack containing your laptop with your friend. And where is she hiding, I wonder? Someplace close? You couldn't have gotten here on your own. We need to invite her to the party."

A chill runs down Helen's spine.

Georgi's tone turns mocking. "You're plucky, Helen, I'll give you that. You survived—twice. Impressive for someone in your condition. But don't mistake survival for winning. I've seen it, you know, where it happened. A linen closet of all places. A lot of blood. His and yours. Well, mostly his. That was some work for us to clean all that up. You put up a hell of a fight. It looked like maybe it was a close thing. Was it? A close thing?"

Helen refuses to answer.

"To tell the truth, I wish I'd seen it live. Must have been thrilling."

It wasn't thrilling. It was terrifying.

"Helen, you've heard of the KGB, yes? Russian intelligence? Of course, you have. So popular in American movies. Hollywood seldom gets it right. How about the NKVD? Heard of that? It's a...specialized branch. What the NKVD is good at—what I'm good at—is getting answers. I've had a lot of practice. Unlike the movies, the good guys don't always win.

"You're paralyzed below the waist, right? Well, I'll just have to keep my ministrations to what's above. That leaves plenty to work with, wouldn't you agree? Skin. Bones. Eyes. Ears. Fingers. Don't worry, though, I won't cut out your tongue. You'll need that. You'll tell me everything I want to know before the end. A messy end. But things could happen more quickly, without the pain, without the mess, if you will just answer me truthfully."

Helen can't help but imagine being strapped down. Tortured. Pieces of her cut away. And she imagines the same thing happening to Juanita.

"Goddamn. You sure can talk. You must really love the sound of your own voice. Before I tell you anythin', I wanna know somethin'," Helen demands. "Why?"

"Why or why now? Two different questions. Let's start with why." Georgi leans in, his voice dripping with amusement. "It all begins when a hard-pressed debtor pays us in silver coins. Very old ones—like the ones your mother cashed in over fifty years ago."

His eyes gleam as he continues. "Then we find out someone plans to sue you for your land." He smirks. "The claim? Your mother's marriage made it community property. That gets us thinking—why fight for a nearly worthless plot with nothing but a collapsed house? Then, his lawyer mentions a decades-old hearing where you were questioned about your father and your mother's missing boyfriend. No charges, but it raised eyebrows."

His smirk widens. "Fifty years later, a man sues for a pitiful tract of land? That's not just strange. That's suspicious. His attorney tells us his client believes something valuable is hidden there. So, we search the house—nothing. Then we dig beneath that strange concrete slab, and the pieces fall into place."

Georgi leans back, stretching out his arms like a man savoring a story well told. "First, a skeleton—dented skull and all. Then, something better—two dozen rotted canvas bags. And beneath them? A hoard of old silver coins, just like the ones we were paid with. No wonder your mother only spent a few at a time. Too many, and people would start asking questions."

He chuckles, the sound low and amused. "Our Mexican friend gets real interested when he sees those coins. He likes the idea of owning a pirate's buried treasure. Doesn't take much to strike a deal—his crew digs up the rest, and we both profit."

Georgi spreads his hands in mock humility. "Today's been a good day. Funds transferred to our offshore account, half the treasure delivered, and our buyer...well, let's just say we sweetened the deal with some 'compelling' videos that proved valuable to his business. All he has to do is pick up the other half, and our deal is done. Honor among thieves, right?" His eyes glitter coldly. "Not that the man suing you will be happy to find the treasure he seeks is gone. Texas law says buried treasure belongs to the landowner. Maybe that's why you refused to sell, or maybe you didn't know. Either way, it doesn't matter now, does it?"

His expression hardens. "Why now? Simple. Letting you live was a mistake—a rare act of mercy, and as I've been reminded, mercy is seldom the wise choice. I never imagined you'd crack that old email sent to Ben, let alone navigate the dark web. But you did, and now you're a risk." He chuckles, shaking his head. "I have to admit, though, watching you seethe as we took over Mustang Manor has been entertaining. Taking the buried treasure without you even realizing? Priceless."

He claps slowly, the sound deliberate and mocking. "And the body? You really thought it would stay buried forever? It was a good hiding spot. We never would've found it if we weren't looking for something else. But once we did, everything clicked. A body buried on land you refused to sell, even when you were desperate? Obvious."

His smirk deepens. "Bravo, Helen. You did what had to be done. As someone who's never shied away from the ultimate solution, I have to applaud you."

Georgi dips his head slightly, his hands coming together to resume the slow, taunting clap.

They found his body. The new evidence; the reckonin'. That's why the attorneys want to meet. I shoulda known—nothin' stays buried forever. Secrets claw their way to the surface. And now, he's come back from the dead. Just like I always feared. Just like I always knew he would.

Helen stays silent, jaw tight, heart pounding. Words won't change anything. Escape is impossible. The only thing left is to stall—for Juanita.

"Oh dear," he murmurs. "I seem to have wandered off track, haven't I?" He exhales, feigning exasperation. "Honestly, I don't care about the remains. Your stepfather? I've heard the rumors—how he beat your mother, how he brutalized you. It's a tale as old as time. Sexual violence is an addiction, a sickness that makes those who crave control lose control. I understand this. I exploit this. But your killing him? Your lies? None of that matters to me."

Helen has so much she wants to say, but none of it will change a thing. Her survival is no longer a real possibility. Now, it's about time. Delay. Anything to stall. Anything to give Juanita a chance to escape. To live.

She doesn't respond, just presses her lips into a thin line and glares.

Georgi sighs. "This unpleasantness is so unnecessary," he says. "If things had gone according to plan, you'd have had yourself a nice, quiet overdose. The backup was a good old-fashioned strangling—a crime of passion if you like. It needed to look personal, not professional. So, I sent someone competent, but not exceptional."

"Not good enough," Helen retorts. Her gaze shifts to the man with the bandaged head. "Your brother—he squealed like a pig when he died. When I cut his throat. You both have the same stupid, fat faces. The scar on your face? Well, guess what? He's got a matchin' one, 'cept his scar is on his neck."

The man takes two steps forward, fists clenched, a deep growl bubbling up.

"Now, now," Georgi chides. "She's baiting you, Will. Why don't you take a break? Fix us up a little cold dinner. Torture is hardest on an empty stomach. You'd think it would be the other way around, but no." He waves a hand dismissively.

Will stomps off, but not before throwing Helen a glare of pure hatred.

Georgi turns back to her. "Admittedly, I should have sent someone better. Clarence was…mediocre. Too many years as an armed deputy made him arrogant. Sloppy. We can agree on that. Good help is so hard to find. Frankly, I'm astonished you survived. You gave us quite the chase. It's all been very thrilling." He smiles. "But now, for you, thrilling isn't quite the right word, is it? Painful. That's more like it."

Helen sneers. "I knew we never shoulda leased this place to you. Told Ben we could find someone else. Knew you were a slimy wad of shit from the start."

Georgi chuckles. "Ah, Benjamin. Your husband. Or should I say, your late husband? Is ten years still considered 'late'? I don't know how that works. At what point does a man simply become…dead?

"They never found who caused the crash, did they? Interesting. Do you know who benefited most from your deaths?" He leans in. "Me? Bingo. They'll never find the truck. Never find the driver. They don't exist anymore."

His words hit her like a sledgehammer knocking the air from her lungs. She suspected, but to hear him say it so casually.

He killed Ben. He fuckin' killed Ben. And the attempt at the Casita? That was round two. The first try was the accident. Which wasn't no accident at all.

"Fuck you!" she screams. "I'll kill you if it's the last thing I do!"

Georgi smirks. "No, the last thing you'll do is tell me what I want to know. We established that, didn't we? You're not a very good listener, are you?"

"You listen!" she snaps. "You're nothin' but a miserable, sick fuck. You and your fucked-up sons. You defiled this house. Built those rooms—the ones with cameras and microphones. What is it, Georgi? You get off watchin'? You use that footage to own people, don't you? Some pay to keep their secrets hidden. Others? They work off their debt. They do whatever you say."

Georgi spreads his hands, amused by her accuracy.

"But let me tell you somethin'," Helen hisses, her voice razor-sharp. "All those people you've got tangled in your blackmail? That's a lot of leashes to hold. And one by one, they're gonna slip loose. And when they do...you'll be right here, just like me—trapped, ruined, with nowhere left to run."

"I agree," Georgi says, surprising her. "The clock is running out. We're leaving soon. Here's an irony for you: if you hadn't opened that email, you'd have gotten Mustang Manor back. I don't even like this place. Too hot in the summer, too drafty in the winter. It's served its purpose, though. We're almost done here. Just a few more loose ends to wrap up."

His eyes lock onto Dmitri, cold and deliberate. "Speaking of loose ends," he murmurs, his voice edged with finality. "We need to deal with Ivan. He's seen too much—he's never really been one of us, has he?" A pause, calculated, heavy. "I'd prefer not to leave him breathing. The Mexicans can handle it. No urgency...but it needs to happen. Soon."

Georgi's gaze switches back to Helen.

"Hiding the computers was a nuisance, I'll admit. But most of what you stashed away has been backed up. The important files, anyway. Chesterfield's old fireproof safe came in handy. Convenient.

"We've hosted some powerful people here—bankers, actors, politicians. Their secrets are valuable. And now, we go digital. Blackmail is only part of the business. Social media disinformation is where the real money is. It's not so different from Soviet counterintelligence ops, just more profitable. The last three presidential elections proved that. Politicians, corporations, governments—they all want what we offer: effectiveness with deniability.

"Our motto? 'We don't invent lies; we bring them to life.'

"Catchy, no? Well, we're still workshopping it."

He leans back. "I get to be like most workers now. Remote. I'll live where I want, with all the protections I need. Maybe I'll find wives for my sons. Grandkids. Mustang isn't the only island, you know. I've already picked one out."

His voice turns sharp. "But before we go, there's one last thing. You had help. Juanita Jiménez, right?" He glances at Andrei.

Andrei sneers. "Yeah. Tried flirting once. She's frigid as hell. Or queer. Fuck, with that nose, maybe even a tranny."

Georgi waves him off. "So, Helen, where is she?"

"How the fuck should I know?" she snaps.

"But you do. And you will tell me."

He smiles. "Fun fact: the video rooms aren't the only rooms downstairs. We have one more. Lefortovo, we call it. It's named after a rather famous Russian prison. One where answers are...obtained. It's soundproofed. Easy to clean. A nice little drain in the center."

Helen says nothing. She knows his patience is wearing thin. She knows what's coming. Even so, she empties her mind, imagines herself untethered. She is liquid. She is gas. She is free to fly away.

Georgi sighs. "Nothing? Not even more foul language? Fine. Have it your way." He checks his Breitling. "Andrei, pick her up and take her to the room. Antonio Lima and his posse will be here in about an hour. I'll want some time to clean up after. Wash my hands, at least."

Helen squawks as Andrei gathers her up in his arms, sheet and all.

He strides toward the stairs that lead down to the basement but stops abruptly.

Curiously, he backs up.

CHAPTER TWENTY THREE

The One Bullet Bamboozle

*"Masters of the bluff and masters of the proposition,
but the enemy I see wears a cloak of decency."*

~Bob Dylan (1941 – present), American singer-songwriter

———————— ••• ————————

JUANITA LOITERS MIDWAY UP THE SHADOWED STAIRS THAT
lead from the basement to the living room. She edges upward, toward
the light, toward the voices. She recognizes one voice as Helen's. The
other is deeper, masculine. Russian accented.

*Must be Georgi. He's here? How? When? Thought they were
supposed to be gone at least one more day. We're in deep shit, now.*

Juanita is torn.

*Retreat back downstairs? Escape altogether? That would mean
leaving Helen to them. Can't do that. What to do?*

"Take her down to the room," she hears Georgi say. "Antonio Lima
and his posse will be here in about an hour. I'll want some time to
clean up after. Wash my hands, at least."
She hears Helen squeak. Someone is hurting her.

*Damn. There's at least one person besides Georgi. One of his sons?
Maybe both? That'll make it three against one. Not the best odds.
Plus, I only got the one bullet. They don't know that, though. Wish I
had time to plan something.*

There's no time to plan. She hears heavy footsteps coming her way. A bulky, vague hunchbacked silhouette fills the top of the landing. Juanita knows she'll never get to the bottom of the stairs before being seen. So, she dashes up the stairs, rifle butt fixed to her shoulder.

Arms full of Helen, the man is about to step down, his eyes fixed on the first of the stairs. He doesn't see Juanita but feels something press against his forehead. That stops him in his tracks. His eyes bulge and cross as he stares at the rifle barrel pressed smack between his eyes.

"You're not going anywhere," Juanita growls, "unless it's to an early grave. Back up!"

The man shuffles his feet, the pressure of the barrel forcing him to retreat backward into the living room. Juanita starts to tell the man to put Helen down, but she realizes it might be better if his arms are full. She pushes harder, not gently, and the man staggers further.

Twin candles cast umbrellas of jitterbugging light onto the side tables. The room is filled with two chairs, a couch, a loveseat, and coffee table atop the largest, most luxurious rug she's ever seen. The room holds even more furniture—a lot—but she can't make out the details since the candlelight doesn't extend that far. She spies Georgi, half in and half out of his chair.

"You!" She yells. "Sit back down."

Georgi hesitates but relents, easing himself back into the chair. Next to Georgi sits another man. He, too, begins to rise up from his chair.

"Dmitri. Right? Never met you before but your brother's a real charmer. Don't you move either. I've got an itchy trigger here."

She turns the rifle's sights on Andrei but switches back and forth between three Kasks.

"You don't want to see your precious baby brother Andrei get his brains blown out, do you?"

Dmitri's glare is venomous, sociopathic, but he eases himself back down.

"This must be the mystery girl," Georgi says. "Jiménez, isn't it? I'd say, 'nice to meet you,' but this isn't very nice, is it?"

"Believe me," Juanita barks. "I'm not thinking nice thoughts."

"No. Don't imagine you are," Georgi says loudly.

Is he hard of hearing? He's damn near shouting. Nerves, maybe?

"So, what's your plan?" Georgi continues, volume be damned. "You think you can come in here with a peashooter and have your way? That's not going to happen. Put the gun down. Let's talk like civilized people. No one needs to get hurt here."

"Ain't nothin' civilized 'bout you," Helen calls out from Andrei's arms. "And you're a fuckin' liar. All you do is hurt people. And you like it, don't you? Shut up already, dickhead."

Juanita scrambles to think of some way out of this. She's only got one bullet. It's chambered and ready to fire. But if she does, then what?

We'll be shot. Best-case scenario, we'll be overwhelmed. Captured. Wait a minute. That's not the best-case scenario. It's the worst.

She recalls Georgi's instructions to Andrei.

'I'll need to clean up after. Wash my hands at least.' That's what Georgi said, wasn't it? Clean up from what? Torture. That's what we'll face. No surrender, then.

Okay. First, barrel whip Andrei? Second, shoot Dmitri? He's the most dangerous. Shit. If I knock Andrei down, he'll drop Helen to the floor. Can't risk that. Shoot Dmitri first? Then what? Turn the rifle on Georgi? Threaten to kill him? That might bluff them. For a while, anyway. How long until they figure out there's no more bullets in the rifle?

"Put Helen down on the floor," she tells Andrei. He hesitates.

"Carefully. Do it now!" she yells. Andrei bends over and deposits

Helen onto the floor.

"Move back! More. More!" she directs Andrei. "More. Stop! That's far enough. Sit down. On the floor."

Juanita resists the urge to look at Helen. She's sure taking her eyes off the Kasks, even for a moment, would be a fatally bad idea.

"You okay?" Juanita asks.

"Yeah. Head's hurtin' pretty good though."

"Nobody move!" Juanita says. She gathers her courage.

"You want to know my plan? Here's my plan."

She moves swiftly, positioning herself behind Dmitri's chair, the rifle pressed firm against the back of his head. Her free hand snatches up a handgun from the table. She considers using it—knows it holds more than a single shot—but she isn't familiar with pistols, and now isn't the time to find out if it's loaded or fiddle with the safety. She cannot afford to show anything less than absolute control. Keeping the rifle steady, she tucks the handgun into her waistband.

"Unless you've got an absurdly thick skull—and you might—you'll do exactly as I say. You'll hand over your car keys. Then all of us are going downstairs to one of your fun little rooms, where I'll lock you and dear old Dad inside. Andrei is going to carry Helen to the car for me, and then we're leaving. He'll ride with us. Soon as we're off the island, we let him go. If not, well... it's going to be the OK Corral in here."

Juanita shifts a few feet, moving behind Georgi's chair. She lays the rifle barrel against his temple, leaning forward just enough to meet his eyes.

"No matter what happens, you'll be my first shot. Maybe we'll win a fight. Maybe your boys will. But you'll never know one way or the other because you'll be brainless and all."

Georgi twists himself around in the chair to look more directly at Juanita.

"Well. Since you put it that way. We could do that...but..."

Georgi's eyes slide to the side and grow wider.

"Not going to fall for that trick, Georgi," she says. "Nice try, though."

"Hmmmm," Georgi purrs. "Yes. Nice."

Suddenly, the rifle is snatched from Juanita's hands. She's spun around and the rifle butt hammers her stomach. Juanita collapses, legs jellied.

She rolls onto her back, gasping for air.

Standing over her is the man she'd fought on the dock. The man she'd thought she'd killed. The scar is still there, and his head is swaddled in bandages. He snatches the gun from Juanita's waist and hands it back to Dmitri who spins the revolver around his finger a few times before putting it back down on the table.

"Remember me?" Will says, looking down at Juanita who's sprawled on the floor. "Sure, you do. Thought you'd get one over on me and walk away? Thought that'd be the end of it? Nuh-uh. Well, you're never going to forget me."

He backhands her, sending her rolling away. He catches up, grabs a fistful of her hair, and yanks her head back. He kisses her hard, biting into her swollen bottom lip so that it breaks open the scabs that had barely begun to crust over.

"We're going to have some fun, sweetheart. You get me? Don't worry. You'll get me all right. I'm going to use you. All of your holes. That'll be your last memory."

Juanita closes her eyes. She whispers a prayer through bloodied lips.

CHAPTER TWENTY FOUR

A Vaquero at the Door

"If you weren't surprised by your life you wouldn't be alive."

~William S. Burrough (1914–1997), American writer
and visual artist of the Beat Generation

———— ••• ————

GEORGI SMILES. THE FLICKERING CANDLES ANIMATE A GRIN that looks joyful, then evil, then back to joyful.

"Goodness, how the tables have turned," Georgi says. "This is turning out to be a most satisfying day. We're all going downstairs after all. Just not according to your plan, Juanita. Time for a different plan. Two birds, one stone. That's the right phrase, isn't it?"

The gravity of Georgi's rhetorical question falls onto Juanita, adding to the weight of Will's knee on her chest.

With attention diverted, Helen eyes the rifle lying on the floor where Will dropped it while assaulting Juanita. She debates whether she might be able crawl to it without being seen or, if not, whether she can reach it before one of the men stops her. *Unlikely*, she thinks.

The silence is broken by booming, rapid knocks coming from deep inside the shadowed entryway. Juanita is motionless, partly because the knocking is clearly unexpected by everybody, it appears, but also because Will has her pinned to the floor.

At Georgi's permissive signal, Andrei goes to answer the door, gun drawn and at the ready. Andrei cracks the door open just enough to see a man standing on the stoop. Rainwater drips from the cowboy hat that shades the man's face.

"Who are you? What do you want?" Andrei inquires.

"My name is Reynaldo," the voice answers in a Texican accent. "I was sent here by Sheriff Conley. I have a written message for Señor Kask. I was told to give it to him personally."

Andrei turns and gives his father a questioning look. Georgi shakes his head 'No.' Andrei turns back to door.

"He's tied up with something right now. Give it to me," Andrei says opening the door a little wider, "I'll make sure he gets it."

"Sure boss," says the man outside.

He extends a folded sheet of paper toward the opening. Andrei reaches out to take it, leaning forward to keep his shoes sheltered from the rain.

Quick as a rattlesnake, the hatted man grabs Andrei's wrist and pulls him halfway through the door, forcing it wide open. Andrei falls flat on his cursing face. The gun Andrei had been holding tumbles from his hand and skitters to the floor.

Two explosions send literal shock waves through the manor. The cowboy steps through the door. Twin smoking pistols, as if by magic, are now in his hands. He steps over the still twitching body and stalks calmly forward into the room, elbows bent, hands thrusting the dual six shooters out in front.

Much of the man's face is hidden under the hat. He's wearing a long overcoat atop jeans and cowboy boots. He's slim but tall, and he walks with just a touch of a limp.

With the man's face covered, Juanita sees what she wants to see. It's Clint Eastwood, reprising the role of William Munny, outlaw and killer. A vengeful antihero. An unforgiven dark angel.

The man spares a swift glance at Juanita. For just a moment, their eyes lock. The light is poor. His face is shadowed beneath the hat. Even so...

Brown eyes. Bushy eyebrows. Hooked nose. A limp.

His gaze swings away but not before Juanita realizes who he is, even as she swears it cannot be.

Abuelo! What? How?

Juanita gasps aloud but realizes she must not distract him, let alone give him away. She turns her attention to Georgi and Dmitri, both of whom appear to be stunned because they haven't moved from their chairs.

Horacio directs his hitched walk straight toward Georgi's eldest son, Dmitri. Nursing a glass of scotch, Dmitri had returned his handgun to a side table, still within reach. He's comfortably stuffed into a chair that is generously appointed. This proves to be his undoing.

The silk pillows are snug against his arms and shoulders. As a result, his lunge toward the gun is a touch slower and a tad more awkward than it otherwise might have been. As Dmitri snatches the gun from table and raises it to aim, he's met by two bullets, one in the abdomen and the other in his shoulder. Dmitri squeezes off one wild shot before collapsing. Blood pools on the Persian rug. Dmitri moans and rolls onto his back showing reddened teeth.

Horacio pivots to face the last man standing. Will, too, is slow to respond. He fumbles trying to draw the gun at the small of his back. Without hesitation Horacio fires, the twin revolvers, again, barking death.

This has all happened in mere seconds, and Georgi has yet to move except for startled jerks when the guns were fired. But Helen can see the realization breaking out on Georgi's face. He's witnessed his sons being gunned down. Will being shot, too.

Georgi raises his hands.

"I am unarmed. I have no desire to see anyone else harmed here. Especially me. You are free to leave. You have my word."

"Fuck your word," Helen says while crawling. "Your word don't mean shit. And you're a bad fuckin' liar," she says. She pauses her crawling to look him in the eye. "I know. Takes one to know one, remember?"

Georgi drops one of his raised hands to reach into his pocket, but

Helen stops him with a wave of Ben's rifle. She'd crawled even faster than she thought she could.

"I want to kill you," Helen says. "Just gimme a reason. Move again and my dreams'll be fulfilled. Me? I don't care if I die. But I reckon you do."

"You're bluffing," Georgi says.

"Go ahead," she nods, "Make my day."

Watching, Juanita can't help but grin.

A one-hundred-pound bag of skin, bones and grit, Helen still makes a convincing Dirty Harry Callahan. Clint Eastwood would've been proud.

"I was only reaching for my phone," Georgi says, moving slowly. "It vibrated. Cell service is back. You can call the Sheriff."

"That feller over there?" Helen yells. "His brother was a deputy, dipshit. Or did you think we didn't know? You retarded enough to think that we're gonna call in more of your thugs just to play into your hands?"

Helen gives Juanita a quick look.

"Sorry," she says. "Shouldn't have said retard."

Helen turns back to Georgi.

"That sorry is for her. Not for you, fuckface. That's your son over there. He's bleedin' all over your precious rug. Your other son? He's a doorstop. And you're tellin' me it's time for 'Let's Make a Deal?' Bullshit! You sheep fuckin' coward. Sons are dyin' and all you can think about is yourself. If anyone else dies here today, trust me, it'll be you."

Juanita watches her grandpa shuffle over to Dmitri who is still twitching and moaning on the floor. Horacio studies him for just a moment before he shoots Dmitri again, all the while staring at Georgi.

Then, Horacio steps over to Will's body and shoots him once again as well.

"If I've learned anything, it's best to be sure," Horacio says as he ambles back to stand in front of Georgi.

Juanita sees her grandpa holster one of his guns. His face is a grimace. With the now empty left hand, he reaches to his side. He brings it back close to his face. The hand is smeared with blood.

Oh my God. He's wounded.

Juanita stands and goes to Horacio. Without taking his remaining gun off of Georgi, Horacio tells Juanita to draw the holstered pistol. She pulls it free and points it at Georgi.

He says in a near whisper, "Two bullets left." Juanita nods her understanding.

Juanita pries Dmitri's gun from his dead hands. She thinks to give that pistol to Helen but recalls Helen doesn't need it since she's already pointing the rifle at Georgi.

"If Georgi so much as moves, shoot him," she tells Helen.

"Gladly," Helen replies. "I'm kinda hopin' he gets twitchy."

Juanita returns to her grandfather, takes the other gun from his hand and helps direct him to the couch. She pulls a coverlet off the back of the couch and knots it around her grandfather's abdomen to staunch the blood flow.

"By the way," Helen says to Horacio without taking her eyes off of Georgi. "Can't say it's good to see you considerin' the circumstances. Still it's, well, good to see you. You're not gonna bleed out on us, are you?"

"Good to see you, too, Helen," Horacio chuckles. "This isn't my first time getting shot. I think I'll make it. Didn't expect to find you here. Still, I figure you're a good one to share the foxhole with. You're tough as a leather boot. You're a survivor."

A jarring shout comes bursting through the open front door.

"No shoot! No shoot!" a Russian-accented voice calls out, sharp and pleading. The hallway leading to the front door is dark, but Juanita's eyes catch a hand waving back and forth, frantic. A head peeks out, eyes wide with alarm.

It's the guard, Igor. He had to have heard the gunshots. I'm not sure I can hit him from here. Need to coax him in closer so I have a better shot.

When all heads turn to the voices, Georgi decides to make his move. He drops his arms and reaches behind himself to pull a pistol from the small of his back. Seeing his movement, Juanita pivots toward him and fires twice. The first shot misses. The second does not. Georgi gasps and drops the gun to put one hand on an arm that blossoms red. Juanita shakes her head, angry at herself.

Stupid. I should have checked him for a weapon. Jeez. Is everybody on this island armed?

Juanita and Helen both turn back to point their guns at the man crouching in the doorway.

"You no shoot," the Russian says again. "I come in. Okay? You no shoot."

Igor is big enough to block out nearly all of the light seeping in through the doorway. After a few paces, she can see he's holding a pistol in one hand, pointed at the floor.

I'll never get a better shot, Juanita decides.

She braces her right arm with her left, lines up the sights and squeezes the trigger. The hammer falls, but her gun doesn't fire.

Shit. No bullets. I thought I had one left.

"No! No shoot me!" the Russian's voice thunders. "I no bad man. I only out," he adds pointing out the door. "I no in," he says, sweeping one unarmed hand around the living room. "You no shoot."

"If you're not a bad man, put your gun on the floor and kick it over here," Horacio says after rising from the couch.

Igor looks out the front door and then back inside. He seems conflicted about something.

"Okay, okay," he says, his voice quick with compliance. He lowers the gun, lets it fall to the floor, then kicks it forward. It skids across the wood, stopping only when halted by the rug.

"Please," the Russian man says. "Bad mans come. More bad mans."

"What bad men?" Helen asks.

"Bad mans! Mexicans. They come now. Please! I close door!"

Sounds arise from outside the still open front door. A car braking in gravel. Doors opening and closing. Spanish words float in through the door.

Juanita keeps her gun pointed at the Russian; he won't know she's out of ammo. Now that he's in better light, she recognizes him for sure.

It's Igor. Definitely the same guy I met years ago.

Juanita is torn between trying to save her grandpa and trying to figure out if Igor is a bad guy who's trying to get them to lower their guard, not to mention who the heck is speaking Spanish outside.

"When?" Juanita demands.

"Uh, I see," he says.

The Russian lurches his way back to the front door and looks out.

"Now! Bad mans here now. No good!" he calls out. "Juanita? You name Juanita? Yes? I help you. Please, I close door."

The Spanish speaking voices are getting louder.

Horacio hisses through clenched teeth, "Let him. I believe him. We need help. Might be...only chance we've got."

The big Russian doesn't wait for Juanita's assent. He drags Andrei's body inside, closes the front door, and locks it.

"Where go?" the Russian asks. "This no good place fight," he adds motioning around the room.

Helen thinks of another room in the Manor, one with a heavy oak desk and bookshelves. They might be able to hide behind them.

"The study. Up those stairs. First door on the left," she says, pointing across the room toward the stairs opposite those leading down to the basement.

Triage is one of Juanita's skills. Realizing there are three people who'll need moving—Horacio, Helen, and the wounded Georgi—she decides to task the Russian with getting everyone into the study.

"Hey you," Juanita says, pointing. "Mister big Russian man. Can you carry hurt people into the study?"

"I no Russian" the man says. "I from Belarus. No Russian. My name is Ivan Novick. I help."

Ivan…not Igor. Well, I was close.

Juanita dispatches Ivan to carry, first, Horacio and then, Helen into the study. By the time he returns for Georgi, Juanita has gathered up the pistols. Arms full of assorted weaponry, she hears pounding on the front door. She quickens her pace, running up the stairs and into the study. She closes and locks the door.

Fat bit of good that'll do. That knob is flimsy as hell.

Ivan has already started building a barricade facing the door. He's swept books and who knows what from the shelves of a heavy book-case and he drags it on its side, placing it at an angle facing the door. He does the same with a second bookcase and drags it opposite the first one.

"Juanita. You help," Ivan says, motioning to the massive desk.

Juanita and Ivan grunt and heave and just manage to topple the heavy oak desk. Together they inch it forward to fill the space between the two bookshelves. It's the final piece of an inverted U, the open end facing the closed door to the study.

Juanita doesn't have time to thank Ivan. They hear the Manor's front door bang open.

"Take your gun back," Juanita says, handing it to him. "Are you any good with it?"

"Yes," Ivan nods, smile beaming. "Yes. I know good."

Juanita makes sure Helen has the rifle. She's lying prone on the floor. Helen has thrust the rifle barrel through the crack left between the desk and one of the bookcases. She's ready. A one-shot sniper.

I'm ready. Gotta be ready. Gotta stay ready. Ain't gonna be like waitin' in the ambulance. I ain't gonna fall asleep this time.

Juanita rechecks Horacio's wound. Blood flows freely but it isn't gushing. She hugs her grandfather gently and resumes her position behind the desk. She clenches two guns, Dmitri's in her right and Will's in her left, making her feel, eerily, that she is, indeed, her Abuelo's grandchild. Ivan slides himself next to her, protecting her flank.

Ivan smiles at her, a face full of teeth.

"I do not forget you," Ivan says. "You go leeetle house. Yes?"

"Yes," Juanita replies. "I remember you, too. Uh, by the way, I'm sorry for trying to shoot you."

Ivan smiles again. He's good at that.

"You want kill me? Is mistake, but I understand. Maybe God say… this good mistake. Make sure no bullet."

Juanita is taken aback. Ivan knows that she'd intended to kill him and, still, it's like water rolling off of a duck's back. He's an enigma.

"What are you doing here, working for Georgi Kask?" Juanita asks.

"I no want work for Georgi," Ivan says. "I have brother. He fight against Russians in Ukraine. He is wounded and, uh, captured. He is in Russian prison. Georgi say I work for him, or he no protect my brother. I no want work for him but I no want brother hurt. So…"

Is there nothing Georgi won't do? Juanita asks herself. *He's got tentacles everywhere.*

Realizing he might have information, Juanita shuffles over to where Georgi sits propped up in a corner, one hand still holding firm to his bleeding arm.

"Unless I miss my guess, those are cartel soldiers. Right?"

"They are," Georgi says. "Sicarios. Trust me, they outgun you. If you give up, I'm sure I can convince them to let you go."

Juanita leans down putting herself mere inches in front of Georgi's face.

"Give up? I don't think so."

He flinches when Juanita reaches into his jacket pocket and takes his cell phone.

"You can't win here, Juanita. Surely you understand this."

"We'll see about that," she says. "If you want to live, you'd better hope we win."

Juanita's first instinct is to make a call, but she freezes at the thought of her voice slicing through the silence. One wrong sound, and the sicarios could be on them in seconds, guns drawn, no questions asked.

She considers recording a video instead, but the night is closing in fast, swallowing everything in shadow. It'd be useless.

Heart hammering, she pivots to the only option left. Her fingers fly over the keyboard, crafting a message in frantic bursts. Each second stretches unbearably long, the weight of urgency pressing down on her.

Beside her, Georgi shifts, suspicion flickering in his eyes. "What are you doing?" he murmurs.

"Shut up," she hisses back, barely glancing at him. When he doesn't, she silences him with a quick, sharp kick to his shoulder. He flinches, sucking in a breath through his teeth, pain flashing across his face.

Finally, the message is done. No time to second-guess. She presses send and shoves the phone into her pocket, pulse thudding in her ears.

Juanita turns and dashes over to the window. She pulls the drapes closed, plunging the study from pretty dark to very dark. She feels her way back to stand between Horacio and Ivan.

"We win," Ivan says in the dark. "You see."

Win? We'd better. Never say die.

CHAPTER TWENTY FIVE

The Texican Standoff

*"Victory is celebrated in the light,
but it is won in the darkness."*

~An opening line from Dune: Prophecy, 2024, HBO and Max

———————— ••• ————————

A SOLITARY VERTICAL LINE OF SMOKY LIGHT—THE LAST remnants of evening—steals in like a phantom between the ever-so-slightly parted drapes. Otherwise, the room is pitch black.

Horacio, who's been put into the wheeled desk chair, uses his feet to navigate himself behind the desk. Juanita makes sure he has his pistol, the one that still has two bullets left. Horacio grins through clenched teeth.

"Don't worry about me," Abuelo says. "Been in tougher scraps than this."

"How did you know to come here?" Juanita asks.

"A man came to the house looking for you. He searched the house even after I told him you weren't home. Said you and Helen were wanted by the sheriff but he wouldn't tell me why. Scared the daylights out of Alex before he finally left. I knew something was very wrong. I also knew you'd left late last night to get Helen. So, I tried to find you ."

"That was you," Juanita says. "Standing outside. Watching the Casita. That was you, wasn't it?"

"Yes. I knocked on the Casita door, but no one answered. I staked it out. I finally gave up on watching the Casita and decided to try the Manor. I saw you and called to you, but you didn't hear me before you went down that hole. With my leg and hip, I knew I couldn't follow. I decided I'd knock on the front door but before I got there, I saw the whole Kask family arrive. They pulled out guns before they even went into the house. I figured, then, you might be in real trouble. When that Kask boy opened the door with a gun in his hand, it told me all I needed to know. I looked past him and saw a man holding you down on the floor. I stopped thinking and started doing. Old habits, you might say."

"Thank you, Abuelo. Thank you. If you hadn't come…"

"Juanita," he says. "You are the light of my life. Of course, I would come. Tell me, what is happening?"

"Long story. A man tried to kill Helen. And me. We've been on the run all day. I'll tell you all about it. If we survive this. The men outside work for a drug cartel. I think. I don't know why they're here or what they want."

Everything keeps getting worse. It's bad enough people are trying to kill Helen and me. Bad enough they already killed Sam. Now Abuelo gets dragged into this, too. And that's not even counting Ivan. What a nightmare.

One hand pressed to his side, Horacio shuffles to and squats down next to Helen who lays prone in the floor. Juanita cannot hear their whispered conversation, but she can imagine what they might be saying to each other.

It's…weird. Abuelo and Helen. Still can't picture it. Don't want to picture it. Who would have thought they'd meet, again, in Mustang Manor? Waiting for a gunfight to the death? Whatever passed between them, it's nothing compared to what we're facing now. God, let him live. And Helen. And Ivan. And me. I can't think what would happen to Alex if Abuelo and I don't survive this. He's already lost his mother and father. How much trauma can one person—even someone as kind as Alex—take before he goes back into his shell?

Juanita sees Horacio squeeze Helen's shoulder and slowly rise back to his full height before retracing his steps back to the wheeled office chair.

Helen's eyes slowly adjust to the near-total darkness. With the rifle in hand, she peers down its length, a sharp wave of déjà vu crashing over her. She's back in the linen closet, waiting for the masked man, just as unsure of how to use the weapon as she is of whether she'll survive.

One more time, Ben. Help me be brave.

Her courage is immediately tested when she hears the study's door-knob rattle.

"Señor Kask?" a voice calls. "Que paso?"

Before anyone can think to silence him, Georgi calls out.

"Help! I am being held hostage."

Juanita hears hushed discussion coming from the other side of the door.

"Rehén? Hostage? Quién lo tiene? Cuántos? Están armados?" a voice asks.

Georgi doesn't speak much Spanish, but he understands the gist.

"Yes. Just one woman and two men," he yells. "They have pistols. If you want the treasure you must rescue me!"

"Estás bien? Uh, you hurt? You sons is dead. Another man, también."

"I'm wounded, you idiot!" Georgi screams. "I'm bleeding out. Hurry!"

Ivan leaves Helen's side and makes his way to Georgi's. He squats very close to him.

"Shut up," Ivan tells Georgi in a terrifyingly calm voice. "You talk, I kill."

Georgi nods, whimpering in pain.

Ivan is back at Juanita's side before the voice outside the door resumes.

"Entiendo," the voice says. "We come soon."

Soon doesn't feel like soon. Already, a good ten minutes has gone by. Juanita weighs whether to speak, thinking through what she might say and how to say it in Spanish. Before she's decided, let alone sorted a translation, Horacio beats her to the punch.

"Estamos armados y mataremos a cualquiera que entre por esta puerta," he announces in a gravelly voice. "Si entras, morirás."

You enter, you die.

Juanita hopes her grandfather's bravado will scare the Mexicans away. No such luck.

With a bang, the door buckles inward. The man holding onto the piece of furniture used as a makeshift ram is the first to die. Ivan dispatches him with a headshot that sends the man tumbling head over heels.

The response is deafening. Automatic weapons spray the room, bullets whacking into the barricade, the floor, the ceiling, ricocheting deadly happenstance around the room. Using the hailstorm of bullets as cover, two men rush through the door.

The first pirouettes, blindly firing as he's pierced by bullets, one each from Helen and Juanita.

The second intruder opts for speed but, unable to see in the dark, he runs straight into one of the chest high bookcases. Horacio half-raises himself up from his chair and shoots the man in the face, knocking him backward onto the floor. He doesn't die. Yet. His shrieks are ghostly in the twilight.

Cordite and copper fill the air. Helen retches, hawks and spits. She knows her rifle is empty. She wonders if she can squeeze herself through the crack between the desk and the bookcase. She figures she can locate the man on the floor and take his gun on account of how he's wailing and all.

Juanita's ears ring, dampened by the echoes of the gun blasts. She opens and closes her mouth, trying to restore some sense of hearing and equilibrium. The relentless chiming in her ears grows stronger, louder.

Am I screaming? Is it coming from me? No. It's coming from outside. It's getting closer.

A siren.

"Policia!" she hears a voice outside the doorway yell. "Vamos, date prisa!"

As footsteps pound away, she finally registers the howling.

"You called the sheriff after all?" Horacio asks.

"No," Juanita replies. "The cavalry."

CHAPTER TWENTY SIX

An Unexpected Exhumation

"...to all the monsters in my nursery:
May you never leave me alone."

~Guillermo Del Toro, *The Strain* (1964–present),
Mexican filmmaker, author, and artist

———— ••• ————

HANDS PULL HER EYELIDS DOWN. THE DAZZLING LIGHT stings her eyes. Helen tries to slap the hands away, to no avail.

"Hold still, ma'am, still checking your eyes," the man says. "I'm going to give you a cold compress for your head."

"Lemme guess," Helen says, shooting a wink at Juanita. "Five minutes on, five minutes off?"

"You got it," the paramedic says. "We'll be taking you to the hospital, too. You might have a concussion."

"Sonny, if'n that's the only hurt I got, I'll be a happy girl."

"Don't you believe her," Juanita chirps through butterfly-bandaged lips. "I've never seen her happy."

"You shush," Helen mouths. "We're alive. You, me, Horacio, even that big ol' Russian feller. Georgi's goin' to prison after they patch him up. Them sicko sonsabitches of his dead. They're outta my house, too. Well, will be soon's them bodies get carted off. And the cherry on top? I'm gettin' Mustang Manor back. What's not to be happy about?"

"Sam's still dead," Juanita says, a touch of anger in her voice. "Plus, there's a sheriff's deputy, his brother, and three Mexicans in addition to Dmitri and Andrei. Eight people dead. Two more wounded, one of them my abuelo. It easily could have been us killed. That doesn't feel like happiness."

Juanita waits for the paramedic to close up his medical kit and step away so she can talk to Helen without being overheard.

"And, unless you forget, there's another man dead," Juanita says in a somber tone. "The one buried on your mama's land. That doesn't feel like happiness to me, either."

Helen is smart enough to be contrite. Or, at least, act like it. She hangs her head.

"By the way, Ivan isn't Russian," Juanita adds. "He's Belarusian."

"Ain't that the same thing?"

"According to him, no. He speaks the Russian language, but he doesn't like Russians. Go figure."

Paramedics swarm over Mustang Manor. Already, gurneys have taken Horacio and Georgi to the trauma unit at Ben Taub Hospital in Houston. An attending EMT reassured Juanita and Helen that Horacio was stable and in good condition "all things considered." Both Helen and Juanita teared up when he was loaded up in the ambulance.

She hadn't thought to inquire about Georgi. Honestly, she doesn't care, other than taking satisfaction in the thought of him spending the rest of his life behind bars, not tucked away on a private island living a life of luxury.

On the heels of the first responding ambulances, law enforcement, too, has arrived. So has the Nueces County coroner. Sheets lay over three bodies in the study and three more in the living room, cadaver bags on standby. Police, already wide-eyed at the body count inside the manor, are astounded to learn of another dead body stuffed into the outdoor oven.

Ongoing conversations between deputies, police, forensic technicians and paramedics make the house buzz. Despite electricity having been restored, portable spotlights illuminate places in the manor where dozens of bullets are embedded into walls, furniture, and, of course, the bodies of the men whose lives they've taken.

Standing alone, speaking to no one, a tall, wrinkled and weather-beaten man waits in the hallway. Dressed in jeans and a wind breaker, he holds a white hat in hand.

Juanita looks up, sees the man, excuses herself from Helen, and goes to him. The man turns toward Juanita. Reflected light winks from a circle of silver with a five-pointed star in the middle. The badge is pinned to his chest.

"You must be Juanita," he says. "I'm Vance. Vance Barrow."

"I don't know how to thank you," Juanita says. "Abuelo has spoken highly of you, but I was afraid you wouldn't believe me. Thought for sure you'd think I was some crackpot. I couldn't trust the Sheriff. Wasn't sure I could trust the Corpus Christi police either. You came to mind."

"Well, I was tempted. But I've heard whisperings about Mustang Manor. And the Kasks? They aren't quite as under the radar as they thought they were. What you texted to me? It sounded crazy. But crazy enough to be true. After alerting EMT and police, got here as fast as I could.

"Even more," Vance adds, "I've known Horacio for a long time. We coordinated on busting up a rustling ring back, oh, damn near thirty-five years ago. That bust was a big one. Opened doors so I could get on with the Texas Rangers. I'll tell ya, I don't forget citizens who helped my get my star. I figured Horacio Jiménez' daughter gotta be made from the same stock."

"I...ahem...thank you," Juanita manages to say. She's never been comfortable with being complimented. "I thought if an ambulance or two could get here before anyone from the sheriff's department did, we'd stand a better chance of getting out of this alive."

"Having me call for multiple ambulances, sirens blaring away? I almost didn't do it. I didn't want to put unarmed first responders at risk against armed perpetrators. But I figured I could give them a little head start. Put the Corpus Christi police right on their heels. They both made it here before anyone from the sheriff's department did, so you didn't have to worry about them getting here first.

"Juanita," Vance says. All of a sudden, his voice is somber, his face serious. His lips are thin, pulled in tight. His eyes bore into hers.

"Tell me the truth," he says. "Did you know?"

Oh my God. He knows. I can see it in his eyes. It was bound to happen. Bodies don't stay hidden forever. If Georgi found it, he can too.

"Did I know what?" Juanita replies. Even she can hear how puny her own voice sounds.

"Did you know they found it? Dug it up after all these years?"

The question is a catastrophe. She feels the growing portent, the foreboding. Vance is asking her about the man Helen killed nearly fifty years ago.

Helen should be the one to tell them. Not me. If I play dumb, they might buy it. But I don't think I can get away with lying. I've never been good at that.

"Found what?" Juanita answers, her voice hollow.

Juanita is too afraid to break eye contact with Vance. He'll know something is wrong. He'll realize she knows more than she's saying. The effort makes her eyeballs sting and water. She is on the verge of covering her eyes with her hands.

It'll be hard to expose Helen when I don't even know the who. Or how. Or why.

"The treasure," Vance says with a broad smile. "We found two heavy plastic boxes in the Manor's butler's pantry. They're full of silver. Coins, most of it. Old coins."

Juanita is flummoxed.

"That's just the half of it. Literally. The other half is in the two containers that we seized at the Wild Horse Lodge. We don't know why, but it looks like the Mexicans had already taken possession of the first half and were coming back to Mustang Manor for the other half. Maybe to pay for it? It's just a theory, for now, but it feels right.

"The ambulance sirens spooked those two sicarios into running. You'll be glad to hear we've got them in custody. We caught up to them at the motel. They were loading up their van with two containers of treasure. Word is the motel manager tipped the containers over and spilled the coins all over the floor of the Wild Horse Roadhouse. They had a boat waiting offshore and might've gotten away if they hadn't wasted so much time picking everything up. We owe a thanks to somebody."

Betsy! Dang. That took some serious guts.

So, he's talking about treasure. Not a dug-up body.

Juanita's blood pressure sinks back to something closer to normal.

"Well, I'll be…"

CHAPTER TWENTY SEVEN

Lights, Camera, Inaction

*"He'd (Reggie Jackson) give you the shirt off his back.
Of course, he'd call a press conference to announce it."*

~Catfish Hunter (1946–1999), American professional baseball player

———— ••• ————

THE CAMERA LIGHTS ARE DAMN NEAR BLINDING. Microphone-wielding reporters jockey for position and the opportunity to ask questions. There are plenty. Of reporters and questions.

To say the story has sparked a feeding frenzy among journalists, including international media, is a colossal understatement.

It has all the ingredients. Sex. Money. Blackmail. Corruption. Gunfights.

And, to top it all off, there's buried treasure wreathed in history, legend and mystery. Historians are already speculating the silver had been buried by Jean Lafitte, perhaps the most famous pirate, privateer, patriot and spy in American history.

Rights to the treasure are being argued. It's pretty clear Texas antiquities law says treasure belongs to the owner of the property on which it's found. That's Helen. Or maybe not. A man claiming common law marriage to Helen's mother, has sued for ownership suggesting the land is community property. Still other attorneys argue the treasure constitutes a national artifact and, therefore, belongs to the people. Exactly who those people are, they don't say.

And, at the center, a cast of heroes and evildoers straight out of Hollywood central casting.

A widowed woman in her sixties, rendered paraplegic by a deliberate hit-and-run crash that killed her husband, fights off and kills an assassin in self-defense—and likely also took down an attacking sicario.

Another woman, a private ambulance driver who'd quit college to take over the family business from her deceased father, doggedly stays one step ahead of the killers; often she does so carrying her paraplegic friend from hiding place to hiding place. She, too, shoots and, perhaps, kills a sicario.

A 76-year-old grandfather who looks like he's stepped out of a Louis L'Amour novel straps on his six guns one last time in order to rescue his granddaughter from death by torture.

A single mother who raised two children on her own in a single room of a weathered old motel risks her life by dumping containers of silver coins onto the floor of the Wild Horse Roadhouse. The distraction takes the drug cartel sicarios so long to gather the coins that law enforcement captures them before they can flee.

An elderly Cambodian immigrant, a quiet man who refused to let his life be defined by violence, is nevertheless caught up in it and killed after sacrificing himself to save his friends.

An immigrant from Belarus, a man who knows very little English and even less about his fellow heroes, joins them to win a desperate stand against dubious odds.

The villains are, indeed, vile.

A former Russian NKVD interrogator and his sinister sons secretly film sexual trysts, drug many of their victims, and blackmail the rich, the powerful, and even the powerless.

A corrupt sheriff's deputy and his brother graduate from being informers to enforcers to murderers for hire.

The Nueces County Sheriff, the man whose voice matches that of a man who'd called himself Top Hat and arranged pursuit and attempted murder of two of the heroes, has been suspended pending further investigation.

Five Mexican nationals, sicarios working for a drug cartel, lose a shootout that leaves three of them dead while the other two flee. The two survivors are later caught attempting to steal half of the recovered treasure.

Rumors run wild. A book deal is done. Movie rights are being auctioned off. Helen Mirren's agent has pitched her to play her name-sake. Edward James Olmos is desperate to play Horacio. Selena Gomez, America Ferrera and Ana de Armas are fighting over the role of Juanita. Charlie Sheen, curiously, wants to play Georgi, proving, once again, that truth is stranger than fiction.

Not to be outdone, lawmen and lawyers have tied up heroes and villains alike in seemingly unending investigations. They've been questioned by area police, state police, Texas Rangers, the FBI, the Department of the Treasury, Homeland Security and, even, the CIA and NSA.

Last but not least, there's the skeleton found on the property. The remains have yet to be identified.

The press conference was Vance Barrow's idea.

"One time deal," he'd suggested. "Let them get their fill. They'll never leave you alone, otherwise."

Helen has been advised by her attorney to make no comment. Horacio has declined all questions as well. Neither are present. Ivan stands nearby but given his limited understanding of English, he's not expected to have much to add. Betsy has agreed to participate, to absolutely no one's surprise.

Juanita steps to the podium bearing the seal of the State of Texas. She shields her blinking eyes.

"Please," she says. "Can we turn off some of these lights? I can't see."

Betsy hops off the stage and shames multiple broadcasters into extinguishing several of the lights.

Under the, now, more civilized illumination, the questions begin.

CHAPTER TWENTY EIGHT

The Dedication

"Darkness cannot drive out darkness; only light can do that"

~Martin Luther King (1929–1968), American Baptist minister,
activist, and political philosopher

A SEARING, BRILLIANT MEDALLION OF SAFFRON YELLOW mutates into tangerine as it kisses the ocean. The sunset marks day's end and the start of the evening's festivities.

For most people, sunset is a time for easing off the throttle, slowing the pace, reflecting on the day. Sunsets are, for Helen, a starter's gun. They make her want to run, make her feel like she must run. Ten years in a wheelchair and, still, the urgent compulsion will not leave her be.

It's early Spring in Texas and, though the day has been warm, the evening promises to be cool. The ocean is calm. The waves are temperate and regular. Flowers in full bloom tempt dragonflies, bees and butterflies. Blue Winged Warblers, long-beaked Green Herons, and red-breasted Painted Buntings rest after stressful, marathon flights up from Winter lodgings on the Yucatán Peninsula. Like their human cohabitants on Mustang Island, spring break ends all too quickly for the migratory birds who'll soon return to their more northern neighborhoods.

Dressed in enough colorful finery to compete with the birds, guests float around the grounds, drinks in hand. Some are inside, adventure tourists of a sort. They look around the living room, tramp through the study, and imagine what the shootouts must've been like.

The bullet holes have been patched. In lieu of seating, the room is full of work desks artfully sectioned off by display cabinets. Inside the cabinets are island creatures of all kinds. Drawing the lion's share of viewers are the cases full of mounted butterflies, with scientific taxa and commonly used names adorning plaques beneath each.

Outside, sedate partiers chat under a large tent staked out on the lawn. The canvas pavilion is decorated with papel picado flags in green and yellow, pink and orange. Dozens of round tables covered in white tablecloths and unfolded chairs fill the interior.

The scents of roasting beef, chicken, fish and all kinds of side dishes waft over guests who look at their watches and wonder how soon dinner will be ready since their mouths have begun to water.

Helen, in her wheelchair, is off to one side, alone. She shuffles through a handful of index cards and nearly fumbles them. She's nervous and fears her speech will not go over well. She's frightened of the thought of addressing the hundreds of people who've come for the dedication.

A large hand grips her shoulder. Helen twists to look up to find the hand belongs to Horacio.

"Tranquilo, Helen," he says. "You will be fine. Go slow. Breathe when you need to."

"Thank you, Horacio. Can't someone else do this? Juanita? How about Betsy? She can talk the ears off a donkey."

"Nonsense. These people have come to hear you. And Juanita has other things on her mind."

Helen looks for and finds Juanita across the way. Wearing a green dress, sandals, and her hair pinned up, she looks beautiful. She's smiling, holding tight to Ivan's hand.

"I did not see that coming," Horacio says.

"Well, not to be a know it all, but I did. Nothin' says romance like a brush with death. 'Sides, he seems like a good man. A gentle giant. If he was ugly, they could be the beauty and the beast. But he's handsome, in rough and tumble way."

"Might come in handy having a beast as a business partner," Horacio says, squeezing Helen's shoulder. "I tell him I am the brains; he is the muscle. But, truth is, he's smart. He has a degree in advanced mathematics. Have I told you that?"

"Only a thousand times," she replies.

Helen recognizes a voice from behind her.

"Let's get those pitchers of water out on all the tables. Need to make sure folks drink water and not just alcohol. I don't want to see anyone falling on their faces or puking on the lawn. And one more thing…"

The voice moves away.

"That's Betsy. Never stops moving and never stops talking," Horacio says. "God bless her."

"There you go again, Horacio. God ain't in control of everythin'."

"Hmmm," Horacio murmurs. "Maybe you are right. Maybe you are wrong. We will all know. Eventually."

Helen studies Horacio's face.

"You're a good man yourself. Handsome, too. Have I told you that?"

"Only a thousand times," he chuckles.

Helen looks around and sees Juanita's brother, Alex. Somehow he's managed to wrangle himself a pre-dinner serving of peach cobbler and he's wolfing it down, smiling at the ongoings. She's come to share seemingly everybody's inability to resist Alex' natural charm and unrelenting goodwill.

A man approaches, professional looking camera in hand.

"May I?" he inquires.

"If you must," Helen replies somewhat testily.

The man takes several pictures, thanks them, and returns to roving the grounds to find and photograph people with more authentic smiles.

"It's time," Horacio says. He wheels Helen up a ramp onto a humble stage where a microphone awaits. Horacio adjusts the height to suit Helen.

"I could use a cigarette about now," Helen says.

"Good thing you gave them up, then," Horacio responds. "Time's a ticking."

Steven Hanson climbs the ramp to join Helen. He's a PhD, a

lepidopterist. Helen can't pronounce the word and wonders why he doesn't just call himself what he is: an authority on butterflies. Thankfully he has his own microphone, set for his height.

"Hello," Dr. Hanson says, tapping his microphone. "Is this on?"

"Yes," a smattering of attendees' answer.

"My name is Steven Hanson. Welcome to the grand opening of the Mustang Island Natural History Museum. If you haven't yet seen the displays inside, I urge you to do so. A lot of hard work has been done by a lot of people, many of them here today."

Doctor Hanson's initial comments cause other conversations to cease. Guests move closer to the stage, eager to hear or, if not eager, at least able to pretend they are.

"I would particularly draw your attention to the butterfly exhibits. This is a working museum, and you'll not find a more comprehensive representation of Southwestern American butterflies anywhere in these United States. The displays here will serve as an annex to the United States National Butterfly Center in Mission, Texas.

"As you may know, gathering zoologists, taxidermists, curators, archivists and exhibit managers doesn't come cheap. Nor should they. Your donations are as necessary as they are welcome. Which brings me to our cornerstone patron."

Hanson smiles, peering at Helen through trifocal glasses.

"So, it is with deep gratitude that I introduce Helen Chesterfield, our primary benefactor. If not for her largesse, we wouldn't all be here today. Ladies and gentlemen, Helen Chesterfield."

Helen interrupts the polite applause.

"Largesse?" Helen says. "Did he just say I have a large ass? That ain't no way to thank a lady."

The crowd roars with laughter.

"Thank you doctor Hanson. You and your team have done a fine job changin' this place from a drafty ol' house into a museum. I can't hardly believe it's the same place."

Helen shuffles her index cards and realizes she's gotten them out of order. Frustrated with herself, she drops the cards onto her lap.

"I ain't good at givin' speeches," she says. "Don't even like hearin' 'em much, neither. My apologies to the, ahem, helpful folks who made so many fine suggestions as to what I oughta say here today. But I ain't gonna read that speech. Since we're all fixin' to have dinner and I'm the only one standin' betwixt y'all and eatin', I reckon you can thank me later.

"What I want to say, need to say is simple and short. Juanita, Horacio, Ivan, Betsy, I am grateful to see you here today. We owe each other our lives. That's no small thing. There's another man not here today. His name was Chan Sam."

Helen pauses to dab her wetting eyes.

"I didn't know him hardly at all. He didn't know me either. That didn't stop him for carin' for me. Savin' my life. If'n there were ever a man what didn't deserve to get killed, it was him. He was a Buddhist. Believed in reincarnation. If right, he might be here today. Maybe one of these butterflies dartin' around us?

"I don't reckon I'm gonna be on this Earth all that much longer. Oh, my friend Horacio believes in the afterlife. I ain't so sure. But I am resolved to live a good life, whatever is left. Be kind to these here butterflies. One day, one of 'em might be me. Wouldn't that be a hoot?

"That's all I got to say. Let's eat!"

CHAPTER TWENTY NINE

Gathering Spilled Memories

"We do not remember days. We remember moments."

~Cesare Pevese (1908 – 1950), Italian novelist, poet,
short story writer, literary critic, and essayist

———— ••• ————

GARISH FLORESCENT LIGHTS FLICKER OVERHEAD. THE STILL
to be renovated old annex room buzzes with electricity, matching the
mood of those assembled.

It's rare for an initial property rights arbitration hearing to be so
intense. Given the stakes—rights to millions of dollars' worth of
treasure—it's not surprising. Four of the seven seats at the table are
filled by eager litigators. One of the chairs, the one at the head of the
table, belongs to the arbitrator. Another belongs to the plaintiff. The
final seat does not resemble the others. A chair has been removed to
make space for a wheelchair.

Helen stares at the blank notepad and pen on the table before her.
Her attorney said they're for taking notes—more likely, they're just
something to keep her hands busy. To her right sits Jimmy Manley,
her lead counsel. To her left, a paralegal from his firm. Across from
them, the opposition attorneys are lined up, rigid and poised, like
pawns on a minimalist chessboard. The match is about to begin.

The man sitting directly across the table from Helen is suing her
for ownership of the plot of land.

"Are you ready?" Jimmy asks.

"As I'm ever gonna be," Helen replies.

The mediator, a small, elderly and baldheaded man weighing no
more than 120 pounds, takes charge.

"We are here today to take depositions as a first step pursuant to exploring whether there is common ground that could render a civil suit unnecessary. This arbitration hearing relates to a dispute as to rightful ownership of property, specifically identified as tract number 1784B in Nueces County, Texas. In lay terms, this is a plot of land on Mustang Island. It is my understanding that the parties in dispute have been unable to reach any compromise. This hearing, then, is a required step before any suit might proceed. Post-arbitration recommendations, if any, are non-binding, but we encourage both parties to be mindful of both time and expense should this suit go to trial.

"You should already be aware that these depositions are recorded and archived. Your testimony must be truthful, as you are subject to perjury penalties, criminal and otherwise, if any person knowingly provides untruthful testimony. Both parties will be required to be sworn in before addressing the arbitrator.

"Mrs. Chesterfield, you have asked to go first. Is that correct?" the arbitrator says taking a squinty-eyed look at Jimmy who returns the look but says nothing.

Helen nods.

"As I mentioned, this hearing is being recorded. Please voice aloud your assent for the record, Mrs. Chesterfield."

"Yes, I would like to go first," Helen answers, hands already fidgeting with the pen.

The arbitrator picks up a card and reads from it despite the fact that he knows the words like the back of his liver-spotted hand.

"Do you solemnly swear or affirm that the testimony you are about to give in this hearing is the truth, the whole truth, and nothing but the truth, so help you God?"

Helen pauses. She considers asking that the mediator retract the part about God, knowing it's no longer mandatory in the state of Texas, but she decides to let it go.

"I do."

After establishing her identity and general bonafides, Helen's attorney consults his notes while shaking his head. Going first is not, typically, an advantage in instances such as this. Usually the plaintiff would be expected to go first. Jimmy is concerned about whether Helen fully understands and has considered the implications of the testimony she's about to give. Even though Helen has executed informed consent documentation, Jimmy worries that Helen will place herself at risk in the event of a criminal trial, which he's told her is a distinct possibility after people have heard what she has to say.

This opening gambit, then, is not what Jimmy counseled. It's what Helen insisted upon.

"Mrs. Chesterfield," Jimmy begins, "you've sworn to tell the truth. You told me that was very important to you. Why?"

"I meant what I said. About tellin' the truth. I done some things. Lied about 'em. I'm done with that. I'll tell the truth, the whole truth…"

Helen pauses to look across the table at her adversary. He nervously looks away, declining to maintain eye contact.

"…and nothin' but the truth," she finishes. There is no give to her steely stare.

"Mrs. Chesterfield," Jimmy resumes, "tract 1784B has been owned by you or your ancestors for how many generations?"

"Counting me, three."

"Would you please tell us who these ancestors are?"

"Well, my great grandaddy, Samuel Holcomb, was from Iowa. He was a soldier who'd come to Texas toward the end of the Civil War. Story goes, he was rich and left a lot of money to his son, my grandpa. It was him, Matthew Holcomb, who first bought the land in 1898. Weren't very long after the Republic of Texas became part of the United States. My granddaddy got killed in France during the First World War. When he died, the land was left to my grandma. When she died, it was passed to my mother. Mama willed the land to me for whenever she died. I was underage at that time, so the deed stayed in a trust until I was eighteen years old. I've owned it ever since."

"Mrs. Chesterfield, the plaintiff asserts he took ownership of tract 1784B. Specifically, he maintains he did so on February 12, 1974. Do you recall the incidents of that day, and do you have a reason to believe that the plaintiff's claim of ownership is invalid?"

"Yes."

"Why?"

"This liar, here, he says the plot of land and house belong to him. That ain't true. That ain't what happened."

"What, then, did happen?"

"It ain't a short story," Helen replies. "But it's time it was told."

Helen closes her eyes, takes a breath. Her hands rest on her abdomen. She swears she feels a tingle. Butterflies. She gathers her courage, sorts her memories, and begins.

———— ••• ————

The sky that day was grey as a cast iron skillet, thick with clouds that looked like they weren't goin' nowhere. The rain warn't comin' down so wild no more—it had settled into a steady drizzle. But the pitter-patterin' on the roof kept on, like it aimed to stick around a while.

I hated it when it rained. It's not so much bein' wet or bein' denied the warmth of the sun's rays that bothered me. More, it was bein' kept indoors. If'n it were up to me, I'd be outside.

Especially if Willy was there.

I couldn't understand what Mama saw in him. Oh, he cut a fine figure. On the outside. Inside, the man few people can see? That's another story.

We'd first noticed Willy in church. Of course, we did. He dressed nice. Smelled nice. Talked nice. Quoted scripture. Everybody liked Willy, it seemed.

His hair was longish, feather cut down to his collar. He looked like an older version of David Cassidy, the teen crush actor who was playin' Keith Partridge on the television show the other girls at school never missed.

I was the first to notice him. It wasn't hard to do given Willy stared at Mama the whole service. Every Sunday. He didn't look nowhere else, even if he were supposed to be followin' along in our hymnal books while the choir sang or listenin' to the preacher's sermon or passin' around the collection plate. I seen he pretended to put money in the dish whenever it got passed around, but he never added so much as a quarter.

Willy had figured out, too, that Mama had some money stashed away. She worked her maid job but that didn't pay enough to feed us and clothe us, cover the insurance premiums and keep up to date on the property taxes. She had a newer car, and we always went to the diner for lunch after church. Mama always had a crisp twenty-dollar bill for the collection plate. Willy said Mama must have herself a pot of gold hidden somewhere and where had she caught the leprechaun? He said it was a joke, but he said it a bunch times and it wasn't funny any of those times.

When Mama told me she'd invited Willy to lunch at the diner after church one day, I was uneasy. By the time we was done, I was worried.

Willy hardly ever blinked. I'd stare at him, countin' the time between blinks in minutes, not seconds like most people. Much as he looked at Mama, he wouldn't hardly look at me at all. It was almost like he was afraid to. If'n he paid me any attention at all, it was to give me a pat on the head like I was the family pet.

So, when I told Mama what Willy had done, Mama didn't believe me. Until it was too late.

Willy had lied and Mama went along with it. Said it was 'cause the congregation at church wouldn't understand. Wouldn't approve. They told people Mama had gotten a divorce and that she and Willy had gotten married by a justice of the peace in San Antonio. It weren't true. Mama was still married to Daddy, but he was gone. Daddy

*had up and left us years before. No word as to where he was goin'
or why, or for how long.*

*When Willy was visitin', everythin' changed. Willy told Mama
and me he was the man of the house, now. It was his castle, and he
was the lord. Said God had seen fit to deliver him to us. Said we
needed to show him respect as was his due. He set down rules. And
punishments for breakin' the rules. At first, it involved gettin'
smacked for breakin' a rule. Then Willy said he could read my
mind, so it became punishments for supposedly thinkin' about
breakin' the rules. And I'd get hit. Eventually, Mama or me was
gettin' hit for no reason at all, just 'cause he felt like we needed it.
Preventive medicine, he called it. Seems like every time it got a little
worse.*

*I was already scared so when Mama told me she was gettin'
scared, I told her she was just catchin' up.*

*It was harder on her. I mostly stayed outside. But Mama? She
couldn't. Even when he was at work off in Harlingen, Mama felt like
he was watchin' her. Dinner. Laundry. Cleanin'. It all had better be
done and ready when he came to visit, even though Mama worked
full shifts as a maid. I felt guilty for leavin' her on her lonesome and
knowin' I wasn't there to get my share of his attention.*

*Sometimes, even though there were punishments, I would take
terrible risks. One of the rules was I had to be in the house by sunset.
I got to where each day I would get a little further away and wait
for the sun to start goin' down. I'd wait until I knew it was gonna be
so close that maybe, just maybe, I wouldn't make it in time unless I
ran pell-mell. Right when the sun touched the ocean I would burst
through the doorway and fall on the floor, heavin' for breath, tremblin' with fear, but proud I'd won today's race.*

*The night it happened I felt like it weren't happenin' to me. It
couldn't be me. It was some other girl. Someone I didn't know. That*

helped me forget. Or pretend to.

I told the preacher at church. He told me lies are sins and Willy would never do what I'd said. He told me I was wicked. Said I should keep my mouth shut and ask for God's forgiveness. Once, I tried to tell a girl who sat by me in class. She wasn't a friend, exactly, but at least she wasn't mean to me. But she put her hands over her ears and said it was makin' her sick and she didn't want to hear about it.

After that, I figured I shouldn't tell anyone. I started to think I must have imagined it. I wanted that to be true. I threw those memories down a deep, dark hole. It worked. For a while.

Not all spilled memories are easily gathered back up. For me, at least. Some dodge, flee at speed. Others hide, blend into the background. Still others favor distance, runnin' as far away as they can. Memories sometimes have to be recaptured. They're slick. And quick. Some of 'em, you swear you can't ever catch up to, no matter how hard you try.

But when you least expect it, they find you.

Mustang Island's mostly sand, so there ain't no natural tide pools—none of those little pockets of water left behind when the tide rolls out. Least, not that I ever found. But I did come across a big, thick concrete slab with a bowl-shaped divot carved out near the water's edge. Don't know who put it there or why. All I knew was that it'd been left to time and tide, forgotten. Now, it weren't nothin' but home to a little round tide pool.

I liked to visit it, see what the waves left behind—tiny, dartin' fish, clear as sunlit foam, slippin' through the water like silver needles. It grieved me, knowin' they were trapped, left behind when the last wave pulled out. I'd reach in, tryin' to catch 'em, thinkin' I could set 'em free, but they were too fast, too slick. My fingers herded 'em in frantic circles, a game of tag I'd never win. The water was warm, the concrete edge hot beneath my wrists. Salt crusted in the creases of my knuckles, dried tight on my skin.

I've done my best not to think about that secret tide pool for a long while. Tried to let my memories scatter, like the little fish in that water. But truth is, that place never left me. Some memories, you don't just remember—you stumble over 'em, like somethin' buried just beneath the sand, waitin' to be found all over again.

Some memories don't just need recapturin'. Sometimes, they need rediscoverin'.

Findin' somethin' long thought lost is harder than findin' it the first time. More powerful, too. Hardest of all is admittin' that I hadn't simply forgotten—I'd chosen to forget. Worse, I lied to myself, pretendin' those memories were useless, that forgettin' wouldn't cost me nothin'. But I know better now. Of all the lies we tell, the worst are the ones we tell ourselves.

I'd chosen to forget so I wouldn't miss it. Wouldn't miss that tide pool. Wouldn't miss the thousand little things only I knew.

The feel of warm summer water lappin' at my sunburned calves as I waded the marsh, my dress hitched up and tucked into my underpants to keep 'em dry. The fine sand shiftin' under my feet, collapsin' into tiny brown clouds with every step. The hoppin', hoppin', hoppin' across sun-scorched dunes, feet dancin' from one patch of shade to the next. The seagulls, laughin' at me, teasin' me, waitin' till I got near before takin' flight, always just out of reach. And me, laughin' right back, chasin' 'em again and again, knowin' I'd never catch 'em but runnin' anyway, 'cause the world was wide open, and for a little while, so was I.

These were things I seen and smelled, heard and tasted, things I'd been grateful for because they gave me somethin' real—a place to be, a place where I belonged. A place where I felt safe.

A place that wasn't Mama's house when Willy was there.

Was a time when I would leave early in the mornin' to walk and run and be gone for as long and as far as I could, as long I stayed on the island, and as long as I obeyed the rules includin' bein' home by dark. And, as long as I obeyed the nighttime rules, too, which were many.

I told myself I needed to get stronger. Braver. I knew, even then, that one day I'd have to get away. Or make a stand.

February 12, 1974 was that day.

I was fifteen years old. I'd begun havin' periods just a few months before. I hated 'em, the pads, the cramps, the sense that things were changin' fast and out of control. Mama said I was becomin' a woman. I'd seen what bein' a woman was like; I didn't want no part of it.

When my periods stopped, I was glad. Until Mama noticed. At first, there was all hell to pay. What boy had done this? When?

It took a long spell for Mama to accept what'd happened. Mama cried up a storm at first but, after her tears dried up, she was stone faced. Willy was not there, which was good 'cause Mama said she'd kill him. I wanted to help her do just that.

When Willy returned home, he denied it all. But Mama was havin' none of that. Willy broke down. Said he'd been tempted by the Devil. Said he'd prayed about it and asked for forgiveness and that Jesus had forgiven him. He even told Mama that I asked for it. That weren't true. I never asked him for nothin', 'cept to leave me alone.

After that, somethin' gone outta Mama. She didn't say nothin'. Didn't do nothin'. She just sat there, blank faced. Catatonic, I later learned it's called.

Willy had the nerve to say Mama was bein' spiteful since he'd already been forgiven his sin and who was she to deny him grace? Willy stormed out of the house, hopped into his pickup truck, and set out for who knows where.

I remember the hours of silence. Even with nothin' bein' said, they were the loudest hours I ever heard.

Finally, Mama seemed to come out of her trance. She told me she was goin' for a walk. Said she needed to be alone.

I wanted to believe her but, for some reason, I didn't. I followed at a distance. I watched Mama walk into the ocean thinkin' she needed a swim to get herself straight. But Mama just kept walkin' until the ocean closed over her head and the water took her away.

I screamed and ran after her. I plunged into the waves, fightin' the current, cold stealin' my breath. I dove down, hands outstretched, fingers graspin' at nothin' but water. I kept searchin'. Kept callin'. Kept swallowin' the ocean.

And then—I couldn't no more. My body gave out before my heart could. The sea nearly took two of us that day.

I crawled onto the beach and lay there throwin' up salt water and heavin' sobs. I couldn't get up. I thought that if I left, whatever little chance there was that Mama might still be alive would be ruined. It would be my fault.

And that's where Daddy found me. He'd come home, out of the blue.

Daddy gathered me in his arms and carried me into the house. He called the sheriff. The lawmen were mostly quiet after they found Mama's body washed up on the beach, lyin' there pale and still, like she'd been part of the tide all along. The ambulance men loaded her up and took her away. I didn't get to say goodbye.

The sheriff asked Daddy a lot of questions. I tried to tell Daddy that I needed to tell the sheriff what had happened. Tell him 'bout Mama and Willy. Tell him 'bout me. But Daddy shushed me, sayin' he would take care of everythin'.

Daddy bathed me like I was a child, not a young woman. I was grateful. I didn't even care that I was naked in front of him. Didn't care that my tummy was beginnin' to swell. He sat me in front of the fire and ran a towel through my hair. I told him that Willy raped me, and I was pregnant. Never once did he cry, or tell me he was sorry, or hold me when I got to tremblin', not because of the cold, but because of what I'd seen Mama do. He didn't have anythin' to say when I told him I was scared 'cause I wasn't ready to be a mother, *seein's how I seen what it done to Mama. Daddy listened to everythin' I said but said nothin' back.*

Willy came home later that same night, drunk.

Daddy had already carried me upstairs to bed. He told me I needed rest, but I couldn't sleep. Felt like I might never sleep again. I stared at the ceilin'. I couldn't move. Could barely breathe. I found myself hopin' I would stop breathin', hopin' my next breath would be my last. If'n I died, maybe I could keep Mama company so's she wouldn't be alone. I kept seein' Mama's empty face, her slumped body, and how she'd walked into the ocean like somethin' out of a zombie movie.

That's when I heard Willy's voice. When I heard that voice in the house, it was like a spell was broke. I crept halfway down the stairs to listen and peek some, too, but I was careful not to let 'em see me.

What I heard, I wished I hadn't.

I thought for sure Daddy would be mad at Willy and maybe he was, but I didn't hear no yellin' at all. I heard Daddy ask Willy how much of Mama's inheritance was left and if he knew where she kept her strongbox. I couldn't hear Willy's answer, but next I heard Daddy ask Willy where the deed to the house was.

Daddy told Willy that he'd come back because he needed money and there were some men who'd hurt him if'n he didn't pay up soon. Daddy said that, with Mama dead, he was the sole owner of the house. If'n Willy wanted it, he'd need to make him an offer. And quick. Next thing I know, they're arguin' 'bout the value of the house and the land, but then they calmed down.

I could see Daddy was sittin' at the table in the kitchen. His back was to me, but I could tell he was writin' somethin' down. Every now and then he'd read what he'd wrote to Willy who'd say somethin' in response before Daddy would go back to writin'.

Wasn't long before Daddy asked if they had a deal and Willy said, 'maybe, but there was one condition.'

'What about Helen?' I heard Willy ask.

'I guess I'll have to take her with me,' Daddy said.

'Nothing doin', Willy said. 'She comes with the house. That's part of the deal. Take it or leave it.'

Daddy didn't say anythin' for some time but, finally, I heard him say, 'okay.'

I crept back up the stairs to my bedroom. I pulled out the only suitcase I had and started throwin' clothes into it. Willy must've heard me 'cause he came upstairs sayin' where did I think I was goin'? I told him I was leavin'. What he said next, I'll never forget.

'You don't get it, do you Helen? Everything has been worked out. I bought the house from your Daddy. Bought you, too. You're mine. Your Daddy knows. He agreed to it. So, unpack your shit and, when you're done, come on downstairs. We're celebratin' tonight.'

It felt like the world was endin'. Here I'd started thinkin' I might be rescued by Daddy. Turns out, I wasn't rescued. I was sold. And to who? Willy.

I'd long known how much I hated Willy. Thought I could never hate anyone else as much as I hated him. But that weren't true. Now, there was one person I hated more. My Daddy.

When Willy wasn't lookin', I snuck out the back door. Daddy had the hatchback of his old yellow Hornet open, and he was puttin' the last of his old clothes—clothes that had been hangin' in Mama's bedroom closet, clothes I used to rub between my fingers and smell, clothes I dreamed he would wear when he returned—into his car. He was in such a hurry to get away he hadn't bothered to take 'em off the hangers.

He nearly jumped out of his skin when I hugged him from behind. I cried and begged until I had nothin' left inside. The whole time he just kept sayin' 'there, there,' while he patted me on the back as though I had stubbed my toe, not that I'd witnessed my Mama die *or that I was pregnant with his grandchild or that Willy had just told me he owned me.*

When Daddy pushed me away and opened the car door to drive away, I lost it. I grabbed the first thing I could find, a shovel that was leanin' against the house. He never saw it comin'. It sounded like a rock strikin' a ripe melon. I hit him just the once. That's all it took.

I thought Daddy would get up. He didn't. He twitched a few times and that made me sick to my stomach. Then, he went still. I told Daddy to get up. Told him I was sorry. But he was dead and couldn't hear me no more.

I...I didn't mean to kill him. I just wanted to stop him from leavin' me alone with Willy. Wanted him to take me away. To care what happened to me. I...

Willy came runnin' out of the house. 'What did you do? What did you do?' he kept hollerin'. He said it with his hands over his ears as he ran in circles like a dog chasin' his tail.

I didn't have no answers until after I'd sat myself down on the stoop for a while. I went inside and looked at the paper Daddy had written. Then I took a meat cleaver from the kitchen drawer and held it in my hand when I went back outside to where Willy was squattin' down next to Daddy's body.

'I ain't leavin'," I told Willy. 'You are.'

He looked at me like I was a retard.

I told him to take the money he'd given Daddy and go. I didn't care 'bout whatever paper or bill of sale Daddy had written. I told Willy that if he didn't go, I'd tell the sheriff he'd raped me and killed Daddy. I told him he wouldn't get away with killin' me so soon after Mama just died so he'd better stop thinkin' on that.

I told Willy he'd be suspect number one. I told him I was a better liar than he was, and people would believe me and not him.

And, last, I told him if he stayed, I'd kill him, too. When he least expected it. When he was asleep. The cleaver in my hand and the bloody shovel layin' nearby might'a helped convince him.

I said, "Willy, 'ain't nothin' here for you. You best just get."

At the end, Willy was relieved to go, I think. He was beginnin' to realize my bein' pregnant would lead to questions, and those questions would lead to him. My bein' fifteen and all, he would probably be goin' to jail whether anyone believed me or not. He climbed into his truck and drove away as fast as he could.
Once Willy was gone, there was two more things to do.

First, what to do about the body?

I dragged Daddy over to the concrete slab—the one with the tide pool—usin' the same shovel I'd laid him out with. Dug deep under the part the tide never touched, packed him in real good, and lined it with rocks so he wouldn't come up. Or be found. Figured I'd put him where no one'd ever think to look.

What I didn't know—what I couldn't have known—was that Mama, or somebody else, had already buried somethin' there first. All that silver hid right beneath him. And me, thinkin' I'd just buried my biggest secret, when all along, I'd gone and laid him to rest on top of another one I didn't even know was there.

Second, there was the baby.

Roe v. Wade had been decided not even a year before when I found myself in trouble. Caught the bus to Corpus Christi, walked straight to the clinic, but no doctor'd do the procedure without a parent signin' off. With Daddy and Mama both gone, that wasn't gonna happen. Heard at school some girls in trouble had gone and done it themselves. So, I did. But after, I got an infection. Learned later I'd never have young'uns of my own.

Daddy was buried, Mama was in the cemetery, and Willy was long gone. That left just me. I lived in that house, learned to balance the checkbook, paid the taxes, stretched what little money was left 'til it wouldn't stretch no more. Even took over Mama's cleanin' job. I stayed, alone, 'til I married Ben six years later.

Ain't never gone back. Not to the house, the slab, or the tide pool. Used to love them places, but love don't stand no chance against ghosts. Bad memories roll in on the tide, washin' all the good ones away. Those memories are stuck there, like the little fish swimmin' in circles. Trapped. Just like me.

———————— ••• ————————

The shock is evident on the faces of everyone in the room including Jimmy. Helen has testified to things he'd never known about. Things he'd normally never have allowed her to say so that she wouldn't incriminate herself. He'd interrupted Helen several times, tried to get her to stop, but Helen was adamant and told him he worked for her, not the other way around.

"Maybe now would be a good time to take a break," Jimmy offers.

Clearly Willy wants a break. He's halfway out of his seat before Helen speaks.

"No," Helen says. "Don't want no break. I got just a few more things to say. Then you can break all you want."

Helen turns her attention back to Willy who's fidgeting and can't seem to stop running his fingers through thinning locks, hair about which he used to be so prideful.

"Willy," Helen says, "you got some nerve tryin' to claim Mama's land. You been sayin' you bought the land? Here's why that ain't true."

Helen, a true believer in lists, raises a finger with each point.

"First, you and Mama, you never got married 'cause her and Daddy never got divorced.

"Second, you never lived with us regular like. You'd show up when it suited you, take what you wanted, and disappear again. Half the time, we didn't even know where you were. And when you did come around, it was mostly when Mama was at work. We both know why. Accordin' to the laws, I expect there's punishments for that.

"Third, that handwritten sale agreement you included in your filin'? Funny how it's signed. 'Cause I seen it weren't signed. And that was after Daddy was already dead. I'm pretty sure a handwritin' expert will tell us his signature has been forged. I expect there's punishments for that.

"And, if that ain't enough, think on this. If'n I'm a murderer, and maybe I am, then you're an accessory. I expect there's punishments for that, too."

Helen places her palms down and raises herself up and out of her wheelchair. She leans over the table putting herself as close to being nose-to-nose with Willy as she's able.

"I'll tell you the same thing now that I told you on February 12, 1974: Willy, ain't nothin' here for you. You best just get."

Willy's attorney got all huffy and started telling Jimmy that it wasn't called for, and that he needed to control his client.

But Willy? He couldn't get up and out the door fast enough.

CHAPTER THIRTY

Free to Fly

"O harmless Death! Whom still the valiant brave,
The wise expect, the sorrowful invite,
And all the good embrace, who know the grave
A short dark passage to eternal light."

~Sir William Davenant (1606–1668), English poet, playwright

———————— ••• ————————

THE STAINED-GLASS WINDOWS ARE PRISMS; THEY SORT the incoming light into blues and yellows, greens and reds, browns and golds. These windows are embedded in stucco walls that, too, are colorfully painted with images that tell stories drawn from both Old and New Testaments.

The windows and multihued walls inside the chapel are a sharp contrast to the outside walls, which are simply, white.

Two tall crosses rise above the petite house of worship. Both crosses were manufactured and installed by Voss Iron Works. Voss is the very same company that cast and bent, welded and shaped the gate and the balconies of the mansion. They'd made the iron bend to their will, confident in their skill as only true masters are. They'd written in flowing iron script: *Mustang Manor.*

Helen, if she'd been there, would have said: 'It's just a coincidence.'

Juanita, in reply, would have said: 'There are no coincidences.'

It's symbolic, she knows. Still, the gate often occupies her mind. Juanita finds herself going out of her way, inventing reasons to drive by. It's rumored the gate is coming down soon, making way for a wider and more practical gate, one befitting a research center and museum. Knowing this is a relief but it also makes her a touch sad.

She remembers a day when the gate was closed. She was locked in. On that day a man told her he was going to rape her, and another man told her he was going to torture her. She feared, first, to lose her own life and then, she took lives from others. She killed and saw Helen kill and saw Abuelo kill and saw Ivan kill and they...

...survived.

She remembers a different day, a day when the gate was open, by accident or provenance, and only by going through it did she discover a man who could barely speak the language but who didn't let that stop him from communicating with her anyway. And he'd smiled at her...

...twice.

Every now and then she's back in the kitchen, hands and ankles bound, zip ties ratcheted tightly across her face and the pressure is truly maddening. She knows the man is coming back and she must get free, and she'll wake up struggling and Ivan will hold her and encourage her to talk about the dream and tell her it's something to understand, not something to fear.

Juanita squeezes Ivan's hand and looks around. The woman who conceived of and had the little church built called it the Chapel of Eternal Light. Juanita can see why.

Perched atop the very highest elevation on Mustang Island and overlooking Port Aransas' old town, this Chapel on the Dunes is a tiny sanctuary, only 250 square feet wall to wall. Finished in 1938, it's Mustang Island's oldest continuously operating church. At the time it was completed, the island already had Catholic, Protestant and Baptists churches. But the woman who had the chapel built, a woman whose poetry and essays were so highly regarded that she came to be named a Poet Laureate of Texas, wanted to offer a place for meditation and reflection that was Unitarian, open to all.

Juanita likes that thought. Open to all. Raised Catholic, she can't help but notice there's not enough room for a confessional. There is no shielded place in which to tell secrets and confess sin. The wooden boards that make up the humble altar are not gilded.

The simplicity...appeals. It's why she'd gotten married here.

Unlike nearly every other church on the island, the little chapel has mystifyingly survived eight decades of hurricanes with nothing more than minor damage, not even to the stained-glass windows. Juanita has rediscovered her interest in history and learned this smallest of all cathedrals might never have been built at all if not for a deadly storm. A tremendous tropical cyclone, the byproduct of a 1919 hurricane that ravaged the Gulf Coast, destroyed most religious institutions on the island. The storm's survivors needed a place to understand and try to accept their losses. Since then, residents of Mustang Island have said they've come to think of this chapel as their own, pint-sized Sistine Chapel.

Juanita has a special respect for survivors of storms.

Inside, there's room for only six high-backed wooden pews, and sitting in one makes you feel like you're riding in an old-timey carved sled, ready to whoosh down the slopes as soon as they hitch up the reindeer. The pews accommodate, allowing for elbow room, about eighteen people. Today, there are fewer than that—six, to be exact. They sit shoulder to shoulder in the first two pews. There were some others who'd heard about it and wanted to come, but they'd been told, politely, this was to be a private, intimate goodbye.

Helen is already in the ground and has been for a week, now. Her friends were not surprised that Helen pointedly declined any graveside services. She'd refused to entertain a memorial service, too. Not even a wake. She was firm and didn't change her mind as she'd approached death.

That was not to say she couldn't change her mind and wouldn't change her mind about other things. Helen had long been set on cremation but, surprising all six of them, she'd changed her mind. She decided to be buried in the cemetery, right next to her Mama.

Even knowing Helen's predispositions, nothing was going to stop Juanita, Horacio, Alex, Ivan, Betsy and Jimmy from coming together at a place and time of their choosing to remember. Time and place were supplied, inarguably, by Horacio.

They're well aware of the irony of assembling in a house of worship, even one as humble as this chapel. It was Horacio who insisted. Rather, he told the rest of them that he was going to the Chapel on the Dunes one week after Helen was buried and whomever else showed up would be welcome.

Given he's a man who, generally, says little, it was unexpected when Horacio said he wanted to go first.

Horacio's gaze shifted between the windows and the faces around him. He spoke of God as a loving, forgiving presence—one who had watched over Helen all her life, even when she hadn't known it. But more than that, he said, God had not just watched Helen's life; He had shared it. Lived it. Felt it.

God was forlorn when Helen felt ashamed, pained when she suffered, regretful when she carried guilt. God had shared in her sorrow, her survival, and in her love, too—the love she had for Ben, the love she bore for her Mama. He had been with her when she found the strength to accept that her mother's suicide wasn't a failure of love, but a tragedy of being human. That sometimes people break, sometimes they run out of strength, and that was never her fault.

Horacio said God had felt it all, every moment, and that He always had been—and always would be—part of Helen, just as she would always be part of Him. And God, he said, knew what the people in this sanctuary meant to Helen. He was grateful that they kept her in their memories.

After Horacio, each had something to say. Even Juanita's brother

Alex, of whom Helen had grown quite fond, told how much he missed her. As Helen's health had declined, Alex was content to sit quietly nearby, if that was what Helen preferred. They seemed to communicate just fine without talking much.

Horacio and Helen were never again lovers but became good friends. He'd begun teaching her Spanish. She'd begun teaching him to play bridge. Turns out, they both loved dominoes and they played often.

Betsy and Helen remained friendly, but they were never close friends. Betsy just talked too much for Helen's liking and Betsy never met a silence she couldn't fill. Helen did see to it that Betsy's son Danny received the best therapy and drug rehabilitation treatment money could buy.

Jimmy wound up spending a lot of time with Helen. He'd gone to battle with a district attorney who'd been threatening to bring murder charges against Helen in conjunction with her Daddy's death. And he'd hinted he was considering whether to charge Horacio over the shootings of Georgi Kasks' sons. Rumors were that Georgi, even from prison, was either bribing or blackmailing the D.A. to do his bidding. Jimmy was outraged. By the time he was done in the courtroom—and the court of public opinion—no charges were filed, and the district attorney had lost his reelection bid by a landslide.

Helen ultimately sold part of the treasure and used some of the proceeds to help fund the fledgling museum on Mustang Island. She donated some more of it to The St. Augustine Pirate & Treasure Museum in Florida. She kept enough money to last her the rest of her life which, in her case, wasn't very long.

Helen's abundant affections—who knew she had it in her?—were mostly reserved for Juanita and Ivan. When they were married—in this very Chapel on the Dunes—Horacio walked Juanita down the aisle. Helen, in her wheelchair, accompanied Ivan, acting as his best woman.

Juanita and Ivan helped Helen move out of her Casita which she donated to the museum, as she'd done with Mustang Manor. She bought a small house very near where Juanita and Ivan live. She planted a butterfly garden and spent hours in it. Sometimes she would call Juanita on the cell phone she'd shockingly decided she needed, to tell her she had seen Sam that day. He had told her to tell Juanita that he chanted each day for the strength and wisdom to forgive any who may have harmed her, and any she may have harmed, and—even—that she learn to forgive herself.

Juanita, with a scholarship bestowed by Helen, went back to school, graduated, and is now working on a master's degree in Conservation Biology. Though she no longer operates it as a business, Juanita kept the ambulance. She and Ivan took turns taking Helen wherever she wanted to go. Helen, having been a homebody in her Casita for so long, surprised everybody with her newfound thirst to see everything—museums, plays, concerts. Sometimes, it was a simple trip to the beach or a park, where she would watch children play and birds soar.

When they've all had their say, the six file out of the church, one by one, their faces marked by quiet reflection. They exchange soft tears, long hugs, and whispered goodbyes.

Ivan and Juanita are the last to leave. They linger at the door, standing side by side in silence. The soft evening light spills through the stained glass, casting shadows that seem to stretch on forever. They wait for sunset, savoring the stillness.

They watch as the sun falls. It finally touches the water, casting a golden glow across the surface. Juanita's hands rest gently on her belly, feeling the soft stir of life within. The tiniest of flutters. Like butterflies.

Juanita and Ivan already know the baby is a girl; she'll be named Helena. The name means the same thing in Russian as it does in Spanish. It means "shining light."

Juanita reaches into her pocket and pulls out a well-worn piece of paper. On the day after Helen had died, Alex had brought the letter to her. Helen had asked Alex to hold onto the letter and to give it to Juanita when she passed. Alex kept his promise.

It's a letter she's already read a hundred times. She unfolds the letter and reads it again.

Dear Juanita,

As you know, I ain't one for speeches. Still, there's so much I need to tell you. You hear some people say they've lived their lives with no regrets. They're liars. We all have regrets. Some are small things. Some are big things. But we all got them.

There's so much to say but I narrowed it down to five things. You know how I like lists.

1. I'm sorry. You didn't ask for and didn't deserve the things I put you through. The fault was mine. If I hadn't held so tight to hate and revenge, things would have been different. Sam would be alive. Some other people would be alive, too. Maybe they didn't deserve to go on living but who am I to say that? The thing with Horacio? I'm not saying it was right, but it wasn't all wrong either. It was one moment in time with a kind man in despair over how he was losing his soulmate bit by bit. He gave himself to me as a gift, a gift to someone who'd lost their own soulmate sudden like. We both understood how that felt. It happened just the once. I may be a liar, but I ain't a cheater. So, I can't bring myself to regret it. I do regret calling Alex a retard. I am ashamed of it. It's something we'd call each other when we were kids. Still, that's no excuse. Alex is special and he's smart in his own quiet way. I'm sorry, too, you had to kill to save me. It's hard to think on, I know. Me, too. I regret lusting after Mustang Manor. I've asked myself why. Easy answer is because it's the home I shared for a long time with Ben. But that wasn't the main reason. I held on because it was the first and only place I'd finally felt safe. It was a world away from Mama's house and all the things that happened there. It felt good to give Mustang Manor up. That's the truth.

2. I've got major Daddy issues. I'm fucked up. I know it. Willy took something from me that I could never get back. Not spilled memories. More like a spilled-out heart. I won't excuse killing my Daddy. Did I mean to do it or

not? I still don't know. When it happened, I felt like Daddy and Willy had become one person in two bodies. I blamed them for what they drove Mama to do. I had so much hurt inside, I wanted to give them their share of it. I regret killing him. I'd long since known I'd have to leave that place or make a stand. I regret not choosing to just leave.

3. Hang on to Ivan. A good man is hard to find. Guess I should say the same thing about women because you're a good woman as well. Ben was the right man for me. Ivan is a keeper for you. Plus, Horacio loves Ivan and their partnership is good for Horacio. It's given him a new lease on life. Go team Horacio & Ivan!

4. Thank you. If I'd had a child, I'd want her to be you. You are smart, tough, beautiful, resourceful. You'll be a good mother. I regret I didn't live long enough to see yours and Ivan's baby born. I am blessed you've decided to name her after me.

5. You are amazing. You saved me that day and even though I was there every step of the way (all your steps, by the way), I remember all of what you did and think it cannot be true. Who could do all these things? You patched me up, packed me up, carted me all over the island and never once considered abandoning me.

I don't know if there's a God, but you, Juanita, are an ambulance driving, cripple toting, wave counting, elephant hiding, boat paddling, heart healing, bullet bluffing, Goddess of Fucking Light. You can do anything.

I love you. I never told you that before. Well, it's true.

~Helen

P.S. - Maybe Sam's right. Maybe there is a kind of reincarnation, a way for pieces of us to carry on in others. If that's true, I hope some little part of me lives on in Helena. If I can, I'll watch out for her, wherever I am.

Juanita refolds the letter and puts it back into her pocket. She dabs her eyes and leans against Ivan who's been waiting patiently, solidly by her side. They both look toward the sea.

The setting sun paints the sky in ribbons of oranges and reds, yellows and pinks, and it sends softened light scattering across the horizon.

Juanita whispers her thoughts to Helen.

Run Helen. As much as you want.

Better yet, fly. Now, you're free to fly.

Afterword

FIFTY YEARS AGO, I WENT ON SPRING BREAK TO MUSTANG Island. I traveled there in a car with three buddies. One of my friends would always claim "shotgun." He would practically refuse to go anywhere unless he got that front seat next to the driver. While positioned there, he had a peculiar stunt he'd pull. Often, when a cop car came into view, he would flip them the bird.

It wasn't funny, yet at the same time, it was hilarious. It was brazen, and we couldn't help but laugh in spite of ourselves. There was something almost voyeuristic about sharing in that little thrill of defying authority—something teenagers, which we were, are naturally drawn to. That he did it so confidently, so casually, and for no particular reason only made it all the more alluring. More fun.

I figured I'd give it a try.

What I likely hadn't fully appreciated was my friend's artistry. Only later did I rethink what I had missed, what with me being tucked in the back seat and all. He had a way of flipping the bird, but he'd disguise the gesture as a scratch of his head or rub of his nose. I had failed to appreciate the nuance.

I, on the other hand, offered no feint when I flipped off a sheriff's deputy we passed while he idled in his car at an intersection. I locked eyes with him and grinned and shot him the bird, no mistake. I saw his eyes grow wide.

Once we passed, I turned and smiled at my friends, expecting grins. They didn't smile back. That was the first clue. The flashing red and blue lights were the second.

Within minutes, my car door was yanked open, and I was dragged out like a rag doll. Spun around, handcuffed and marched over to the back door of the squad car and was thrust inside with great care.

When I say *great care*, know that I mean he showed great care to be sure I received a glancing blow to my face from the topmost part of the door opening before being shoved fully inside. I got his point.

Saying nothing, he drove me at urgent speed to the jail and had me promptly thrown into the can or clink or slammer, take your pick. I say I was arrested, but the deputy never said what I was to be charged with and he never read me my rights. A twisted part of me wanted to know what it was like to be on the receiving end of a Miranda warning. What was the charge? Criminal salute? Disorderly demonstration? To this day I have no idea.

It took a while for my friends to catch up to me at the sheriff's station since the officer who'd arrested me refused to slow down so my friends could follow. The only time he spoke was to inform me that my friends' challenge of finding where he was taking me was my problem, not his.

Long story short, I spent a couple of hours in a group lockup trying to keep from straying into some vomit that lay unattended in the middle of the crowded cell. I had to scrounge cash from my friends to pay a fine and get out, none of which made me popular since we were all, now, broke. I was given a piece of paper that told me how I might go about appealing the fine but that would require a future court appearance back there. I decided not to push my luck.

I don't remember his name, only the bulk of his arms, thick as my grudges. To me, he'll always be Officer Bicep. Even now, I send him a silent, defiant salute, childish or not. Incidentally, my finger-flipping friend? He went on to be a decorated undercover vice cop in Hawaii.

The lesson burned deep: small-town law dances to its own rhythm, and sometimes, that rhythm pounds with the echo of frontier justice. You've heard its beat in *Of Light & Lies*.

Acknowledgements

FIRST AND FOREMOST, I want to thank my wife, Mika. This book wouldn't be what it is without you. From being my sounding board to tirelessly editing, laying out the pages, and designing the cover, your talent and patience have shaped every part of it. Your support, insight, and eye for detail have made all the difference. I'm endlessly grateful—for this and for everything.

To my incredible children—Mallory, Hayley, Nolan, and Drew—thank you for reading drafts, offering thoughtful feedback, and helping shape this book into something better. Your insights, encouragement, and honest critiques meant the world to me. I'm grateful not just for your contributions to this story, but for the joy and inspiration you bring to my life every day. In particular, special thanks to my oldest daughter Mallory for the thoughtful reading and important comments on plot development and rationalization of characters' actions. You've helped make this a much better book.

To my mother, Katherine Justice, whose unconditional love and unwavering support have always been a source of strength—thank you for believing in me every step of the way. And to my father, Davis Denny Jr., who sparked my love of reading and opened the door to countless stories. I am forever grateful.

To my brother Dave Denny III and sister Diana Ross—thank you for braving the very rough early drafts, offering encouragement, and always believing in me. Your support, honesty, and friendship mean the world to me. I admire you both, not just as siblings, but as the incredible people you are. I'm lucky to have you in my corner.

A heartfelt thank you to my mother-in-law, Guida Quon, and my aunts, Betty Ann Chase and Merry Wennerberg, for your love, support, and encouragement. Your kindness and wisdom mean so much to me.

Endless gratitude goes to Anita Mitchell, Editor-in-Chief of the *Copperas Cove Press*, who gave me my first job as a newspaper reporter. Your corrections and encouragement—always in equal measure—taught me the value of perseverance and precision. I will forever be grateful to you for setting me on this path.

I am deeply grateful to the many colleagues and mentors I've had the privilege of working with over the years. A special thank you to Marsh Freeman, Tom Kemp, Don Pazour, David Nussbaum, David Loechner, and my teammates at Stevens Publishing, Miller Freeman, Penton Media/Informa, Emerald Expositions, and Inquiry Management Systems. I miss you all and think about you often.

A most sincere thanks as well to my fellow journalists and editors at the *Copperas Cove Press, The Killeen Daily Herald, The Lufkin Daily News, The Waco Tribune-Herald,* and *The Austin American-Statesman.* Your support, collaboration, and shared passion for news reporting and storytelling have been invaluable.

I also want to express my profound appreciation to Joseph and Chela Banuelos. My closest friend, Joe, passed away less than a year before I finished writing this book. Both Joe and Chela embody true artistic dedication. They have lived their craft with passion and purpose, and their commitment to creative expression inspired me to write this book. I carry that inspiration with me always.

Finally, a special thanks to my friends and neighbors in the Floral Park and West Floral Park neighborhoods of Santa Ana, California. Your words of encouragement kept me going, and I appreciate your patience with me as I wandered through the streets on my afternoon walks, lost in thought and furiously typing on my phone—thank you for not running me over!

www.ingramcontent.com/pod-product-compliance
Lightning Source LLC
Chambersburg PA
CBHW061118100726
47911CB00013B/598